THE
AMBASSADORS

DREW AND KIT COONS

Enjoy the adventure!

Kit & Drew

Good Reading James

DREW AND KIT COONS

THE
AMBASSADORS

The Ambassadors

© 2018 Kit and Drew Coons

ISBN: 978-0-9995689-0-3

Library of Congress Control Number: 2017916733

Edited by Jayna Richardson
Illustrations by Julie Sullivan (MerakiLifeDesigns.com)
Design: Julie Sullivan (MerakiLifeDesigns.com)

First Edition

Printed in the United States

23 22 21 20 19   1 2 3 4 5

Principal Characters

Molly Powell | Early-thirties reporter for DSC, a major television network

Paul Sanders | Mid-thirties NASA scientist at Kennedy Space Center

Fitzgerald and Isabella | Ambassadors to Earth

Harry Thompkins | NASA's Director of Kennedy Space Center

Dr. Ginger Peters | NASA Medical Specialist at Kennedy Space Center

Tom and Becky Sawyer | Paul's former in-laws in Oregon

Beth Sawyer Sanders | Paul's deceased wife and Tom and Becky's daughter

Dr. Ben Finkle | Founder and owner of Future Tech, a bioengineering firm

Dr. Laura Holdridge | Geneticist who works for Future Tech

Jeff Holdridge | Laura's son

George Baker | DSC Network News Director

Bill Samuel | Opinion Show host on DSC

Steve Wilson | DSC Network News' anchor

• • •

This novel is dedicated to all
who put their self-interest aside
to cooperate for the good of others
including future generations.

• • •

Acknowledgments

• • •

We would like to thank our partners for their invaluable help on this, our second novel. Jayna Richardson provided professional editing and proofreading. Julie Sullivan provided artwork and formats for publishing. Leslie Mercer and Margaret Zimmerman read the manuscript and made valuable corrections and suggestions.

Chapter 1

• • •

A flash of darkness as if light had escaped the universe occurred in the plane of Earth's solar orbit. Light re-illuminating the vicinity revealed a capsule the size of a delivery van in solar orbit. An encrypted radio signal reported, "Transport within acceptable limits."

More flashes of darkness followed, from which other sections arrived. Two beings emerged from the capsule to begin assembly of the pieces into a spacecraft.

Eighteen Months Later

"NASA's Orion mission to Mars has been repeatedly postponed due to budget constraints. There are also continuing concerns about the effects of cosmic radiation on the flight crew during long-term space flight," Paul Sanders explained to a group of career-day visitors from a high school in Titusville, Florida.

Most of the teenagers acted more interested in a day away from the classroom than a career-day visit of headquarters offices at Kennedy Space Center. Boys and girls standing in the back snickered and jostled each other. But in every group a handful always paid rapt attention. One of these raised her hand. "What is cosmic radiation?"

"Good question. Cosmic radiation is made of electromagnetic waves, sometimes called gamma rays, produced by nuclear reactions on the sun and elsewhere in the galaxy. They can slowly cause genetic damage to humans, which can lead to cancer or nerve damage perhaps even to the brain. Earth's magnetic field and atmosphere shield us from most cosmic radiation. But the crew of a spacecraft going to another planet would be exposed."

"Can't we protect the astronauts?" another attentive student asked.

"Yes, but shielding is very heavy. We make each spacecraft as light as possible to get them off the Earth. The shield would require a much bigger rocket. More fuel would be needed in space to accelerate the heavy spacecraft toward Mars then slow it down to Mars orbit speed. The fuel is heavy itself. Even larger rockets are needed to..." Loud voices in the hallway distracted Paul and caused everybody to look toward the door. Running footsteps sounded out of place for the Space Center headquarters.

A boy from the back of the group held up a smart phone. "Hey guys, look at this! A big meteor is headed toward the earth."

The group of kids crowded around him staring at the tiny screen. One boy quipped, "I hope it hits Mr. Farcus." All the teenagers laughed.

Paul spoke above the noise, "Don't be worried. The earth is huge. The odds of a meteor hitting near us are minuscule." The teenagers appeared disappointed as if nothing exciting ever happened in their world.

A security guard opened the door and spoke to Paul, "Mr. Sanders, you are needed in Launch Control." To the students he continued, "Please follow me back to your bus for return to the Visitor Complex. The tour is finished for today."

The teenagers looked to see Paul's reaction. He began, "I'm sure this is a routine precaution. There's nothing to—"

"Director Thompkins wants you right now, Mr. Sanders," the security guard interrupted. He gestured toward the hall and spoke to the students, "This way, please."

Paul stood flummoxed for a few seconds, then collected himself and walked purposefully to the parking lot. He got into his car and drove to Launch Control near to the Vehicle Assembly Building famous from Apollo and Space Shuttle missions. Entering the firing room depicted in so many real and fictional missions, he found a pick-up crew staring into consoles. NASA's director of Kennedy Space Center, Harry Thompkins, talked urgently with a group of senior managers. Paul joined the group to hear, "...maintain security and don't alarm the public until we know what is going on. The news media are already trying to create a story to boost their ratings. Let them run with the meteor strike for a while."

The engineers dispersed, leaving Paul.

"Where have you been?" Harry demanded.

"In the headquarters offices. My turn came up to meet a group of career-day high school students."

"Never mind. What have you heard?"

"A meteor is headed toward Earth."

"That's what we thought at first. Remember what I'm going to say in case you are ever called on to testify. NASA didn't lie to the media." Harry took a deep breath as Paul waited. "At first, we thought the object was a meteor. Then radar showed that the object separated into two parts as it approached Earth. The larger part accelerated toward the Pacific Ocean, broke up, and burned in the atmosphere. The smaller part slowed and went into low Earth orbit. If I didn't know better, I'd say the smaller section pushed off the bigger to de-accelerate."

"How could a meteor do that?" asked Paul.

Harry answered with irritation, "That's for you to tell me!"

An administrative assistant hurried toward them and spoke to the director, "The administrator wants you on the phone with him and the president starting three minutes from now."

Paul watched Harry rush away. The director could be a stern and authoritative man. He had recognized potential in Paul while he had been a graduate student at MIT. After Paul's graduation, Harry hired him as a personal assistant. Paul, in turn, admired and respected his mentor. He knew Harry still got excited about exploring space. Harry's life-long passion had sustained him through all the government politics necessary to keep America's space program viable.

• • •

In the telemetry section, Paul found a technician punching directions into a keyboard for a tracking telescope. "Have you gotten a look at the smaller hunk of the meteor?"

"Not yet. The small piece is on about a fifty-minute orbit. We missed it on the last pass. It should be back in range about fifteen minutes from now, give or take a few. The orbit path should pass about sixty miles south of our location. I don't know if we can see much through these clouds, though. And we're handicapped since the PDL closure after the shuttle program."

"See if Houston can get anything from the TDRSS satellites."

Paul tried the radar technicians next. "How big is the orbiting section?"

"About half the size of the space shuttle. It's oddly shaped, though. Not what you'd expect from a hunk of rock."

"What about the bigger section?" Paul stared intently at the scope.

"We didn't get much on it before it fell into the Pacific. From the tapes, I'd say twenty times bigger."

A man shouting drew everybody's attention. "Listen! Listen! I've got a signal."

Paul and several others moved over to a radio console. "Maintain your decorum," the superintendent of Range Operations ordered the technician.

5

"A UHF signal is coming from the damned rock!" The technician tore off his headphones and hit audio.

" . . . requesting permission to land," a raspy female voice said. After a pause, "Calling the National Aeronautics and Space Administration, or NASA. Calling NASA at Kennedy Space Center. This is a diplomatic mission requesting permission to land."

"Unidentified object, please identify yourself," the superintendent answered.

"This is a diplomatic mission. We do not have flight numbers or a transponder signal. We are the vehicle in orbit above you."

The NASA team looked at each other. Someone repeated, "Vehicle in orbit above us?"

"Where are you from?" the superintendent persisted.

"Someplace different. Requesting permission to use the Shuttle Landing Facility at Kennedy Space Center."

"This is not a commercial airport."

The female voice responded, "We are not a commercial flight. This orbit is deteriorating. We need to land somewhere almost immediately. We are asking for the protection and security of NASA."

Paul broke in, "When can you land?"

"The second orbit after this one. One hundred and four time increments you call minutes. We already have your coordinates. We can attempt a visual landing."

"How can you avoid being burned up in the atmosphere on entry?"

"We have an ablative under-coating."

The superintendent reasserted control. "Landing here is not permitted. You could be terrorists or carrying a nuclear weapon. Try aborting in the ocean."

"This vehicle will break apart and sink on impact. We will die. We're coming into Kennedy Space Center or diverting to a commercial airport. Our diplomatic mission is imperative."

Paul felt his stomach knot up. "Permission to land is granted," he said. "Shut down all power and do not leave your craft after landing."

"Understood. On the ground, we will wait for your instructions. Ending transmission."

An unknown male voice on the radio added, "Thank you."

The radio went silent. The superintendent turned to Paul in anger. "You didn't have the authority to do that. You're just a smart-ass kid."

"Acknowledged. I'll take full responsibility."

"What the hell is going on?" The group looked to see the director running back into Firing Room Four in response to a summons he had received. He paused a few seconds to catch his breath. "Can somebody tell me what is happening? I had to hang up on the president."

Nobody spoke. All eyes turned to Paul. "The smaller portion of the meteor may be a vehicle of some sort. I gave them permission to land on the shuttle runway."

"You gave them permission?"

"This is an emergency, Harry. They would die otherwise or could jeopardize commercial airline flights at the Orlando airport. They entered orbit west to east to minimize vehicle-to-ground speed like our Apollo capsules. The craft should

7

come down in about an hour and a half." Paul continued to tell all the details they knew. The director looked at the others to confirm or deny Paul's account. They all nodded except the superintendent who, although pouting, didn't disagree.

"Okay, we'll let those chips fall later." The director then spoke to the superintendent, "Right now call the security chief. Tell him I said, 'Maximum Alert.' And have him tell the Air Force at Cape Canaveral to scramble a couple of interceptors. Paul, you review everything we have. *Everybody!* Keep a lid on this! I've got to call the president again."

Everyone frantically prepared for the next fifty minutes. More data came in from the TDRSS system of satellites and Houston. Paul reviewed all the data revealing the approach of the meteor toward Earth, the separation, and the radio signals. Radar showed the orbiting vehicle altering its course slightly to pass directly over east-central Florida and Kennedy Space Flight Center.

On the next orbital pass, the female voice stated, "We will begin descent in twenty-seven minutes. Reestablishing radio contact could be possible in about forty-six minutes."

NASA's Landing and Recovery director had been summoned. "You are cleared for landing. Wind is north by northwest at eleven miles per hour. Light cloud cover at twelve-hundred feet. Emergency vehicles and personnel are standing by. Two Air Force jets will accompany you down to five hundred feet. Make a straight approach. Remain in your vehicle after landing."

"Understood."

• • •

An event this dramatic couldn't be concealed. The high security alert told everybody something big was happening. NASA employees, many of whom had no idea about the circumstances, called home to speak to their loved ones in case of a catastrophe. Rumors in the nearby community ran wild. The press smelled an engaging story. They reported every rumor they heard with the caveat "unconfirmed." Local news reporters relished the spotlight as their local affiliates uploaded on-the-spot reports to national networks.

Technicians in Launch Control maintained more external discipline. They simply made up rumors in their own heads. *A hoax? Terrorist attack? Space aliens? No, that last one is too silly.*

Radar picked up a vehicle approaching over the Gulf of Mexico and vectored the Air Force fighters toward it. An F-18 pilot reported, "I have a visual at about 70,000 feet," as the unknown vehicle passed over the west coast of Florida.

"What does it look like?" the Recovery director asked.

"Glowing red from heat. Otherwise, I can't tell yet."

A couple of minutes later the pilot came back on the radio. "The vehicle looks like a swept-winged aircraft coming in on its stomach like the shuttle. The bottom appears to be burning. I've never seen anything like this."

An Air Force controller came in. "Do you see any weapons?"

"Negative. Now the vehicle is leveling off and starting to maneuver. Vents are opening. A flame is coming from the rear. The vehicle must have started an air-breathing engine. I see a contrail."

"Follow it down."

"Affirmative."

Cameras recorded a stubby swept-winged aircraft breaking through the clouds at about six miles. The first approach to the runway was too high and a little off angle. Using its engine to maintain flight, the craft circled the runway at a radius of five miles, corrected the altitude and angle, and touched down on wheels at about 280 miles-per-hour on Kennedy Space Center's shuttle runway. The engine reversed thrust to brake. Once stopped the vehicle closed the vents and then remained motionless. The female voice came back on, "Ambassadors on a diplomatic mission to Earth waiting for instructions."

Chapter 2

•••

Better to be in Orlando during January than in New York, thought Molly. She lay on her hotel room's bed watching the world's hottest current story on TV. The Russians had won more medals at the previous summer's Olympic Games than the next two nations combined. People had become suspicious and demanded an investigation. Molly mused, *Actually, people are always suspicious of Russian cheating.* Testing had revealed no evidence of drugs, blood doping, or steroids. The Russians steadfastly denied breaking any rules and attributed their success to superior training schedules. But a Russian national had recently come forward offering inside details to the Russian Sports Federation's system in exchange for asylum in the United Stated and five million dollars. Speculation ran wild in the media.

Her cell phone rang in the late afternoon. "Is this Molly Powell?" Molly identified the voice as George Baker, the recently appointed news director for DSC, a major TV network and her employer.

As a lowly field reporter for an exposé show, Molly had only met George a couple of times. She considered him arrogant and totally self-serving. Getting a direct call unnerved her a bit. She assumed he would inquire about her slow progress researching a likely cover-up of a scandal by Orlando's city government. "Yes, this is Molly. I have some good leads. I'm meeting with a possible whistle blower tonight."

"What about? No, don't tell me. I don't care. We need you at Kennedy Space Center as soon as you can drive there. Something big is happening at NASA."

"But I've worked for weeks gaining my contact's confidence. Can't this wait a few hours?"

"Forget about whatever you're doing. And get over to NASA. Our local DSC affiliate will provide a cameraman." George then spoke deliberately, "Ms. Powell, I want you to leave for the cape *now*."

"I'll be on the road right away."

"That's a good girl."

George's sexist language irritated Molly, but she usually knew better than react. She fumed over missing her meeting with her carefully cultivated informant. *This had better be worth it*, she thought.

In fifteen minutes, she had checked out of the hotel and had joined traffic traveling east on Florida's Bee Line Expressway in the rush hour twilight. An hour later she joined a throng of reporters converging on the Kennedy Space Center Visitor Complex just west of NASA's entry gate. The

12

network had already secured her entrance to a hastily called press conference. Molly took one of the last seats at the Astronaut Encounter Auditorium just before the meeting began. The local cameraman had to wait outside. A NASA representative passed out a sheet of paper with quickly prepared bios on those who might be part of the press conference.

A NASA public relations spokesman began, "President Truman Johnson will address you all in a minute."

The president? Molly wondered.

A huge screen dominated the wall back of the stage. The screen played a channel tuned into a national TV network. The famous news anchor, Steve Wilson from Molly's network, attempted to fill air time with meaningless chatter. He appeared relieved to announce, "Here's President Johnson."

The network picture switched to show the president in the familiar White House hallway setting used to make dramatic announcements. "Good evening," the president began. "This afternoon an unidentified aircraft landed at NASA's Kennedy Space Center facility. The occupants remain inside. Let me emphasize that the unknown aircraft has posed no threat. Also let me caution about jumping to any conclusions. NASA is determining the facts. Now we'll switch to a news conference with Director Harry Thompkins of NASA in Florida." The president paused. "And I'll be watching this with you," he added.

The picture switched to the Astronaut Encounter Auditorium. Molly could see the scene before her on the screen including the screen itself. The picture receded into an infinite number of reproductions disappearing into obscurity.

The director stepped into the picture and stood behind a podium. Molly saw a tall, balding man wearing a tie but without a coat. She glanced at the handout sheet to see that Director Harry Thompkins had graduated from Georgia Tech with an MS in Aerospace Engineering in 1990. He joined NASA in the later days of the Space Shuttle program and spent most of his career managing projects for unmanned deep-space probes. Three years earlier NASA had promoted him to manage the Florida launch site.

Director Thompkins began by repeating the president's words about no apparent threats and announced, "And here is a live picture of the unidentified aircraft." The screen switched to a closed-circuit feed to reveal an odd-looking aircraft sitting idle on a runway. Lights from several ground vehicles illuminated the craft from all angles. The bottom of the aircraft appeared scorched. Observers saw no activity.

The director resumed speaking. "We know you all have questions. But we need to keep this short so that we can concentrate on finding more answers for you. Using seat numbers, we have randomly preselected ten of you to ask a quick question. The seat numbers will be displayed on the screen behind me."

Along with all the other reporters, Molly looked behind her to find her number, seat M114.

B26 appeared on the screen. Director Thompkins continued, "Seat B26 is first."

The reporter in B26 stood after a moment's hesitation. A camera focused on him as he asked, "Is this a real UFO?"

"Maybe, yes. The vehicle did fly and is unidentified in respect that we don't know where it came from."

As the remaining nine seat numbers appeared one at a time on screen, members of the press stood up to ask their question.

"Who or what is inside?" asked seat D14.

"We don't know," said Director Thompkins. "But they spoke English."

"Was the landing a surprise?" inquired D71.

"Certainly, we didn't anticipate it yesterday. But the occupants requested permission to land. I believe we have a tape."

The closed-circuit TV switched to a video of the aircraft landing while an audio played of the conversation with Launch Control giving permission to land. The final exchange between Paul and the superintendent had been edited out. The F-18 pilot's initial observations followed.

Seat F22 asked, "What security measures are being taken?"

"Let me introduce Security Chief Ben Wilkins."

The security chief came to the podium and described the directions given to the occupants to remain in the craft. "A SWAT team is on standby. Quarantine quarters like those used on the first Apollo moon flights are being prepared."

The next reporter asked, "What do the occupants look like? And how many are on board?"

"We don't know the answer to either question," answered the director. "We heard both a female and a male voice."

"Why are they here?" asked seat G28.

"You heard the recording. They claimed to be 'ambassadors.'"

G28 wouldn't sit down. "From where?"

"We don't know. Next."

Seat H31 asked "What will you do next?"

"When the quarantine quarters are ready, we'll invite our visitors to disembark."

"What are the occupants doing now?" asked J13.

"They asked permission to rest. We think they are sleeping."

Seat K91 asked, "Is the military involved?"

"No, this doesn't look like any known military aircraft, American or otherwise."

"I meant is our military involved in case this is an alien invasion?"

"The US Armed Forces are aware of the situation. But we see no immediate threat."

K91 started to persist. "What if—"

The director cut him off. "Last question, seat M114."

Molly immediately felt the eyes of the entire world on her. For the briefest of instants, she was tempted to ask a safe question. Then her instincts directed her. "How do we know this isn't a hoax?"

Director Thompkins smiled at her directness. "A good question! Let me introduce Dr. Paul Sanders. He is a NASA scientist with a bachelor's degree in mechanical engineering from the University of Oregon and post-graduate degrees in both physics and biology from MIT. He led the analysis team."

Molly saw a fit-looking man about six feet tall in his mid-thirties approach the podium. The NASA man nodded to the projectionist. The screen immediately revealed a PowerPoint presentation. Paul started by showing slides of the radar records of the craft coming from a distance greater than the moon. Using simple layman's charts and terms, he explained a reverse sling-shot maneuver around the moon to de-accelerate and approach Earth. Then a push-off technique from an apparent service module allowed the landing vehicle to enter descending Earth orbit. He continued, "They used a burn-off coating to absorb the heat of entry to the atmosphere. We used something like that for the ablative shield on Apollo. Inside our atmosphere, the landing vehicle employed an air-breathing engine to navigate to a safe landing. No Earth-built spacecraft has ever done that."

The scientist's voice sounded familiar to Molly. *He is the one who said, "Permission to land is granted,"* she realized. Despite her professional self, she noticed his curly dark hair and blue eyes. *You're pathetic*, she told herself.

Paul finished and stepped back. The director returned to the podium and concluded, "We know you have a thousand unanswered questions. We do also. But this is all for today. The videos and recordings will be posted on the NASA website and shown on NASA Television. I suggest you go get some rest. Tomorrow will be an eventful day for everyone. Our first press conference will be about 10:00 a.m." All the NASA representatives immediately exited through a door at the back of the room.

• • •

"I'm glad you reassured the public about quarantine quarters, Ben. But we don't have any designed to keep germs in," Harry started as soon as the reporters couldn't hear. "The Mobile Quarantine Facility used after the first Apollo moon flights is at the Smithsonian."

The security chief shrugged. "Yeah, I know. They made those in the sixties from an Airstream camper. I sent an engineer to a local RV dealership in Coco Beach to buy a new one."

"Can't we do better than that? The late-night comics would have a field day."

"Maybe in a couple of months."

Harry looked at the NASA team around him. "Does anybody have another idea?"

Paul cleared his throat before speaking. "Don't we have a clean room available in the VAB? They are virtually airtight and the air brought in is already filtered. To be certain nothing got out, we could reverse the pressure from positive to negative with a suction pump. We could use ultraviolet irradiation to disinfect the air and water both in and out."

"Where would our guests sleep?"

"We could set up partitions and beds."

Harry pondered a moment. "Okay, call in whomever you need, Paul. Overtime is authorized. Ben, your team can get that camper ready as a backup. If we must, we'll put the camper inside the clean room."

• • •

Molly met the DSC affiliate cameraman outside. She recorded an impromptu report to be uploaded to her network. She knew that technicians at the network would use pieces of it together with the videos downloaded from the NASA site to create a segment for the morning news shows. Then she stopped at a fast food restaurant for a meal to go and found a chain hotel.

Inside her room, she turned on the TV. Replays of the NASA press conference competed for air time with an explosion of alleged UFO sightings across America. Local reporters showed people flocking to gun stores to get ready for an anticipated invasion. Others stocked up on canned goods and other survival supplies.

• • •

By 2:00 a.m. Paul had technicians working to set up an improvised quarantine facility. "After all, we're NASA," he told the workers. "We can accomplish whatever is needed in a hurry."

After returning to his office and removing his necktie, Paul picked up a framed photo from his desk and sighed. A picture of an exceptionally attractive young woman in an evening dress reminded him of his empty and lonely apartment in town. *You should get some rest too*, he realized. *Might as well stay here*. As Harry's personal assistant, this wouldn't be the first time he had spent the night in his office. He even kept a pillow in a filing cabinet just for such occasions.

Chapter 3

• • •

At 5:00 a.m., Paul woke aching from lying on the hard floor. He made some instant coffee from a hot water dispenser at the water fountain and grabbed a packaged donut from a lower desk drawer. After eating the stale donut and drinking the wretched coffee, he grabbed some bathroom things and headed toward the men's toilet. There he washed his face, used an electric razor, and brushed his teeth.

After checking on work he had started on the quarantine facility, Paul entered Launch Control. Nothing had changed. Closed-circuit TV showed the spacecraft dark and inactive.

At 7:00 a.m., he listened as the Landing and Recovery director gently prodded the visitors by radio. "Good morning. Are you receiving this?"

The male voice, also raspy like the previous female voice, came back immediately, "We hear you. Thank you for your hospitality."

"Are you doing well in there? Did you get some rest?"

"We are fine. But we've been in a confined space for a long time. When can we get out?"

"Probably later today. Our protocol is to quarantine for a period anybody possibly exposed to an unknown environment. We want to make certain they don't inadvertently carry harmful microbes."

"A good precaution. We understand."

The NASA man continued, "There appears to be a door just behind the cockpit on your aircraft. Is that where you'll emerge?"

The female voice came back, "Yes, we can open the door from the inside when you tell us to do so."

"That will take a few hours. Our ground crews are going to approach your craft and attach a containment vessel around that door. Once you've left your craft, you'll be able to sit down in the containment vessel. Then we'll seal off the entrance and transfer you inside to quarantine quarters. NASA also quarantined our own astronauts when they returned from the moon. A camera will be inside the containment vessel. We would like to record your exit from the aircraft."

Every last person listening said to themselves, *and see what you look like.*

"That is agreeable," the female voice responded. "Our muscles may have atrophied from a long period of weightlessness. We may need some assistance."

"That can be arranged. How many of you are there?"

"We are two," the male voice answered.

"Do you have names?"

"We like the names Fitzgerald and Isabella. We have diplomatic passports, if you would need to see them." The

22

male voice added after a pause, "Sorry we don't have visas. There wasn't an American embassy near where we started." The listeners, tight with uncertainty, didn't know whether to laugh or not.

"Uh...just show your documentation to the camera and take everything you have into the quarantine quarters with you. Close the door to your craft after exiting."

• • •

At 10:00 a.m., every major media outlet carried the NASA press conference. Molly had arrived at the Visitor Complex auditorium by 7:00 a.m. to get a seat nearer the front. A public relations spokesperson initiated the meeting by rehashing the news from the previous night. Then she calmly announced, "The visitors are expected to exit their aircraft today at about 8:00 p.m. Eastern Standard Time." Her words caused a tumult of talk and questions among the reporters present. The spokesperson shouted for quiet and then carefully explained NASA's stringent isolation procedures and quarantine quarters.

Molly spent the day studying NASA's releases and preparing for every contingency to comment for DSC during the evening broadcast. At 7:30 p.m., nearly every TV in the world displayed the NASA broadcast. Those headed toward their mountain apocalypse cabins in case of an alien invasion listened on radio. The video feed showed a person wearing a hazmat suit standing in the containment vessel facing the spacecraft's door. Molly's network news anchor spoke to her over the picture, "Molly, who is that waiting in the suit?"

"Steve, that's Dr. Ginger Peters, a NASA medical specialist. She volunteered for this assignment and could be the first human to ever encounter alien life." As they waited, Molly added details about Dr. Peters. "Dr. Peters received her medical degree from Baylor University. Ten years ago, she joined NASA after interning at a hospital in Dallas. She is married to Dr. Bill Peters, who practices internal medicine locally. They have two pre-teen children. Her job is to keep America's astronauts healthy and to provide emergency healthcare at Kennedy Space Center when needed. She's known as a stickler for procedure and safety of her patients."

Molly filled air-time during the lull by praising all those like Dr. Peters who took chances for the good of others. Her words froze as the spacecraft door cracked and slowly swung open. A human-like figure wearing a baggy green flight suit crawled out dragging a bag the size of a large purse. The figure, who looked like a young man with boyish good looks, a light complexion, sandy hair, and a crew cut, gingerly stood erect. He glanced around and located the camera. He smiled at the lens and raised one palm outward in a friendly gesture. He stepped toward Dr. Peters and stumbled. She caught him and helped him to stand. "I'm sorry. I've been in space a long time," he said.

The world's expectations deflated. People everywhere had expected to see aliens with tentacles. They wanted to see something slither out. Or at least a creature that looked like ET. Around a hundred million TVs at least one person in every viewing party said, "I knew it. It's just a NASA hoax."

While Dr. Peters helped Fitzgerald to a seat, a female figure crawled out also dragging a bag. Isabella had an olive complexion, earlobe-length straight black hair, and a round,

24

wholesome face. She turned and closed the spacecraft door, which locked from inside.

Dr. Peters helped Isabella to a seat and strapped each of them down with safety belts. She sealed the containment vessel side that had faced the spacecraft then nodded to the camera. The vehicle carrying the vessel lurched just a little and headed toward the quarantine quarters. Molly, watching and listening with the others through the camera, saw Dr. Peters give each of the visitors a cursory examination and take a saliva sample from their mouths with a sterile swab. Each of the swabs she sealed carefully in an airtight container.

Fitzgerald gestured toward the bags he and Isabella had brought. "I know that American procedure is to check over luggage. Would you check our bags, please?"

Dr. Peters picked up each bag, rifled through the contents, and held them open for the camera. The contents appeared to be a couple of thin electronic devices and a few personal possessions. "I don't see anything here that wouldn't be allowed on a jetliner," she said to the camera.

"Our passports are also there," Fitzgerald said. Dr. Peters picked out the passports modeled after human passports and held them up to the camera. "Don't we get them stamped?" Fitzgerald attempted to joke.

• • •

Every network and news agency wanted an exclusive interview with Dr. Ginger Peters the next morning. Molly stood in line for two hours to get a five-minute segment. She told Molly the same thing she had said to all the other interviewers:

"Both of my patients are somewhat slight of stature, probably a little taller than five feet. But even though they staggered a little at first standing in our gravity, they have firm muscles. They felt strong and even reminded me of gymnasts. If they lived in space a long time, I'm certain they worked out a lot inside that capsule."

Molly, true to her confrontational nature, could not help but try creating some controversy. "Didn't you violate their constitutional rights by taking that saliva sample?"

Dr. Peters looked at her in surprise at the unusual question. But the doctor said, "I suppose that if that sample links them to a bank robbery in Des Moines, it can't be used as evidence. But they know that we're just trying to be cautious about health. They both opened their mouths willingly."

Afterwards, Molly chastised herself. *Tone it down, girl. Not everybody is up to some sinister plot.*

• • •

The next day Paul found an e-mail only ten minutes old on his computer. "Urgent meeting in my office at 3:30 - Director Thompkins." Paul looked at the clock. Only three minutes remained until the meeting. He violated NASA safety rules by running through the halls. In the director's office, he found a dozen key scientists and managers standing around Harry.

"Fitzgerald and Isabella are the real deal," the director told them. "DNA tests from the saliva sample Ginger took prove that they're not human. Chimpanzees are closer to human than our guests are."

"Is the lab sure? There can be a lot of variations between

individuals on those tests," someone said.

"They have twenty-four chromosome pairs. Humans have twenty-three."

Nobody wanted to comment after that revelation. They all stood pondering the significance of the analysis. Finally, the director asked, "How are they doing in the quarantine quarters?"

Paul spoke up, "I went by to see them through the glass. They're moving around with the kind of walkers used for elderly people and getting stronger quickly. Dr. Peters is starting them slowly on human food; bullion in distilled water, some glucose taken orally. So far, no problems. They are enjoying watching TV. Our guests, particularly Fitzgerald, know some of the programs well."

"How can that be?"

"I don't know."

"Well, Paul, I want you to find out. Go down there and debrief them. Find out where they're from, how they got here, and what they want. Go alone; they're more likely to talk without a big audience."

Paul tried to hide his eagerness to do so. "I'll get right on it, Harry."

He first returned to his office and made out a list of questions. Then he went by Dr. Peters' office and explained Director Thompkins' instructions.

"Okay, tomorrow morning," she approved. "But I'll be observing over the monitor. And I won't take chances. If my patients show any signs of stress, I'll terminate the meeting."

"Fair enough."

● ● ●

The following morning at the quarantine quarters, Paul tapped on the window and spoke into the intercom. "Did you have a nice breakfast?"

Both Fitzgerald and Isabella turned away from the TV and hobbled over to the window. They sat down in the folding chairs provided. "We had something called 'chicken soup' for a meal. The food had tiny bits of meat. A chicken is a bird this big, right?" Fitzgerald held his hands about a foot apart as he spoke with his raspy voice.

"That's right. How do you know that?"

"One of my favorite TV shows is called *The Beverly Hillbillies*. Ellie May had a chicken as a friend. Do we get 'possum tomorrow? Grannie was always talking about 'possum stew."

Paul had to smile. "No, the opossum stew was meant as a joke. People don't really eat opossums."

"But you eat chickens?"

"Yes." While Fitzgerald considered that, Paul added, "How have you seen American TV?"

"We picked up an electromagnetic signal."

"Where were you then?"

"Somewhere a long way away."

Isabella broke in, "I recognize your voice. You're the one who gave me permission to land. And I saw you on this television explaining to people about our arrival. You must be an engineer. What do they call you?"

"My name is...they call me Paul Sanders. I know you're Fitzgerald and Isabella." He nodded at each as he spoke their names. "Do you have second names?"

Fitzgerald and Isabella looked at each other and shook their heads back and forth in an over-exaggerated negative gesture. "You could call us Fitzgerald and Isabella Benevolent."

"Could I ask how you got here?"

"You saw us come in. You even explained our arrival on your television," said Fitzgerald.

"I mean, before that."

"That's very complicated."

"Then why have you come here?"

"We are ambassadors to Earth."

Paul reacted in frustration at the evasive answers. "From where?"

Fitzgerald stared at Paul through the window for nearly a minute. Then he spoke deliberately, "We came to Kennedy Space Center because we knew NASA had the best facilities and would help introduce us to Earth. We are on a diplomatic mission to mankind. A mission that we hope all the people of Earth will accept. But we can't let people around the world think that NASA or the United States is receiving exclusive information from us. We know you must have a lot of questions. So we'll give a television interview that all the nations can see to someone who is perceived as being independent."

Dr. Peters appeared beside Paul. "I think we need to let our guests get a little rest now." To Fitzgerald and Isabella she said, "This afternoon I think we'll let you try a little egg of the chicken and some fruit juice." Both brightened.

Chapter 4

• • •

"They want to give a public interview?" asked Director Thompkins while sitting behind his office desk. He motioned for Paul to take a seat.

"That's right. Contrary to what we expected, they're looking for a big audience." Paul sat and repeated what Fitzgerald had said about being ambassadors to the entire earth and avoiding the appearance of exclusivity for the United States.

"Lord help us. There are so many ways that could go wrong."

"He speaks well of NASA. And we're smelling like a rose so far. I think it's worth the risk."

"We smell like a steaming pile of manure to a lot of people. The internet is exploding with conspiracy theories. The talk shows are crowded with so-called 'experts' who are denying the reality of the situation. That political talk show guy on DSC, Bill Samuel, is having a heyday and boosting his ratings through the ceiling." The director covered his face with both hands. "He's like a god to the conspiracy nuts."

"What about the DNA results?" asked Paul.

"We released them last night. The naysayers are claiming the DNA results are proof of NASA's complicity in some sort of hoax. I just wish that Fitzgerald and Isabella looked more alien." The director sat quietly thinking for a minute while Paul waited. "Where would we get an independent interviewer?"

"There's really no such thing as a completely independent interviewer. But that woman reporter the first night did bring up the issue of a hoax. She could have some credibility among the deniers. And she's even from the same network as Samuel."

"Or she could join the conspiracy theorists."

Paul persisted, "I've seen her on various news programs. She comes across as a major pain in the ass. But she has a reputation for truthfully exposing hoaxes."

"She is a pain in the ass."

"Maybe that's what we need now for credibility."

"Okay, you go talk to her. And see what the audiovisual guys can set up using the camera already inside the quarantine quarters."

An e-mail from Dr. Peters waited for Paul on his computer. "Fitzgerald has proposed a list of questions appropriate for a live interview with him and Isabella." The questions followed:

a. *Where are you from?*
b. *How did you get here?*
c. *What is your purpose here?*

d. *Are more of you coming?*

e. *Why do you look so human?*

f. *When did you learn English?*

g. *What are your plans?*

Paul whistled out loud and thought to himself, *these should reveal a lot.* He phoned NASA's Public Relations department to find the name and contact information for the "pain-in-the-ass" reporter. With that information, he researched her online. The DSC Network gave her age as thirty-one. Pictures on the website revealed a strong face with handsome, not necessarily pretty, features. The biography reported that she had been a volleyball star in college. The network used the words "relentless pursuit of truth" to describe her.

● ● ●

Molly sat idly along with more than a hundred other reporters in Kennedy Space Center's Visitor Complex. She hated the part of her job that involved waiting for possible developments. Fortunately, the complex, designed for tourists, contained plenty of concessions for sale. The ring of her cell phone came as a welcome diversion. "Hello."

"Am I speaking to Molly Powell?"

"Yes."

"Ms. Powell, this is Paul Sanders at NASA. I answered your question at a press conference several days ago. You had asked about a hoax."

Molly's heart leaped to her throat. Could this be a possible informant to reveal a cover-up? She responded, "I remember.

I thought your answer was thorough." She left the opportunity to confess unstated.

"Thank you. Would you be willing to meet with me in my office?"

In your office? Molly had expected an underground parking garage or a dark booth in the rear of a bar. "Sure. Can I bring my cameraman?"

"No cameraman this time. Are you available right now?"

"I could be. Yes."

"Okay, if you're willing, don't say anything to the other reporters. But leave the visitor complex and drive toward the employee entrance Gate 3. The KSC Badging Office where they issue temporary passes is the building on the right. I'll meet you there to bring you in. Say in fifteen minutes?"

Molly managed to promise, "I'll be there." Fifteen minutes later she waited at the security building outside the gate.

Paul drove up, parked, and spotted a strong-looking woman nearly his own height with the thick waist of an athlete and brownish-blond ponytail. He walked up to her to offer a firm handshake. "I'm Paul Sanders. Can I call you 'Molly'?"

"Of course," she answered with a husky voice. "Do you go by Dr. Sanders?"

"Only when NASA wants to impress someone. Please call me Paul." He took her inside where a security guard handed Molly a sign-in sheet on a clipboard and a ballpoint pen. Molly filled out her name under "Visitor" and signed where indicated. Paul then signed next to her under "Responsible." Paul handed the form back to the guard, who passed Molly a clip-on visitor badge.

34

In his car, Paul drove her past the entrance gate to the KSC Headquarters. To Molly the space center seemed quiet, even sleepy in the warm sunshine. She saw alligators sunning themselves alongside drainage ditches next to the road and egrets stalking frogs. Paul parked by an office complex and held the entrance door open for Molly to enter. "Is this your first visit to NASA?"

"It's my first visit behind the scenes. I expected more activity."

Paul's voice revealed regret. "There's more excitement on days when a rocket is launched on one of the smaller pads. But we certainly aren't busy like the Apollo and Shuttle days. A lot of our space initiatives are made by private enterprise now. SpaceX and Boeing are leasing some of our launch facilities."

Molly's eyes searched as they walked down halls past offices and copy machines. Aside from posters depicting rocket launchings and a few nerdy science fiction mementoes, NASA operated from a complex of ordinary offices, many of which dated from the 1960s. Finding his office, Paul motioned her to a cushioned seat and closed the door. Molly noticed a picture of a rather pretty and petite young woman on his desk.

Taking his own seat behind the desk he asked, "Molly, what do you know about our guests, Fitzgerald and Isabella?"

She first repeated the things NASA had released including the DNA test results. Molly could not conceal the hope in her voice as she asked, "Can you tell me more?"

"Actually, you already know about as much as we do. We're hoping you might help us discover more."

"How could I help?" Molly's voice revealed her doubt.

"First let me ask about how you interpret what you've heard so far?"

Molly stared right at Paul. "My experience is that when something is fantastically incredible, it usually isn't true. All we know right now is what NASA tells us, which isn't much. That creates an environment for people to make up stuff to fill the void."

"Fair enough. Then if Fitzgerald and Isabella agree, you could help us to learn more by interviewing them directly on live TV." Paul proceeded to explain Fitzgerald's offer.

Molly forced herself to breath. This was like winning the Powerball jackpot.

Paul extended the e-mail from Dr. Peters toward her. "We have a list of questions—"

"Forget it! NASA isn't going to dictate questions to me!" Molly immediately regretted her outburst. "I'm sorry. That was a knee-jerk reaction. People try to manipulate the news media all the time."

Paul sat back and blinked. "Honestly, that was premature. These questions aren't from NASA. They are from Fitzgerald." He re-extended the e-mail.

Molly took the page and looked at the questions. Her mouth went dry at their content. She tried to swallow. "I can use these," she managed.

"I'm thinking tomorrow night at 9:00 p.m. eastern time. We'll go with a split screen, you on one side through your cameraman, Fitzgerald and Isabella on the other side through the camera in the quarantine quarters. NASA will stream the interview live for your network and others to pick up."

"I can work with that," Molly repeated in semi-shock.

"Alright. You and I have agreed; let's go talk to the others."

They found Dr. Peters at her desk reviewing culture studies from the saliva samples and waste products she had collected. Seeing Paul, she started, "Good news. There's no evidence so far that Fitzgerald and Isabella are carrying anything that would be harmful to humans. We'll need to wait for..." Dr. Peters broke off when she recognized Molly as the reporter who had asked the question (a stupid one, in her opinion) about constitutional rights.

Paul said to Molly, "We're giving you the interview of the millennium. Don't scoop us. Wait until NASA releases the lab results to everyone."

Molly nodded her assent.

"Dr. Peters, I believe you've met Molly Powell." Without waiting for a response, Paul continued, "She has agreed as a non-NASA representative to ask Fitzgerald and Isabella the questions you e-mailed to me." He then explained the arrangements and concluded with, "What do you say?"

"We could do that. Our guests are getting stronger in Earth's gravity every hour," the doctor said. "But I'll limit the interview to twenty minutes. Let's go ask the interviewees."

She led the way to the quarantine quarters. Through the window, they saw Fitzgerald and Isabella working out. "Could we interrupt you, please?" Dr. Peters asked through the intercom. Her patients, both breathing slightly hard from the exertion, came to the window. "This is Molly Powell from DSC News. She's independent, not part of NASA. She could conduct the interview you requested."

Molly noticed that Fitzgerald showed some stubble from not shaving.

Fitzgerald framed Molly with his fingers to mimic a TV screen and smiled. "We saw you on TV."

Isabella reached out to pull down his hands and smiled herself. "We are happy to meet you, Molly. What is your job?" she asked.

"I'm a reporter. I love to expose people who are lying or taking advantage of others."

"So you protect the less fortunate? That is very nice," said Isabella. "Is Paul your mated one?"

Fitzgerald made a silly expression toward her and corrected, "That's not appropriate to ask in this situation, Isabella."

She gave him a little playful shove and explained, "Sorry. He studied human culture, while I was studying engineering and learning how to pilot."

Fitzgerald became more serious. "Would the interview be available to everyone using the questions I suggested?" After listening to Paul's assurances of a live-streamed broadcast with his questions, Fitzgerald asked, "When would this occur?"

"About thirty hours from now," Dr. Peters answered.

"We'll be ready."

After that, Paul took Molly to meet Director Thompkins, who gave the final approval. He instructed NASA's Public Relations to inform the media and make the arrangements. Molly couldn't believe her luck.

Chapter 5

• • •

As with the departure from the spacecraft, nearly every TV on Earth tuned in to meet the aliens. Critics branded the event as "another NASA publicity stunt." On hearing that Molly Powell, not a NASA publicist, would conduct the interview, some critics softened their stance. Diehard skeptics insisted, "She must have sold out."

Lacking anything else to talk about leading up to the broadcast, commentators talked about Molly herself, her confrontational style, and those whom she had offended. Pundits debated her record and qualifications. Nobody could challenge her integrity.

Paul hardly recognized Molly when she took her chair under the lights and camera provided by her network and crossed her long legs. *That's one handsome woman*, he realized. Her bosses had insisted on makeup and hair styling. She had been wardrobed in a fashionable and modest dress appropriate for a talk show hostess.

Inside the quarantine quarters, the lighting wasn't as bright on Fitzgerald and Isabella as that on Molly, but it was adequate. The new arrivals had dressed themselves in the green flight suits in which they had arrived. Dr. Peters had gotten those clothes sterilized, cleaned, and pressed. She had even provided Fitzgerald with a razor to shave. She and Paul stood nearby watching the monitor. Harry Thompkins came to observe the monitor with them. Dr. Peters stood ready with a stopwatch in her hand.

The broadcast began with a NASA Public Relations communicator speaking in a grave voice. "We are coming to you from Kennedy Space Center in Florida. This will be the first live interview with Fitzgerald and Isabella, who arrived so dramatically nearly a week ago. They are currently living within NASA's quarantine quarters. A period of isolation is just a precaution against the unlikely event of introducing harmful microbes into our environment.

"Tonight's interview will be conducted by Molly Powell of DSC News. Ms. Powell attended Cornell University on an athletic scholarship. She graduated with honors as a communication major. She joined a Chicago DSC affiliate nine years ago. Then Molly moved to the network where she has worked for five years as a field researcher and reporter. Molly, let's see what our guests have to say."

The monitor screen switched to the split view Paul had proposed. Without preamble, Molly smiled at the camera and spoke to the lens as if she were seated directly across from Fitzgerald and Isabella. "Thank you, Fitzgerald and Isabella, for speaking with us tonight."

Fitzgerald and Isabella smiled back at their own camera. Fitzgerald spoke for both, "Thank you Molly and NASA for this opportunity."

"How has your time on Earth been?"

"We are happy to be out of the cramped space in our vehicle. We'll always be grateful to NASA for taking such good care of us. We hope to someday reimburse them for their expenses."

Paul whispered to his director, "I told you they would speak well of us."

Around the world skeptics said, "See that. This so-called 'Fitzgerald' is a NASA shill."

Molly started using the questions provided verbatim. "Where are you from?"

"We are from a planet you can call 'Benevolent.' What the inhabitants call themselves can't be said with human tongues. But we aren't certain where that planet is relative to Earth. It may be in another galaxy, a different time, or even a parallel universe. Their scientists haven't figured that out yet."

"Then how did you come here?"

"Advanced physicists and engineers figured out how to break through time, space, and dimensions. Isabella and I don't understand the technology behind the transport. But it's very expensive, requires a tremendous burst of energy, and can only send small amounts of matter."

Molly knew a term from science fiction movies. "You mean a wormhole?"

"Maybe it is."

Molly realized that Isabella had not spoken and deviated

from the plan. "Isabella, I understand that you piloted the spacecraft that brought you to Earth."

"That's right. I received training as a pilot and engineer for our mission." She turned her head and smiled at Fitzgerald. "He is trained in human culture and as a linguist to be a diplomat."

Molly redirected the conversation to Fitzgerald. "How did you study human culture?"

"I had tutors who have made study of Earth a lifelong passion." He made a comical face. "Then I watched years and years of television and movies our probe had picked up and re-transmitted."

Isabella broke back in, "Molly, don't get him started. He can talk for hours about Earth's movies and TV."

"Okay. You mentioned your mission. What is your mission here?"

Fitzgerald became serious again. "We are ambassadors of good will. The inhabitants of Benevolent want to be your friends and to help you."

Molly deviated from the plan again. "Can you tell us about the inhabitants of Benevolent?"

"They are living, organic beings like humans. They are born, live, and die like humans. Their intelligence averages about the same as humans. Most are very curious and friendly. More about them at another time, please."

"Well," Molly persisted, "do they look like you?"

"No, we are very different from them. We are genetically engineered to be ambassadors and to survive in your environment. Our creators saw that human movie, *War of the Worlds*, where the aliens die of Earth's microbes. They designed Isabella and me to survive on Earth."

Molly could not hide her surprise. "You were created to come here?"

"That is correct. What you call DNA is made of four amino acids in various combinations as a blueprint for a living creature. Benevolent's geneticists put the acids together in an arrangement to make us like humans."

In her surprise, Molly forgot she was conducting an interview. "Didn't you have a mother and a father?"

Isabella answered, "Molly, we have dozens of genetic parents of different species. The geneticists took gene sequences from wherever they could find them. But we are still thinking and feeling beings like you."

Molly paused and looked back at her notes to reorient herself after that revelation. She read the next question. "Are more of you coming?"

"No, we are the only ambassadors Earth will receive," Fitzgerald answered.

"When will you go home?"

"We can never return to Benevolent. Earth is our home now."

Molly let that sink in to her listeners before asking, "How did you learn English?"

"We grew up speaking English with our tutors. They had studied your language from Earth's electromagnetic signals."

"Your tutors can monitor Earth's signals?"

"They will certainly be listening to this broadcast."

Isabella spoke again, "Fitzgerald actually speaks sixteen additional human languages. Try him."

Molly took the challenge. "Spanish." Fitzgerald demonstrated.

"Russian." He spoke Russian with a smile.

"Arabic." Fitzgerald was fluent in Arabic.

"Navajo."

Fitzgerald returned a boyish grin. "You've got me."

Paul nudged Dr. Peters and whispered, "The designated time is up."

She hadn't noticed. "They're doing fine. Let's let them go a few minutes longer."

Molly continued with the questions. "What are your plans when you leave NASA's quarantine quarters?"

Mimicking a moment he had seen on TV, Fitzgerald said, "We're going to Disneyland." Involuntary laughter could be heard from NASA's off-camera observers.

Turning serious, Fitzgerald looked directly into the camera. "With permission from Earth's authorities, we would like to speak to the United Nations General Assembly. We have an offer to make to all humans."

Behind the camera, Dr. Peters signaled by a finger across her throat for Molly to wrap it up. But Molly felt something missing. The interview would not have been convincing to skeptics. A side of herself remained leery. "I've got one more question, please." Fitzgerald nodded. "A lot of people think you're really from Earth and playacting to fool everyone. What could you say to prove that you are true ambassadors and not from Earth?"

Fitzgerald grimaced a little and said, "I'm not sure what we could say. We came from space and provided DNA samples. But how about this?" He looked at the camera and winked with an inner eyelid that passed left to right across his eyeball.

Then he winked right to left with the other eye. Finally, he stuck out his tongue and closed both inner eyelids together. "Isabella," he said. She did the same. Then they both laughed out loud with a throaty, raspy chortle.

The split screen showed Molly visibly recoil in surprise. She recovered quickly and laughed with Fitzgerald and Isabella. "That will do, I think. Thank you."

• • •

Never had Molly experienced such an outpouring of gratitude from those she investigated. NASA personnel mobbed her, offering congratulations and shaking her hand. "Great work! Thanks!" Director Harry Thompkins told her.

Paul observed the group around Molly and instead moved to the window of the quarantine quarters. He placed a palm against the glass above his head.

"What does this mean?" Fitzgerald asked through the intercom.

"This is called a 'high-five.' It means you did well. You're supposed to slap your hand against mine." Paul slapped his hands together in demonstration and returned his palm to the glass.

Fitzgerald grinned broadly and tapped the glass opposite Paul's hand. Isabella moved closer and followed his example. NASA and network personnel, having finished congratulating Molly, crowded Paul away from the window. They chatted with Fitzgerald and Isabella and made selfies through the glass. Dr. Peters allowed the greetings for a few minutes and then, observing fatigue growing in her patients, shooed the well-wishers away.

Paul wandered to where the crowd around Molly had thinned. "Nice job!" he said.

Molly found accepting compliments difficult. "All I did was read the questions. Fitzgerald and Isabella are the stars."

"You helped them shine."

Gratitude didn't come easily to Molly either. "I heard you selected me to do the interview. Thanks for your confidence."

"I respect truth seekers."

● ● ●

"Your bodies are adapting amazingly well to Earth foods," Dr. Peters said to her patients after virtually everybody had departed.

"We are genetically engineered to digest a wide variety of organic compounds," Isabella explained.

"So it seems. Is there anything special you would like to try?"

Fitzgerald and Isabella readily alternated requests.

"Ice cream."

"Shrimp."

"Asparagus."

"Crow."

"Crow?" the doctor questioned.

"Apparently, humans 'eat crow' as part of a learning ritual. We are eager to learn," responded Fitzgerald.

Dr. Peters couldn't be certain anymore when Fitzgerald was kidding. "I'll have a menu for you to choose from tomorrow."

Chapter 6

•••

Could the questions get any sillier? Paul thought. The bubbly TV hostess had just asked Fitzgerald and Isabella if they had participated in the 1947 UFO incident in Roswell, New Mexico.

"That must have been some other aliens," Fitzgerald responded with good humor.

"Will you be returning the abducted humans soon?"

"We don't have the humans. Try the Roswell aliens."

After Molly's interview, every media outlet had wanted an exclusive with those commonly referred to as "the visitors from outer space." Dr. Peters limited Fitzgerald and Isabella's exposure to eight ten-minute interviews a day. Her lively patients entertained all interviewers in the short segments. Assigned by Harry as NASA's point man, Paul had been forced to set up a lottery to randomly award interview opportunities. At Fitzgerald's request, Dr. Peters allowed sixteen additional interviews to media representing peoples who spoke the other languages he knew.

Initially, some interviewers expressed frustration as Fitzgerald and Isabella deferred answering serious questions about their mission or the planet Benevolent with promises to explain more fully, if allowed to speak to the UN. Interviewers satisfied their viewers by asking about the aliens' impressions of humans, Earth food, and media entertainment. Isabella frequently queried the interviewers with questions about human culture. Some interviewers requested that Fitzgerald and Isabella repeat the clowning they did with their inner eyelids, to which they always complied.

Paul carefully read the transcripts of two somewhat revealing interviews.

An interviewer for an entertainment channel that frequently interviewed Hollywood celebrities asked, "Are you two an item? I mean all that time in the spaceship, alone and all."

Fitzgerald and Isabella looked at each other in confusion. Fitzgerald answered slowly, "We are a mated team. Is that what you mean?"

Isabella chided him, "I thought when we met Molly you said that was an inappropriate question to ask."

"I did think so. But maybe humans speak differently in different circumstances," he responded to her. Then they both looked back at the interviewer.

"I mean, did you have sex in space and all?" the interviewer persisted.

"These human bodies are wonderful. We are learning to use them," Fitzgerald admitted.

"How did you two get together?"

"She was the only one for me," Fitzgerald quipped the obvious.

Since Paul was from a Christian background, the second interview interested him even more. A religious network interviewer had asked, "Do you believe in God?"

"We believe in the Great Creator," Fitzgerald answered simply.

Isabella elaborated, "The Benevolent species has many ancient legends about deities. In the beginning, the stories explained the unknown and gave a belief structure. But as our science developed, most came to realize that the universe has an underlying order in complexity and is too well organized to be random. Our concept of the Great Creator is of one who gave us the marvelous opportunity for life and cares about our welfare."

"Do you have the Bible?" the interviewer continued.

Fitzgerald answered, "You mean the collection of holy writings associated with the Hebrew people, correct? No, we don't have that. But I've read it. I like the prophet Jesus who said, 'Do for others what you would have them do for you.' And Jesus' follower, Paul, who wrote, 'Consider each other more important than yourself.' These ideas are how we believe the Great Creator would have us live. And they should apply to future generations as well as those currently living."

"Do you believe God sent Jesus?"

"The Great Creator could do that. Who am I to say the Great Creator didn't?"

Next, Paul looked over the medical report from Ginger Peters. Although the inner eye trick had surprised her, a thorough physical exam indicated Fitzgerald and Isabella to be anatomically human except for minor differences. For example, their body temperature was 100.1 versus 98.6 for humans. Cultures from their saliva and waste products continued to be negative for any dangerous microbes. And the subjects tested negative to effects of ordinary Earth microbes. Her conclusion: "Approved for release from quarantine seven days from now." Paul forwarded her e-mail to Public Relations.

• • •

Molly had quickly tired of the celebrity status her interview with Fitzgerald and Isabella created. She turned down numerous requests for interviews by saying, "I report the news. I am not the news." To cut off the media pursuit, she turned off her cell phone.

Molly's network had hired an assistant for her and rented several temporary offices in Titusville near Kennedy Space Center. The assistant came into Molly's office. "You'll need to take the next call on your cell phone. It's the boss."

Molly sighed and turned her phone back on. It rang almost immediately. "Molly, this is George. Anything new down there?"

"No, pretty quiet. The aliens are giving interviews like crazy."

"Your interview came first, though. And your interview found out more than anyone else's has." Molly had to concede the truth of that. Her boss continued, "Are you convinced that they're legitimate extraterrestrials?"

"All the evidence supports that. And my scandal nose doesn't whiff any odor of duplicity at NASA. I've become a believer."

"Okay, you know who Bill Samuel is? He asks the questions

in people's heads."

Or plants crazy ideas in people's heads, Molly thought, but acknowledged she knew about Bill.

George continued, "He's asking the questions that bring viewers. His program's ratings are through the roof."

"People love conspiracy theories. I'm glad DSC is still committed to real journalism."

If George noticed Molly's sarcasm, he didn't react. "Good. So I want you to go on the *Bill Samuel Report* here in New York. Tell him the truth. This will be a simultaneous broadcast of his show and a DSC special."

Molly was astounded. "Are you kidding me?"

"This is part of your job for DSC," her boss said simply.

• • •

Once again, the network insisted on makeup and fine clothes for Molly's appearance. She waited off camera while Bill Samuel made his regular opening comments. She had brought notes documenting all the evidence NASA had released. After his preamble, Bill Samuel stood to welcome Molly to the chair on the opposite side of his stage desk. He grabbed her fingers in semblance of a hand shake.

"Welcome to the Samuel Report. You've become quite a celebrity."

"I'm just a reporter."

Bill got right to the point. "Do you actually believe the NASA poison about these so-called 'visitors'?"

"Well, actually the evidence is rather strong supporting their claim."

"But doesn't all the evidence come from NASA? And aren't they getting plenty of publicity just before appropriations hearings in the US Congress?"

"Yes, but—"

Bill cut her off, "And has anyone looked inside their supposed spacecraft?"

"The vehicle is still in quarantine itself. Opening it could pose a threat if any harmful microbes were present."

"We'll get to that later. What one piece of evidence can you give that could not have been tampered with by NASA?"

Molly started to feel herself heating up. "Who else do you know who can blink their eyes like that?"

"How do you know NASA didn't play a specially created optical effect? Weren't you looking at a monitor? You didn't eyewitness anything."

"NASA didn't know I would ask that question. Nobody could have anticipated Fitzgerald and Isabella's response."

"Unless they had planned it for an opportune moment. Didn't NASA give you questions to ask?"

Molly sat speechless. *This is a planned ambush. Does this jerk just have lucky guesses? Or is some insider collaborating with Bill?* She sat in silent rage.

"Uh-huh." Bill grunted in satisfaction. "I thought so."

He changed his tone to one of magnanimous victory. "Let's just suppose that you're right. This pair is really from another planet. Couldn't they possibly carry bacteria or viruses that could start a plague and kill millions of people? They could bring a contagion that would wipe out mankind?"

"That's why NASA has quarantine protocols to—" Molly started.

"Then why is NASA turning them loose?"

"What?"

"Didn't you know?" Bill sneered. "A NASA press release an hour ago said that they had been approved for release in seven days."

Molly didn't know what to say. But she felt anger about to boil over. Bill continued, "The way I see it, one, these are imposters who deserve to be in jail. Or two, they could carry diseases that could wipe out humankind. Either way they should be kept under lock and key!" he shouted.

Molly stood up opposite her attacker. "They have rights..." her words diminished as Bill's producer turned down the volume on her microphone.

Bill's volume went up accordingly. "Criminals and health risks don't have any rights!"

Not able to answer back, Molly reached across the desk and slapped him.

• • •

Back at her hotel, Molly didn't know whether to be angry or start mourning the end of her career. Losing self-control on camera was a death sentence for a journalist. On the walk from the studio, she had purchased a fifth of scotch. She sat sipping the liquor out of the bottle. *A few hours ago, I was on my way up. Now?* Her cell phone resided in a trash dumpster she had passed.

A light tapping at the hotel room door made her look up. She ignored the noise. The tapping intensified. An accented immigrant's voice followed, "Ms. Powell, there's an important call for you on the hotel phone."

"I don't care."

"Please, Ms. Powell. The man promised me $500 if I could get you to answer. My wife is pregnant. We need the money."

At least I can cost some bastard $500. She picked up the phone. "Hello."

"Molly, this is Paul Sanders at NASA."

"What do you want?"

"I just thought you should know that I really respect you."

"I'm guessing that you saw the show."

"We all watched, including Fitzgerald and Isabella." Paul hesitated. Not knowing what to say he added, "That was some haymaker you landed. Did it feel good?"

"It sure as hell did." Molly laughed a little through some tears.

"Wait a minute, there's someone else who wants to speak to you."

Molly waited while some mechanical noises came over the phone. "Hello, Molly? Thank you for believing in us," Fitzgerald said. Apparently, Paul had passed his phone into the quarantine quarters.

"You're welcome, Fitzgerald. Thank you for calling. Could I speak to Isabella, please?"

"Here is Isabella."

Molly told Isabella about her fear and frustration.

Chapter 7

...

"What are we going to do now?" Director Thompkins asked Paul and a group of department managers. They all stood looking at closed-circuit TV of the protesters outside NASA's gates.

NASA had never experienced picketers on this scale. Police barely kept the roads open for incoming and departing traffic. Bill Samuel's followers had coalesced into the No Release Movement. Some protesters carried signs demanding "Jail for Imposters." Others waved "Stop the plague before it starts." The most ominous signs simply had pictures of Fitzgerald and Isabella with cross hairs superimposed. Many protesters had secretly armed themselves.

Polls clearly showed that most Americans believed NASA. But many NASA employees started calling in sick or taking vacation. Some simply wanted to avoid getting entangled with the No Release radicals. A few stayed away in sympathy with the demands.

"I can understand people could have legitimate concerns. But this group is close to a mob," one of Harry's managers commented.

Paul suggested, "They aren't really that worked up over the imposter claim. Why would they care if a scandal embarrassed NASA? But fear of a contagion is driving their emotions. People are concerned about their children. Mix that with distrust of scientists and medical testing in general encouraged by fear-mongering agitators and you get the group you see out there."

Director Thompkins spoke more urgently, "I repeat, what are we going to do?"

Paul thought out loud, "We need to assuage the legitimate fears of people who want to believe that Fitzgerald and Isabella are extraterrestrials. And because of all the interviews, their popularity is sky high. Most people will trust them, if only they can find reason."

"What do you propose?" asked Director Thompkins.

"We need a demonstration. Somebody needs to enter the quarantine quarters and live with Fitzgerald and Isabella without bad effects."

The expressions among those present demonstrated that fears resided even in that room. "Doesn't that violate NASA safety standards for isolation?" one of the managers asked.

"Fitzgerald and Isabella's quarantine time is almost over. This would be in addition to our normal protocol."

"Then who would we send inside?"

After moments of silence, Paul volunteered, "I'll go in." Nobody argued with him.

"We should send a woman in too," said Director Thompkins. "Do you suppose Molly Powell would do it? Fitzgerald and

Isabella trust her. And, God knows, she earned the right by trying to stick up for us in that interview with Bill Samuel. That is, if she wants it."

Paul sighed. "Molly disappeared the day after the interview in New York. We don't know where she is now."

His boss answered, "Leave that part to me. President Johnson wants to avert a crisis, and I think I can get him to help us out."

●●●

Molly slept in a cheap hotel along I-95 somewhere in Virginia. She had unplugged the room's phone. A partially eaten carton of chocolate ice cream dripped in the bathroom sink. Pounding on the hotel door woke her. "Go away, I'll call the police," she yelled back.

"Molly Powell, this is the desk clerk. I recognized you when you checked in. You need to turn on the TV right now."

Molly rubbed her face and picked up the remote. The White House had released a request from the Oval Office. She had missed the original release, but the news networks replayed the short blurb frequently. On the clip the president requested, "Molly Powell of DSC News, please call the Kennedy Space Center immediately. Use your Social Security number as authentication."

Two days later, Molly sat with Dr. Peters, Harry Thompkins, the security chief, and Paul in the NASA site director's office. "Molly, nearly everybody at NASA thinks you got a crappy deal in New York. You can still opt out of this, if you aren't ready," the director said. "For what it's worth, I've also been blind-sided by reporters."

Molly acknowledged his comment with a nod. "I've blind-sided a few people myself. I appreciate NASA giving me a chance to redeem myself."

"Okay then. What's the status, Ginger?"

"Our trial subjects should be safe according to all our tests," the doctor said. "I guess this is the test that really counts."

Director Thompkins asked, "How do Fitzgerald and Isabella feel about our proposal?"

The doctor leaned forward. "They're watching the news about the protests on TV. They're chagrined to spend another two weeks in quarantine, but understand the situation. And they'll be happy for some company. If you're ready, at 10:00 a.m. tomorrow, we'll insert Paul and Molly."

"Is there anything we should bring?" Paul wanted to know.

"Personal communication devices, reading materials, a favorite pillow if you have one. Everything you need should be inside. You'll have Wi-Fi."

"Have Public Relations tell the press," Director Thompkins ordered. "The last thing we want right now is any secrets."

"Do either of you want a priest beforehand?" The security chief's question revealed the uncertainty many in the group felt. Neither Paul nor Molly did.

• • •

Molly drove back to the temporary DSC Network offices in Titusville. Network employees there avoided eye contact with her. When she nearly ran into a coworker in the hallway, his face turned bright red as he stammered a nervous "excuse me" before hurrying out of her way. The office was eerily quiet as Molly packed away her laptop and gathered a few office supplies for her coming internment. She rolled her eyes and thought to herself that at least she wouldn't have to put up with these people for the next couple of weeks. She ignored the stacked-up messages. An assistant came into Molly's office, punched the lighted button on her desk phone and ordered, "Take this."

On the phone, she heard DSC's News Director George Baker again. "Molly, have you seen the ratings? We got a 69% market share. Your interview with Bill Samuel was the third most watched TV airing ever. Only the opening of the spacecraft and your first interview with the aliens were watched by more people. The YouTube video of you and Bill has had over a billion viewings and is still climbing."

"You could have warned me."

"Molly, we didn't know Bill would have the agenda stacked like that. And there are millions of people who love the aliens and love you for sticking up for them. That slap you delivered will be one of the all-time greatest moments of TV."

"I'm just a reporter digging for and defending the truth."

"Yeah, sure. Listen, we'd like you to do a report from inside the bubble, or whatever it is. You can carry in a camera and have the male guinea pig film you with the aliens."

Ah, Molly realized, *he's heard about the human trial.* "We would play it straight, right? We look for and report facts," she responded.

"Of course. Oh, and if you get this done, DSC will double your salary plus a million-dollar bonus."

"Thanks. I'll think about it."

• • •

Paul arrived at the medical area at 8:00 a.m. carrying a duffel bag and the pillow from his office. Dr. Peters waited to give him a thorough physical exam and take blood and urine samples. "We'll use these as a health baseline," she explained.

After Dr. Peters' exam, Paul saw Molly being led in by a NASA Public Relations representative. She had insisted on pulling her own roll bag. He noticed that she had scrubbed off any vestige of makeup and wore her hair in a shaggy ponytail. He liked this Molly better than the striking Hollywood version. "I see you're going with the natural look," he attempted a tease.

"That makeover was the network's idea. The hell with them."

"Good for you," said Dr. Peters. "Please step in here for your physical." She directed Molly to an inner examination room.

Outside the quarantine quarters, Paul watched the NASA communications specialists checking out the camera to document their entry. He knew it would be streamed live over NASA's website and TV channel.

Director Thompkins arrived a little early to observe. "I trust this will be non-dramatic. No scripted words for posterity, right?"

"What do you mean?"

"Actually, this is a historical moment. The first flesh-to-flesh meeting of humans with an extraterrestrial species. The press will expect a profound sound bite. But I think we've had enough theatrics lately."

Paul nodded in agreement. "The thought never occurred to me."

"What about Molly?"

Paul remembered her toned-down appearance. "I think she's had enough of publicity. I wouldn't worry about her today."

"Good."

"Are you ready?" Dr. Peters arrived followed by Molly.

The insertion procedure was surprisingly anticlimactic after all the preparations. Once past two air locks, Paul and Molly found themselves inside.

Fitzgerald and Isabella waited for them at the entrance. The internal camera recorded Paul stepping forward and extending his hand to Fitzgerald. Initially Fitzgerald reached out and gently clasped Paul's hand. When he felt Paul squeezing, he returned appropriate pressure. "They press hands firmly," he said to Isabella. The media recorded those words for posterity.

Isabella mimicked an expression she had picked up on TV. "Welcome to our home."

After the two pairs had exchanged handshakes, the NASA communications specialist spoke through the intercom. "Let's have a group picture."

Paul and Molly took places on either side of Fitzgerald and Isabella. Both stood nearly a head taller than the extraterrestrials. Following an impulse, Paul put his arm around Fitzgerald's shoulders. Seeing his example, Molly did the same to Isabella. "Smile for the camera," Paul whispered.

Nearly every newspaper in the world would feature that picture on their front page the following morning.

Director Thompkins nodded in satisfaction. "Okay, everybody. Let's give them time to get acquainted. Cut off the cameras. Dr. Peters and her assistants will monitor them."

Chapter 8

• • •

Three sleeping compartments opened from the general room. "Fitzgerald and I sleep in here," Isabella indicated the right compartment. "Would you like this one?" She pointed to the center.

An awkward silence followed. "We aren't a mated team," Paul explained using terminology he had picked up from their Hollywood-style interview.

"Does that mean you would not sleep in the same compartment?"

"I think that we would prefer individual compartments."

"This is so confusing to us," Isabella complained. "First asking about being mated to each other is impolite. Then an interviewer asks us on camera if we had sex in space." She looked accusingly toward Fitzgerald. "You're the expert on humans."

"Don't ask me," he said. "On TV, an attractive man and woman always sleep in the same bed whether they are mated or not."

"You aren't alone in your confusion, Isabella. Relationships between men and women are even more confusing to humans," Molly remarked.

Paul and Molly moved into different compartments while their hosts watched the news reports of their meeting. Returning to the common room, Paul saw the photo of them all together on the TV screen. "You both have nice smiles."

"We practiced on each other during the long space flight. I thought I'd never get it right," Fitzgerald responded.

"This is what he looked like." Isabella made a grimace. "I had trouble learning to laugh."

Molly joined them. "Don't you laugh naturally?"

"Yes, but it sounds like an Earth monkey screaming." Fitzgerald made a loud monkey noise. "In the first tapes we reviewed from Earth, we thought the monkeys laughed and the humans coughed."

Paul and Molly laughed, trying not to sound like coughing.

"How do you like the quarantine quarters?" Molly asked.

"Oh, it is nice," said Fitzgerald. "We have everything we need right now. But the best part is the water toilet! It is so funny!"

"Really?" Molly said, surprised. *What could possibly be funny about the toilet?* She and Paul followed Fitzgerald and Isabella as they led them down a short hall to the small bathroom. Fitzgerald opened the toilet lid and dramatically pressed down the handle to flush. They watched Molly's face with expectation. She smiled politely as the toilet performed its unremarkable task.

"Did you see?" asked Fitzgerald. He pressed the handle

again. "Watch the water! There it goes in a circle!" He then laughed. "Why does it do that?"

Isabella answered him, "This happens because of angular momentum and the Earth's rotation. Humans call it 'Coriolis force.' The water is still funny, though."

Molly raised her eyebrows at Paul. He shrugged. "So you don't have toilets on Benevolent?" she asked.

"Not like this!" Isabella said.

"Can I show you around?" Fitzgerald offered. While Isabella remained in the bathroom admiring the wonders of Earth plumbing, Fitzgerald led Molly and Paul on a quick tour of the remainder of the quarantine quarters. There wasn't much to see. The quarters had been equipped with a kitchen area containing a functional dining table with four chairs, a few pots and pans, silverware, a small range, microwave, and a refrigerator. The general room had some upholstered furniture, a TV, games table, and a desk.

Paul pointed at the TV. "So you mentioned that you like *The Beverly Hillbillies*. What other TV shows or movies did you watch to prepare for coming to Earth?"

"Oh, lots," said Fitzgerald. "Human TV and movies are very entertaining. We especially searched for movies about aliens because we wanted to prepare ourselves for how humans might react to us. Unfortunately, most movie aliens are cruel and aggressive."

"E.T. was nice," Molly countered. Fitzgerald nodded in agreement. Molly continued, "I think as the world gets to know you, people won't be afraid. You two seem so...normal... compared to our movie aliens."

"Yes! Exactly. We don't want humans to be afraid of us. We are just normal. Very normal."

Just then, Molly and Fitzgerald heard Isabella cackling from down the hall. "Fitzgerald, come watch!" she called. They poked their heads into the bathroom again to see Isabella adding drops of food coloring to the toilet bowl. The colors swirled together in an artistic display before disappearing down the pipes.

"Wow!" said Fitzgerald. "Now let me try something," he said to Isabella. Leaving the toilet paper on the roll, he pulled the end of the paper and draped it into the water. When he flushed, the pull of the water began unraveling the toilet paper. Fitzgerald and Isabella howled with monkey-like laughter.

Paul snuck up behind Molly. "I'm not sure if 'normal' is the exact word I would have used for them," he said quietly.

When they all returned to the general room, Paul opened a box he had brought in his duffel bag. "Hey, I've got a present for you. This is a laptop computer. It can connect to the internet. Do you know what the internet is?"

"Yes, that's where all the small computers connect into a common source," Isabella answered. "Our technical experts on Benevolent used it to know the human genetic structure. Response times were slow due to the distance, but a series of computerized instructions sped up the process."

"Aren't those protected files?"

"Your primitive binary computers are not so hard for our experts to...do you say 'hack'? Humans are more protective of their Social Security and credit card numbers."

Fitzgerald added, "Finding your DNA genome is how our

creators made us look like humans."

"Where did you get the inner eyelids?" Paul asked.

"Part of our DNA was taken from a desert-dwelling creature. Our creators thought it might be useful if Earth's atmosphere had irritants to us."

Isabella tapped at the laptop keyboard with one finger. "Let me teach you to type," Molly offered. After a couple of lessons and a half hour of practice, Isabella could do basic typing. She taught Fitzgerald, who took a bit longer but learned quickly himself.

Lunch arrived. The extraterrestrials enjoyed the food while demonstrating woeful table manners. As Fitzgerald raised his soup bowl to drink, he noticed the humans lagging. "Don't you like the food?"

"We eat differently," Paul answered.

Molly spoke more directly, "If you're going to be ambassadors, you'll need to learn human manners. This is how we eat soup." She demonstrated with her spoon.

"We saw somebody on the television drinking from a bowl," said Isabella.

"TV often shows people behaving poorly. Also, different places in the world eat differently and behave differently. When you aren't sure what to do, watch the most important person present. And never play with toilets in public."

After lunch, they all watched the news. The media had moved on from the morning's insertion clip to more dramatic events. Bill Samuel appealed to all using God, country, and family values. "Don't let our way of life, the very lives of our children, be destroyed." A cable news service showed Bill's followers staging a sit-down demonstration blocking the gates to NASA. Some fought with police. Local police had brought in tear gas trying to disperse the mob.

"People are already afraid of us," Fitzgerald lamented.

Other radical broadcasters struggling for media market share took even more extreme positions. At a minimum, they urged permanent sequestration of Fitzgerald and Isabella. One suggested execution followed by incineration of their bodies for the safety of all. Another urged, "Let them go back where they came from."

Fitzgerald and Isabella slumped in despondency. "We can't go back," whispered Fitzgerald to no one.

Paul asked, "Why can't you go back?"

Isabella answered, "The apparatus needed to break through time and space and dimensions with just a small amount of matter is huge. By your measurements ten miles across to send our spacecraft even in pieces. And tremendous amounts of energy are required. Benevolents and other species explore the universe by sending out probes. The probes can transport back electromagnetic signals which have no mass. But the probes aren't large enough or powerful enough to send back more than a piece of sand."

"Even if we could return," added Fitzgerald, "they created us for this mission. We would not return until the mission had been completed."

"What is your mission?"

"To save mankind."

Despite gentle prodding by Paul, Fitzgerald would reveal no more.

"Do you know what we need?" All their heads turned to Molly. "We need a publicity campaign."

"What do you mean?" asked Isabella.

Molly pointed at the TV where angry and frightened people denounced all of them with apocalyptic terms. Then she tuned in to the NASA feed which featured uninteresting explanations of trajectories and lab reports. "What we need to do is get our message out in a more convincing manner."

"We gave interviews," said Fitzgerald.

"That was a good start, but not enough. You need a Facebook account. And Twitter. And Instagram. And a blog. And a website. And then more interviews."

Molly took the computer Paul had given them and started typing. "Paul, use your cell phone to take a couple of head shots of Fitzgerald and Isabella."

"Don't forget to smile," he said taking the pictures. In fifteen minutes, they all admired the new Facebook page.

"How will people find this on the huge internet?" Isabella wondered.

"Just you watch. Paul, use your own computer to send out a link to Fitzgerald and Isabella's Facebook page to everybody on your e-mail list. I'll do the same."

A few minutes later, people started to friend them. "Answer those who write to you, Isabella," Molly urged her. Each response Isabella made became a trophy for somebody. When the recipients forwarded their trophies, the friends began to multiply.

"This is wonderful, Molly!" said Isabella.

"You forget I'm a reporter and majored in communications

in college. I know how to grab people's attention. And you haven't seen anything yet." To Fitzgerald Molly said, "Do you have anything to add to the Facebook page? Something people would like to see?"

He went into the compartment he shared with Isabella. In a minute, he returned with a tablet-sized device. After he entered a few instructions, photos of alien lands, planets, and strange creatures started to scroll.

Paul looked with amazement. "Why haven't you shown this before?"

"We were saving this until we could use it to the best effect."

"I think we need it now. Can you download these to a computer?"

"Isabella can move them to your human computer."

Fitzgerald traded with Isabella for the laptop and started chatting online with new friends. Some started to question whether he was really Fitzgerald. "What pose would you like me to give you?" he responded.

"Put your thumbs in your ears and stick out your tongue," one doubter demanded.

Paul took the picture using his cellphone. In less than one minute, the picture of Fitzgerald so posed had been posted. The doubter wrote back for all to see, "Wow! Wow! Wow!"

Isabella entered some instructions to the device and then downloaded over 500 photos to the laptop through Wi-Fi. "Your blog is ready," announced Molly, who had been working on her own computer. "Pick out just one picture."

"Why not all of them?"

"We want people to look at your site every day to see a new picture," Molly explained.

Isabella selected a photo of her and Fitzgerald clinging to a large lizard-like creature.

"What's that thing?" Paul asked.

"That's our mother." Seeing Paul's shock, Isabella explained, "Not our mother the way you understand. This animal is called a snark. The geneticists took the genes for our inner eyelids from her. The species isn't sentient."

In a few seconds, Molly had uploaded the picture to their blog. Fitzgerald typed in a friendly greeting and a description of the snark without any mention of common genes or heritage.

Paul was getting into the spirit of a media campaign himself. "Now watch this." He put the blog site address onto the Facebook page. In an instant, the blog started receiving hits. "Next I'll create a separate web site for you."

The foursome spent all afternoon setting up other social media accounts and linking them together. Heavy traffic slowed some sites down and crashed a couple of others. These caused the news media to report the problem, which alerted more people to the phenomena. The crowning piece was when Paul opened the "Planet Benevolent" website with the photo of Fitzgerald and Isabella and the snark. In addition, Paul had added all of NASA's evidence supporting Fitzgerald and Isabella's extraterrestrial claims and the negative lab results for harmful microbes on the website in easy-to-follow laymen's terms.

By suppertime Fitzgerald and Isabella had over four million followers on combined social media doubling every few hours.

After supper, the foursome brainstormed more publicity ideas. "You need to do more interviews," Paul suggested. "Dr. Peters is convinced that you're healthy now. She'll approve as many as you have energy to do. Molly and I can give interviews as well."

Molly frowned. "I conduct interviews, not give them."

"Of course. But you and I are in a unique position to reassure the public about safety."

"That's true. All I ask is that if Bill Samuel requests an interview, I'll handle that one."

• • •

All the positive goodwill excited Fitzgerald. "Do you think we'll get an invitation to the UN now?"

"Fitzgerald is anxious to start his mission as ambassador," Isabella explained.

Neither Paul nor Molly could predict the UN's response. After chatting a bit more with new friends online, Fitzgerald and Isabella departed to rest together in their compartment, leaving Paul with Molly. He could not help but mentally contrast Molly's verve and vitality to the frailty of his beloved and deceased Beth. He felt awkward around her. "You did a good thing today," he managed. "I couldn't have done what you did."

Molly likewise felt uneasy. "I couldn't have interpreted and explained the evidence the way you did. You're not bad for a science geek." *Why did I call him a geek?* she thought. "I didn't mean that you're..." she trailed off.

"Yes, you did. And you're right. My life is pretty much all about science."

"My life is all about digging up dirt on creeps. I guess that's pretty different."

"Not so much," Paul returned.

"How do you mean?"

"We're both about finding the truth."

The sincerity made Molly uncomfortable. She headed toward her compartment. "See you tomorrow."

"Good night."

Chapter 9

•••

The following days passed quickly. All the "internees," as they had started to call themselves, enjoyed being busy. The goodwill created by their media blitz had swept away much of the public's fear of Fitzgerald and Isabella. Opinion polls indicated that 70% of Americans believed them and looked forward to their release from the quarantine quarters. Even detractors like Bill Samuel muted their criticism when they saw their ratings falling. The No Release demonstrators in front of NASA diminished in numbers and intensity.

Each day Isabella, aided by Molly, selected another picture to be posted on the blog. She proudly proposed a picture of herself and Fitzgerald next to several bumblebee-like creatures. That is, if bumblebees grew as big as ponies and had dexterous appendages. "These are some of our tutors," she said. "They love us like human parents love their children."

"This is the species who created you?" Molly asked.

"Yes, they are the only sentient species on Benevolent."

"I'd save the pictures of your tutors or other Benevolents until later," Molly advised.

"Why?"

"Let the suspense build. Use them as a finale."

● ● ●

At night after giving interviews during the day, the internees entertained themselves playing games. Fitzgerald and Isabella knew chess and had played each other frequently during their long space flight. Neither Paul nor Molly could compete with their skills. But the extraterrestrials preferred games like Monopoly and Backgammon that included an element of chance. Occasionally they forgot to laugh properly and shrieked like monkeys in response to an unlikely turn of fortune.

Isabella used these times of relaxation to subtly investigate Paul and Molly's lives. During a game of Monopoly Isabella threw the dice and moved her piece. "Are your biological parents alive?"

Paul picked up the dice. "My parents retired and moved to Arizona. My father had been a mathematics professor at a local college in Oregon. They're now over seventy years old and have enjoyed good health."

"Do you have siblings?"

Paul rolled the dice. "Only one older brother. He's in the navy based in Okinawa."

"How about you, Molly?" Fitzgerald asked.

"My mother died of cancer two years ago. No brothers or sisters."

"How about your father?"

"He left my mother and me when I was six. Said that he could make more kids if he wanted them. We never saw him again. Mom had more rotten luck with men after him."

"Is that why you don't trust males?" Isabella asked.

"What makes you think I don't trust men?" Molly responded more from curiosity than irritation.

"The night of your distress on television you only wanted to talk with me, not Paul or Fitzgerald."

Molly held the dice without saying anything else. Isabella looked at Fitzgerald. "Was that an inappropriate question in human culture?"

Molly answered for him, "Yes, that would be inappropriate, except for between you and me. You are my friend. So, I don't mind. Maybe my mother's experience does prevent me from trusting men."

Molly rolled the dice and moved, followed by Fitzgerald. While Paul moved, Isabella asked, "Is it wrong to ask if you are mated to somebody, but not to each other?"

"No, that's a safe question," said Molly. "I've never been married."

They waited on Paul. "I was married once. Her name was Beth. She died of Cystic Fibrosis." Seeing Fitzgerald and Isabella's incomprehension, he added, "That's a genetically inherited disease, and it's incurable. I knew before we got married."

Fitzgerald spoke without thinking, "Why did you take a mate you knew would die?" Then he added, "I apologize. You don't have to answer that."

Everybody forgot the game as Paul cleared his throat. "Beth and I grew up on the same street. She was my best childhood friend and my teenage sweetheart. Getting married meant so much to her. When she knew she was dying, she asked me to marry her. So I did. We had six months as man and wife, though she was sick most of the time. She was four months pregnant when she died. Her last words were, "I'll have a baby ready for you in heaven.""

The extraterrestrials sat still in amazement. "I didn't know humans could act that way," said Fitzgerald.

Molly looked away to hide her teary eyes. "Not many humans can."

• • •

After a week of social media and interviews, Fitzgerald and Isabella had nearly a billion followers on their daily blog and other social media. Photography experts analyzed the photographs. "These are real, or they're magic," reported one. The extraterrestrials' approval rating soared to 80%.

Molly wasn't satisfied. "Either public support goes up or sinks down. Let's keep going up."

"What did you have in mind?" Paul asked.

"My network wanted a report from within the quarantine quarters. I'll bet we could make them pay." Molly explained her idea.

"What would we do with the money?" asked Fitzgerald.

"What would you like?" The foursome discussed the possibilities until Fitzgerald and Isabella chose their favorite.

Molly then used her cell phone to call her DSC Network boss, George Baker. "George, do you remember that exclusive you wanted from inside the bubble? How about a two-hour special?"

"Sure, when do you want to air?"

"Wait a minute. Fitzgerald and Isabella want compensation for this."

"What?"

"You heard me."

"Listen, Molly, the aliens have been doing interviews for everybody for free."

"Yeah, but this is an exclusive special. And get this, Fitzgerald and Isabella will show the first photos of the Benevolents, the alien species who created them. They would show ten pictures and talk about them."

"Okay, how much do they want?"

"A hundred and twenty million dollars. One hundred million would go into a foundation to help at-risk kids get a good education. Fitzgerald and Isabella really believe in that. Also, Fitzgerald insists that they compensate organizations who help them. Otherwise they might be perceived as beholden to special interests. Twenty million would go to NASA for their unbudgeted expenses caring for Fitzgerald and Isabella."

"Whoa, Molly, get real."

"Maybe you're right. They should bid this. Thirty-second Super Bowl ads go for five million. This is bigger than any football game. And production costs will be zilch. Somebody will want an exclusive. Do you happen to have the phone numbers of the other networks handy?"

"How about fifty million?"

Molly then used a different angle. "George, think about the public relations. DSC giving money to educate kids? DSC supporting NASA? The publicity alone would be worth the mils."

"Prime time? Three commercial breaks? You and the other guinea pig participate?"

Molly thought, *I've nearly got him now.* "Okay. But ninety million for education plus fifteen to NASA."

"Three days from now?"

"You drive a hard bargain, George."

● ● ●

Three days later, all had been readied and rehearsed for the TV special. Molly stood before her crew of three. "No makeup for anybody, right?" Since only she had ever used makeup, they all laughed.

At Paul's request, NASA's Director Thompkins took one minute welcoming the viewers and thanking DSC Network and Fitzgerald and Isabella on behalf of NASA. Paul manned the lights and camera provided by DSC.

TV ratings vied with the earlier broadcasts to set a record. The first segment featured Molly in an upholstered chair interviewing Fitzgerald and Isabella, who sat on the couch at a right angle to her. Paul had set up the camera to capture the scene at forty-five degrees. "This is different," Molly started. "We looked at each other through a monitor during our first interview."

"We are so happy to have shared our quarters with you for nearly two weeks, Molly," Fitzgerald answered.

"The two of you have become quite a sensation on social media. Over a billion followers worldwide."

"We only wish that we could meet all of our friends in person."

"I believe that funds generated by this broadcast are reimbursing NASA for the expenses you incurred while here at Kennedy Space Center."

"That's right, Molly. And NASA has agreed to store and protect our vehicle indefinitely."

"Now, Isabella, this broadcast has also initiated a program for educating at-risk children named the Benevolent Foundation. Can you tell us about that?"

"Yes, Molly. There is no loss on Earth greater than the loss of human potential. Therefore, Fitzgerald and I would like to do what we can to minimize those losses. Earth is our home now. We hope to be good human citizens."

Molly looked directly at the camera and gave a phone number and website where viewers could contribute to the foundation. DSC overlaid the contact information onto the picture along with the foundation's new logo. She looked at Fitzgerald and Isabella again. "You've been in quarantine for nearly five weeks now. I understand that the test results show that you carry no microbes that could be dangerous to our environment."

Fitzgerald answered, "That is correct. Benevolent scientists removed anything from us that could have been harmful to life on Earth. But the quarantine period was a wise precaution by NASA. We appreciate you and Paul joining us, to make absolutely certain."

"And you have suffered no ill effects from Earth's environment or foods either."

Isabella answered, "We were engineered to digest almost anything organic and to have a strong immune system. Except that I think we are gaining weight on Earth's delicious food."

"What is your favorite food?"

"Chocolate. Fitzgerald likes salmon."

"Could you show us around your quarters?"

Paul picked up the camera and followed them as they toured the limited space. Isabella even showed all the sleeping quarters. Following the tour, the network went to a commercial break. Surprisingly most of the sponsors expressed support for Fitzgerald and Isabella as part of their product or public relations pitch. Several sponsors announced participation in the Benevolent Foundation through a portion of product sales.

After the commercial break, the special featured Paul and Isabella explaining to Molly all the evidence to support the extraterrestrial claims. The DSC program director inserted the appropriate charts Paul had prepared. Fitzgerald ran the camera.

When they deliberately got overly technical near the end, Molly interrupted them. "Hold it! That's getting over my head. What I remember is the inner eyelids." The program director inserted the segment showing Molly's initial recoil. "Isabella, could you?" Isabella reprised her ability. "Can you now explain how you got that ability?" Isabella explained about the gene insert and showed a picture of the snark.

Another commercial break came. When the picture returned, Molly, along with Fitzgerald and Isabella, sat back at the chair and couch. "Now," Molly began, "our guests will take calls from viewers." A phone number blinked at the bottom of the screen. With half a billion viewers, not many got through in the next twenty-five minutes. Most began with, "I can't believe I got through." Fitzgerald and Isabella chatted with all who connected.

The last segment began with the chair and couch view of the internees again. "I believe you have some more photos for us," Molly said. "Can you tell us about them?" Ten previously unshown pictures followed, most including at least one Benevolent being. Fitzgerald and Isabella described and explained each photo and told stories related to the subjects. They had practiced their timing to coincide the finish with the end of the special.

Molly started to wrap up. "Thank you both. That concludes our—"

The monitor view suddenly split in two. DSC showed President Truman Johnson from the Oval Office opposite of the extraterrestrials. "Fitzgerald and Isabella," the president said, "I understand you'll be ready to exit NASA's facilities in two days."

"Yes, sir," Fitzgerald answered for them both.

"I'll be at Kennedy Space Center to welcome you to the United States."

"Thank you, Mr. President."

Chapter 10

•••

"I can't believe he's coming here," said Dr. Peters. "He has opposed every NASA program." She and Director Thompkins watched the TV coverage of the presidential motorcade making its way from the shuttle runway to NASA's Florida headquarters. Separate cars conveyed other officials including Harry's boss, the NASA administrator.

"And why wouldn't he come?" responded Harry. "You don't become a president without some sense of theatrics. Plus, another election is always coming. Fitzgerald and Isabella's approval ratings are at 95% this morning. You couldn't get that many Americans to approve of the Pledge of Allegiance."

"Just don't forget that they're my patients until I release them."

"What time do you think they'll actually exit the decontamination quarters?"

"I told Public Relations they would come out about eleven. All the lab tests are negative for any dangerous microbes for both themselves and Paul and Molly. I'll go inside the decontamination quarters early and give all of them a last physical exam."

Harry turned in surprise. "You'll go inside without a hazmat suit?"

"Why not? I'll be exposed to them shortly after anyway. Do you want to keep the president waiting while I examine them?"

"No, of course not. I'll be meeting the motorcade and giving a tour of Kennedy Space Center's facilities. I'll have President Johnson in front of the camera at the exit at eleven."

Ginger chided her boss, "I guess you don't become a NASA director without a sense of theatrics."

"Don't get me started."

● ● ●

"May I come in?" Dr. Peters asked through the intercom.

The extraterrestrials and their guests stood at the window. Fitzgerald spoke for all of them, "Certainly."

The doctor passed through the airlocks and stood among them. After handshakes, she explained, "I need to give you all a last physical exam. The president will be here in about an hour to meet you."

The exams showed nothing new. NASA's Public Relations director brought a White House protocol manager to the window. They came to the intercom where the protocol manager, acting as a stage director, gave Fitzgerald and Isabella instructions for the historic meeting. "Let the president initiate all the movements. He'll be the first one to shake your hands as you exit. Then you'll pose with Fitzgerald and the president holding a handshake with Isabella standing alongside. Don't forget to smile for the cameras. He will then introduce Fitzgerald and Isabella to some others. Only shake the hands of those the president introduces. Ms. Powell and Dr. Sanders, you can come out while the president is introducing some members of his administration to Fitzgerald and Isabella."

"Welcome to showbiz," Molly whispered to all inside. Isabella wanted to ask what showbiz meant, but there wasn't time.

"Did you vote for this guy?" Paul whispered back to Molly.

"No way in hell."

"Me neither."

They all watched as a flood of people entered the room adjacent to the quarantine quarters. Secret Service men took up strategic positions. Lights came on as the president waited by the exit. The door lock opened. Paul saw Director Thompkins tilt his head ever so slightly toward the exit. Paul nudged Fitzgerald and Isabella gently from behind. They walked through for the first time into uncontrolled Earth air. "Welcome to the United States of America," said President Johnson and shook Isabella's hand first. Then he held the handshake with Fitzgerald and pulled him into an optimal camera angle.

Next the president introduced Fitzgerald and Isabella to key members of his administration starting with the secretary of state and working down the hierarchy to Director Thompkins. Paul and Molly emerged and stood quietly. The president turned to them. "And these are our brave American heroes." He shook their hands and posed for a photo, this time holding the handshake with more-famous Molly.

The protocol manager guided the president along with Fitzgerald and Isabella and pre-selected officials to a private meeting room.

There Fitzgerald and Isabella chatted with the president and other high-ranking administration officials while deferring probing questions. Soon NASA coordinators summoned them all to an executive dining room where lunch had been provided. At one end of the room a long table held various dishes buffet style. A beautiful centerpiece of flowers decorated the table. "Our custom is for guests to go first," said President Johnson to Fitzgerald and Isabella. Seeing their confusion, he added, "You select the foods you want and bring them on your plate back to your place next to me at the table."

Never had Fitzgerald and Isabella seen such a variety of delicious-looking edibles. They followed instructions, returned to the table, and waited to see how to proceed. The president served himself and returned to sit by them. America's secretary of state, Don Cummins, sat on the other side. Fitzgerald and Isabella waited to watch the most important person as Molly had advised them. They began to eat when the president did.

"This smelled so good that I had to try it," remarked Fitzgerald, biting the head off a rose. "I like it much better than the plain lettuce Dr. Peters gave us."

Isabella passed him a lily. "Try this. But the stem isn't so nice. Like the shell of the shrimps we had."

President Johnson and Secretary Cummins made eye contact across the extraterrestrials. *Should I tell them?* Secretary Cummins' eyes asked.

The president shrugged ever so slightly. Then he gave an almost imperceptive shake of his head. "We are glad you're enjoying lunch," he said to Fitzgerald and Isabella.

"Do you have mated ones?" Isabella asked the question Molly had described as safe.

President Johnson had been accused of various sexual improprieties, before and during his time in office. His marital difficulties real and imagined always served as favorite tabloid fodder. He hesitated before answering, "My wife is taking care of our children in St. Louis." Secretary Cummins merely nodded.

Fitzgerald finished the last bite of food on his plate and leaned back in his chair. "That was delicious," he said. "But I think now we all need to try skinny dipping."

Heads around the table whipped up in surprise. The president glanced over at Secretary Cummins, wondering if he had heard Fitzgerald correctly. The stunned expression on Secretary Cummins' face told him he had.

"I'm sorry... could you repeat that?" President Johnson asked.

Fitzgerald smiled politely, unaware of the stir his comment had caused. "Skinny dipping! I hear that many humans do it, even though it doesn't sound like much fun. Maybe it would be easier to do with a group like this for support."

The table had fallen silent as everyone wondered how to respond appropriately to the rather undignified topic. Isabella noticed the sudden atmosphere of discomfort. "Fitzgerald," she said, "I don't know this phrase, 'skinny dipping.' What does it mean?"

Fitzgerald brightened, eager to show that he knew about human culture. "Many humans are quite health conscious," he began. "To become skinny is the opposite of being overweight.

So to go skinny dipping means for your weight to dip."

"Oh!" Isabella said. "I can see how that might not be much fun with so many wonderful foods available."

"Another term is used more commonly," Secretary Cummins interrupted. "We usually call losing weight 'dieting.'"

Fitzgerald nodded. "Yes, there are often many English terms that describe the same thing. It's very confusing, but I'm learning more and more every day."

Isabella beamed at him proudly.

Secretary Cummins coughed discreetly to cover up a laugh that was trying to escape. "Actually, skinny dipping is… well… it doesn't have anything to do with dieting," he explained. "It means going swimming without any clothes on."

Fitzgerald and Isabella's eyes widened. Then Fitzgerald laughed. "Well, that does sound like more fun than dieting!"

Harry Thompkins, seated at a secondary table, observed the exchanges. He smiled to himself in amusement. *Lord help me, but this job does have some perks.* Then he realized, *Fitzgerald and Isabella are going to need someone trustworthy to help them learn human ways and function among important people.*

● ● ●

Following the luncheon, the protocol manager led them all to a NASA conference room for a press conference. Two podiums stood side by side in front of the NASA emblem. President Johnson stood behind one and motioned for Fitzgerald to take the other. The protocol manager counted down seconds on his fingers for the president and the program director: five, four, three, two, one. He pointed to the president. At that signal, the president looked into the camera and began, "This is a historic day for mankind. We have contacted another intelligent species besides our own. On behalf of the United States of America and the entire world, I welcome Fitzgerald and Isabella...Benevolent." He paused and nodded to Fitzgerald, who smiled in return.

The president resumed speaking. "Along with Secretary Cummins, I am pleased to announce that the United States is granting full diplomatic status to the ambassadors from the planet called Benevolent." Applause erupted from the reporters and NASA personnel present. The president garnered the applause with his palms held outward and a self-effacing expression. "Would the ambassador from Benevolent like to comment?"

Fitzgerald had been created and trained for this purpose. With an equanimity that surprised everyone who had observed him eating roses and doing eye tricks, he responded, "Isabella and I would like to thank all at NASA who have taken care of us. Your television staff members have allowed us to greet people from every part of the world. And for our many friends established by computer connections we feel affection and love. We wish that we could meet every one of you personally."

Applause interrupted him for a few seconds, to which Fitzgerald nodded in acknowledgment. "As ambassadors, we request the privilege of speaking to your United Nations General Assembly. We have an important offer to extend to mankind."

•••

Paul watched the press conference from his apartment in Titusville. *We have contacted?* thought Paul. *President Johnson makes it sound like his administration is to thank for bringing Fitzgerald and Isabella.* After the presidential delegation had left him along with Molly and Dr. Peters, Paul had excused himself by citing personal responsibilities. In truth, he simply felt deflated. After two exciting weeks, he wasn't needed. The apartment offered a sanctuary to debrief himself. Paul turned off the TV and realized, *I'm going to miss living with the others.* A memory of Molly teaching Isabella how to floss her teeth popped up. *Molly,* he thought. *Why do I feel so strange around her? Is it attraction?* He had to admit that her boldness and athleticism carried a sensual quality. Fear? He doubted his ability to relate to women so unlike Beth.

Then he put those thoughts away. *What I need is a good long run.* He changed clothes and headed toward a local park. While running, his thoughts kept returning to Molly.

•••

Molly had hated to leave NASA's facilities. The end of her experience there seemed so abrupt. *Why didn't I propose lunch with Paul and Ginger?* But she had somehow felt relieved when Paul excused himself. Molly checked out of NASA and returned to her rental car. *DSC will pay for two full weeks of it being parked,* she thought. That thought didn't displease her. Having nowhere else to go, she drove toward the temporary DSC offices. *Why was Paul so eager to leave?* She realized that she felt a bit hurt. *Forget that guy. Entanglements only lead to trouble.* Still she wondered what it would be like to have someone love you enough to marry you knowing you were dying. *I'll probably never see him again anyway.*

•••

"Get Paul and Molly back in here!" Director Thompkins demanded of his secretary. "Who let them leave?" He slammed the door to his office and almost immediately opened it again. "And call the hotel where the president took Fitzgerald and Isabella. I want to talk to our guests."

Two hours later, Paul and Molly again sat in front of Director Thompkins' desk, only this time chagrined. Dr. Peters sat nearby in support of her boss. "What were you two thinking when you left?" Harry scolded. "Fitzgerald and Isabella still need you."

Molly objected, albeit meekly. "Remember that I don't work for you."

"I'm not talking about work. I'm talking about doing the right thing. Young lady, I have a headstrong daughter like you. Sometimes a person, even as talented as you, needs a kick in the butt. And you..." the director sat glowering at Paul. "You need two butt kicks."

Both Paul and Molly looked pensive. The director finished with, "I want the two of you to go to this hotel. I've talked to Fitzgerald and Isabella already. They're waiting in room 118 for you. Paul, consider yourself on indefinite assignment to host and coach them. Since DSC is giving NASA money on their behalf, I'll cover all your expenses while in Florida. You know how carefully our expenses are scrutinized by the naysayer lobby and how tight appropriations have been. Stretch the money." Harry then remembered one more thing. "Oh, Molly, I called your network. You're still being paid by DSC but on temporary assignment to NASA. So you *do* work for me, at least for a while."

After Paul and Molly left, Dr. Peters remained with Harry for a few minutes. "They left the Space Center to get away from each other, you know."

"They don't like each other?"

"No, that's not it."

● ● ●

Fitzgerald and Isabella opened the door together. Their faces revealed relief. "We are very happy you will be our guides," said Isabella. "Earth is a strange place to us."

"We're honored," Molly returned. "You're our friends."

"Has an invitation come from the UN yet?" asked Fitzgerald. He deflated a little when Paul shook his head.

Molly never had trouble with candor. "I don't think you're ready."

"But I've spent years in preparation and—"

She cut him off. "You'll be taken more seriously when you learn about human ways. Otherwise humans will laugh not at your jokes, but at you. You should be grateful for this delay."

Chapter 11

●●●

"Where are Fitzgerald and Isabella?" Paul asked when he and Molly met on a grocery aisle the next day.

"Didn't they follow you when we came in?"

"I thought they went with you. We'd better find them."

Their guests weren't hard to discover. An amused group of onlookers watched them sampling various fruits in the produce section. "This place is even better than the buffet we had with the president," said Isabella. "We couldn't find the plates, though."

Fitzgerald, his lips stained with blueberry filling, carried a partially eaten pie from the deli section. "Where are the forks?" he asked.

●●●

Freed from the confinement of their spacecraft and the quarantine quarters, Fitzgerald and Isabella became irrepressible in their desire to sample human culture. But whenever offered opportunities separately from each other, the extraterrestrials consistently declined. *They really don't want to be separated*, Molly concluded to herself. *I can't blame them. They have each other as their only familiar connection in a very confusing world.*

And so Paul and Molly together guided them and coached them on visits to a shopping mall, museums, NASA's Visitor Complex, an open-air concert, a swim in the ocean, a hike, a deep-sea fishing excursion, a college basketball game, full-screen movies, a church service, and the zoo. Paul and Molly found themselves having tremendous fun through Fitzgerald and Isabella's reaction to new experiences.

One human trait confused Isabella. "Why do humans carry their larva with them?" she asked Molly.

"What do you mean by larva?"

Isabella pointed to where a young mother cradled an infant. "The very young humans unable to eat or move on their own. They are the human form of larva, correct? Why are they not cared for by others when the parents leave home?"

"Raising children is usually personal for humans. And what you call 'larva,' we call 'babies.' Many mothers love their children so much that they don't want to be separated from them except for short intervals. But you should avoid using the term 'larva.' Most people would think it uncomplimentary."

Isabella still watched the mother and her baby. "Whatever you call the new ones, their mothers are very fortunate to have one to care for."

...

Director Thompkins invited them all to his home in Titusville for dinner. Harry's wife, Marilyn, no stranger to hosting important people, greeted them warmly. Three teenagers, normally not interested in their parents' guests, all waited to meet these celebrities. The youngest daughter overcame shyness to take Isabella to see her bedroom, decorated in pink and stuffed animals. Harry's son, the middle child, taught Fitzgerald about basketball and soon had him playing one-on-one in the driveway. Harry's first-born daughter sensed a kindred spirit in Molly and asked career advice. *This must be the headstrong one*, Molly figured. The girl confirmed that by confiding her frustrations at her father's limitations on her. *If you only knew the value of having an attentive father,* Molly thought. She did her best to explain Harry's love and motivations for his daughter.

While Marilyn bustled about in the kitchen, Paul and Harry drank beer and manned the grill. "Have you learned anything more from our guests?" Harry asked.

"A little. Isabella is the technical expert. She held command until they reached Earth. Then Fitzgerald took over to serve as ambassador. Evidently, there are other sentient species. But I think this operation to Earth is a first for the Benevolents. They somehow transported the vehicle and support systems in pieces near Earth's path. Isabella, with Fitzgerald's help, assembled the pieces and waited for Earth to come to them. Everything was apparently tricky and dangerous."

Harry flipped a burger. "Considering relativity, I can't even imagine the complexity. Have they explained more why they came?"

"Fitzgerald said 'To save mankind.'"

"What does that mean?" Paul only shrugged. Harry continued, "Well then, how did they find Earth?"

"Their equivalent of NASA sends out probes that can relay radio waves home. When they picked up our earliest radio signals, who knows how many light years away, they homed in on them and sent probes closer until they found us. They've listened for decades. Eventually, they felt the urgency to create Fitzgerald and Isabella to send here. Their entire planet got behind the project, which involved tremendous expense."

"How is Molly doing?"

"She's perfect for this. Molly has a zany side under her take-no-prisoners public personality. She makes everything we do fun. And she's a great teacher for Fitzgerald and Isabella."

"Uh huh. You act like you're loosening up a bit yourself."

Paul turned a little red. "Maybe I am."

After dinner on the way back to their hotel, Molly explained, "Human families can take many forms. But a male and female couple living together and raising children like the Thompkinses is the most common."

"Are the four of us a form of family?" Isabella asked.

"I suppose we are."

• • •

"Molly Powell! We went to Cornell together. Do you remember me?" The man's breath reeked of alcohol.

Molly paused on the sidewalk just outside the restaurant

where she and Paul had introduced the aliens to an authentic Italian dinner. The man addressing her was short and stocky with reddish hair and baggy clothes. He swayed slightly as he grinned lecherously at her. People often recognized her from her TV presence. Her job required politeness. She swallowed her revulsion and replied, "No, I'm sorry. I don't."

"Well, maybe we should have a drink together and get reacquainted?"

"I don't think so."

"What! Are you too good for regular folks now? Your old classmates?" The man grabbed one of her elbows and jerked. Molly tried to pull free and failed.

Unexpectedly, someone from behind Molly pressed a thumb deeply into the inner side of the wrist holding her. The inebriated man howled and let go. "Ow! What's the big idea?"

"Hey! Didn't we go through Army Ranger School together?" Paul stepped between the man and Molly, giving her a chance to back away. "Don't I remember you from hand-to-hand combat training?"

The man looked Paul up and down and decided Paul wasn't someone he wanted to provoke, especially since he had apparently received special combat training. The man stepped back. "No. No. I was never in the army."

"Sorry. My mistake. I thought you were an old army buddy." Paul turned away and hurried after Molly, who was leading Fitzgerald and Isabella to Paul's car.

Inside the car, Molly felt embarrassed and reacted with indignation toward her protector. "Why did you do that? I can take care of myself!"

Paul agreed with a bashful smile, "I'm sure you can. You could take care of all of us if you needed to. But it's better when we take care of each other. Didn't you tell Isabella that we're a family?"

The car remained silent as Paul drove. Fitzgerald's voice came from the back seat. "So you've had special training in fighting?"

"No, I haven't. My brother and I used to poke a thumb in each other's wrists to make the other release something we both wanted. I've never been in the army."

"Then you lied?"

"I'd call that a bluff to avoid trouble. That man was drunk and out of control."

"What would you have done if the man started to fight?"

"Once all of you were safe, I would have outrun him."

After another silence, Isabella volunteered, "Fitzgerald cannot lie, except maybe when trying a joke."

"Why not?" Molly asked.

"My credibility as a diplomat is dependent on truthfulness. If ever I am found lying, the humans will not trust me," Fitzgerald explained.

● ● ●

The next morning Paul and Molly took their human-behavior pupils to Disney World. People waiting nearby them in lines for entry and attractions readily recognized Fitzgerald and Isabella. The extraterrestrial couple joyfully chatted and posed for selfies with everyone. Several mothers asked Isabella to hold their babies for photos. Obvious to all, Isabella loved the babies and held them a little longer than necessary.

Unconsciously, Molly started watching Paul while Fitzgerald and Isabella entertained those around them. He stood quietly observing nearby. Occasionally, Paul politely helped Fitzgerald and Isabella to disengage from overeager admirers. *He's watching over them like a sheep dog watches a flock*, Molly realized. *Over all of us!* The thought made her uncomfortable. *Am I afraid he'll expect some sort of repayment? Or am I just embarrassed to have someone looking out for me? Why would I be?* Molly admitted to herself a wordless feeling of security. *Paul is a different sort of man. He has...?* She wasn't sure what Paul had.

Disney employees soon noticed groups forming around the extraterrestrial celebrities and summoned an official representative. "We have VIP passes for you," the likeable young man explained to Fitzgerald and Isabella. "You won't need to stand in any lines."

Molly had taught her pupils how to politely decline an invitation. "No, thank you very much for the offer," Fitzgerald answered.

"But you'll be able to do more, to see more, if you don't stand in lines."

"We wouldn't meet as many lovely people that way," Isabella explained.

The Disney representative appeared bewildered for a moment. "Then would you consent to stay at one of our Disney resort hotels as our guests?"

Fitzgerald looked at Paul, who nodded nearly imperceptibly. "Could our friends Paul and Molly stay as well?"

For the first time, the Disney representative noticed Molly. "You're that reporter, Molly Powell. Certainly, we would also offer a room to Ms. Powell and her companion."

"No, they'll need separate rooms," Isabella injected.

"That will be no problem. Could I suggest the Grand Floridian?" the representative offered. "Just go to the hotel on the monorail when you're ready. I'll have reserved three rooms under Ms. Powell's name."

After accepting their thanks, the Disney representative looked embarrassed. "There's just one more thing, if you don't mind..." he pulled out a cell phone, "...for my kids."

Many of the Magic Kingdom's rides had paired seats. Since Fitzgerald and Isabella always rode together, that forced Paul and Molly to sit together. On a miniature roller coaster, Paul could feel Molly's thigh pressed against his own as she anticipated the ride. *Is she leaning against me more than she needs to?* he wondered. Through the closeness, he could sense her vitality and energy. *You idiot. You're here at Disney World with a beautiful, unattached woman. Just enjoy the time.* Paul put his arm around Molly. *This is what you do on a ride with a girl. Not to do so would be rude*, he told himself. Within seconds, they were laughing together at the exhilaration of speed and turns. *Wow, this is fun!*

Next Fitzgerald and Isabella started eating their way around the World Showcase at Disney's Epcot. The internet filled with posts by guests who had taken pictures of them at various attractions. Attendance surged as guests hoped to meet the extraterrestrials. Fitzgerald and Isabella enjoyed greeting people even more than the Disney amusements.

• • •

After checking in at the front desk of the Grand Floridian, Molly led the group through the elegant lobby themed to feel like a 19th century Victorian beach resort. Fitzgerald and Isabella stopped to admire the chandeliers, Italian marble floors, and potted palm trees. When they came to the elevators, Fitzgerald and Isabella paused in confusion.

"What is this?"

"This will take us to our rooms," Molly replied.

The doors opened, and Molly stepped in followed by the others. Paul pressed the button for the fourth floor. The doors closed, and Fitzgerald and Isabella stared at each other wide-eyed as they listened to the low rumbling sound. When the doors opened again, they gasped.

"It's like magic!" Isabella whispered. "Not even the most advanced planets have invented teleportation."

Paul and Molly couldn't help but laugh. "You think we just teleported?" Paul asked.

Isabella glanced back and forth at them. "We started in one location... the doors closed... and when they opened, we are somewhere completely different."

"Sorry to disappoint you," Paul said as the group stepped out and began walking down the hall, "but elevators aren't nearly that exciting. Basically, a counter balance system with a steel cable attached to the top of a box pulls us up. But a lot of people reacted the same way when elevators were first invented—they thought it was magic. Actually, this reminds me of a joke I heard once."

"We love jokes!" said Fitzgerald.

"Okay. Well, a grandfather and his grandson went into a big department store and saw an elevator for the very first time. They watched an old woman walk in, and the doors closed. Moments later, they watched as the doors reopened and a beautiful young woman walked out. The old man looked down and said, 'Boy, go get your grandmother.'"

Fitzgerald and Isabella both giggled and even Molly smirked. "I wouldn't want my Isabella changed, though," said Fitzgerald.

Paul glanced at Molly after the romantic comment. He found her looking at him.

Molly quickly looked away. "Here's your room, you two," she said, opening the door for them and ushering them inside. "Have a good night. We'll see you in the morning."

"Can we ride the elevator again tomorrow?" Isabella asked.

"Yes, please!" Fitzgerald agreed.

"Sure," Molly said. "We'll ride the elevators as many times as you want." She gave a final wave and closed the door behind them. She turned to look at Paul, standing a few inches behind her in the hallway. "All the rides we went on today, and they're most excited about the elevator!"

• • •

After three wonderful nights at Disney World, the foursome departed. An urgent message waited at their hotel near Titusville. "Hello, Ambassador Benevolent, this is Secretary General Tibor Iscaderian from the United Nations. You are invited to speak to the General Assembly in New York next week."

Fitzgerald hung up the phone. His demeanor had changed. He looked at Paul and Molly with gratitude. "Our mission begins in earnest now. Thank you for your help. Will you also please accompany us to New York?"

"You try leaving us behind!" challenged Molly with a smile.

Ever the practical one, Isabella asked, "Doesn't Earth operate on a transaction basis? How will we pay our hotel and other bills in New York?"

Paul opened his laptop to start looking for airline flights. "I'm sure that somebody will sponsor you." Fitzgerald shook his head. "Do the other ambassadors have to pay their own expenses?"

"Yes. At least, their home countries pay for them," Paul admitted.

"Then we must also pay. We cannot have people think we are in debt to anyone."

Molly suggested, "I'll bet you could get a book contract. The publisher's advance could pay for your expenses as ambassadors." Paul nodded in agreement.

"What would we write?"

"You wouldn't need to write," Paul explained. "You would simply talk to a ghostwriter. Tell stories about your lives. Throw in some of your pictures. A best seller for certain. I think our best negotiator could arrange something for you." He looked at Molly.

Molly nodded as Paul had before. "I'm sure I can. But we'll have to keep good records. All income will be taxed."

"Taxed?"

"Welcome to Earth," Paul said.

"So all humans must pay taxes on their money?"

"That's right."

"What happens if they don't pay taxes?"

"Well, they could end up in jail."

Fitzgerald paused to think for a moment. "Hmm… and who pays for the jail?"

"Um…they're paid for by taxes," Paul replied.

"So if humans refuse to pay taxes, they can live off taxes instead?"

Chapter 12

• • •

"You have diplomatic immunity," Paul explained on the way to the airport a few days later. "They won't search your bags."

"What are they looking for?" Isabella wondered aloud.

"They're screening for drug smugglers or weapons that could be used to hijack the plane."

"We aren't a threat to steal the plane. Where could we take it?" Isabella persisted.

"Well, theoretically anywhere you wanted. And if you did, you couldn't be arrested afterward. That's also part of diplomatic immunity."

"What if we murdered someone?"

"They couldn't put you in jail. But they would deport you to your home country."

"To see them try to deport us would be interesting."

• • •

Plenty of pageantry greeted their arrival in New York. The mayor personally met Fitzgerald and Isabella at the airport. He basked in the media attention the extraterrestrials attracted. "Tomorrow you'll have a ticker-tape parade so that all of New York can welcome you. For today, let me show you around our magnificent city." He hustled his guests into a stretch limo.

Paul and Molly, as they expected, had been relegated to a follow-on vehicle. New Yorkers knew that the mayor would be conveying Fitzgerald and Isabella. Already crowds lined the street hoping for a glimpse of "the visitors from outer space." After the mayor's limo passed, some people stepped into the street hoping for a closer look. These pedestrians slowed the follow-on vehicle. Soon Paul and Molly's transport became hopelessly separated from the police-escorted motorcade. Taxis jockeyed in front of them.

"The mayor will entertain Fitzgerald and Isabella today. Let's hope our students are ready for some solo time handling human culture," Paul reasoned. "I guess you and I have the day off. Should we go to the hotel where we'll all stay?"

"I know the best pizza place in New York. A guy named Julio owns it," Molly answered. "How about lunch?"

"Sure." Paul looked at the traffic nearly locked down. "Maybe we could get out and walk." Molly opened her car door immediately. "Would you drop our bags at the hotel, please? If anybody asks, we'll be there later," he told the driver.

On the sidewalk, Molly acted a little giddy. She spun around. "I feel like we've just sent our teenagers off to their first dance."

"We should have taken pictures!" They both laughed.

Molly wanted to take the subway. Lunch hour crowds pushed into their car, crushing Paul and Molly together. They both pretended not to notice, but neither tried to step away when crowds thinned after a couple of stops. "This is our exit," she announced too soon for Paul's liking.

The proprietor of the storefront pizzeria recognized Molly from past visits. "Ah, Ms. Powell, a long time since you've visited us. And I've been seeing you on the TV. Could I..." he pulled out a camera and gestured toward the walls of his establishment.

Molly saw dozens of photos of the proprietor along with various celebrities. "Of course, Julio."

Paul lingered back. "No, I want you both," Julio insisted. "I recognize you as the NASA guy. Handsome fellow," he said to Molly. A waitress snapped the picture with Julio between Paul and Molly.

After the photo, Paul and Molly argued amicably about toppings. Never reaching an agreement, they eventually ordered two medium pizzas reflecting their individual tastes. Waiting for the pizzas, they talked about all the fun they had shared the previous weeks. They laughed at Fitzgerald and Isabella's sweet naivety and antics.

Paul then turned more serious. "We don't know how this UN visit will play out afterwards. Molly, I just want you to know that I haven't had so much fun in a long, long time."

"I may never have had so much fun," Molly confessed.

The pizzas arrived. They laughed when Paul burned his tongue and reached for the water. After a few minutes, Paul admitted that he had never tasted pizza as good as Julio's.

After lunch, Molly took Paul on a tour of the city. They visited all the famous sites, went to the top of the Empire State Building, and admired the Statue of Liberty from The Battery. In the early evening, Paul invited Molly to dinner. Molly suggested a fine French restaurant. Over dinner and wine, they talked about their childhoods, careers, and hopes for the future. Paul wasn't surprised when the bill came to well over $200.

A horse-drawn carriage idled in front of their restaurant hoping for customers. "Why don't we take a ride?" Paul asked and held out his hand to help Molly up.

The carriage carried them slowly under the myriad of city lights. Molly didn't object when Paul put his arm around her shoulders. And then Paul, overcome by the moment they shared, leaned over and kissed her lightly on the lips. To his surprise, she put her arms around his neck and kissed him passionately. More passionately than he had ever experienced. "About time," she whispered in his ear.

After the carriage ride, they walked hand-in-hand eleven blocks to the hotel where they expected to stay with Fitzgerald and Isabella. They collected their bags and checked into the rooms that had been reserved for them. The desk clerk reported that Fitzgerald and Isabella had gone to their room hours earlier. If it weren't for the bellboy, Paul would have kissed Molly again on the elevator ride up.

After they had tipped and dismissed the bellboy in the hall, Molly lingered by her opened door. "Would you like to come in?" she asked in her husky voice.

Her meaning was clear to Paul. A flood of emotions struck him: acceptance, desire, and then overwhelming memories of a love lost. "I… I can't."

"What do you mean? You're not capable?"

"No, I mean that I'm not ready. You see, Beth and I…" he couldn't find the words. "Beth gave me…" But his words didn't matter. Molly had closed the door, leaving him in the hall.

● ● ●

Isabella could tell that something had happened between Paul and Molly. During breakfast in the hotel restaurant, Paul gave Molly little compliments and overreacted positively to whatever she said. She, in turn, ignored Paul's compliments and acted polite and businesslike toward him. Human male/ female relationships had so far been inscrutable to Isabella. She guessed that she should not interfere.

Paul finally gave up attempting to thaw Molly and turned to business. "I got a message last night from an American genetic scientist. Dr. Ben Finkle won the Nobel prize in biology for his work associating certain gene sequences with genetic diseases or tendencies. He's the founder and president of Future Tech. That's a biogenetic laboratory in the Research Triangle of North Carolina."

Paul noticed Fitzgerald and Isabella paying intense attention. He placed the offer before them. "Dr. Finkle is a billionaire. He promised ten million dollars to the Benevolent foundation for a private meeting with you. That money could help a lot of kids—"

Fitzgerald uncharacteristically interrupted, "Yes, we will meet with him." Isabella nodded.

Hiding his surprise at such a quick response, Paul added

details. "Dr. Finkle came to New York with his protégé Dr. Laura Holdridge in his private jet just hoping to meet you. If you're willing, I'll have him come to the hotel this afternoon after the parade."

"That is acceptable." Fitzgerald's curtness surprised Paul further.

The mayor's envoy found them at the breakfast table. "There you are. The mayor is in the limo outside the hotel to take you to the parade."

Fitzgerald and Isabella hurried away. Paul turned toward Molly, but all he saw was her back as she walked away.

• • •

The parade started at 10:00 a.m. Police motorcycles with sirens led the way down Broadway. A high school marching band playing patriotic tunes followed the police. Spectators filled the air with tons of confetti.

Fitzgerald and Isabella waved and smiled from on top of a vehicle hastily converted from a Macy's Thanksgiving Day Parade float. The mayor, who aspired for a national office, rode with his wife in front of them. Loudspeakers on the float played the Star Trek theme music at top volume. Police squad cars ended the short procession followed by street sweepers.

Molly watched alone from the hotel window. She had recognized Paul's overtures of friendliness and regretted the necessity of rebuffing him. Her feelings of rejection and fear of hurt overrode all other emotions. *Mom trusted men. I can't make that mistake.*

•••

The mayor had arranged a lavish banquet after the parade. Political supporters made up most of the guests. Asked to say a few words, Fitzgerald thanked everybody and made a few self-deprecating jokes about their experiences in American culture. The limo dropped them off at the hotel just after 2:00 p.m. Paul waited in the lobby.

"Is Dr. Finkle here?" Fitzgerald immediately asked.

"Yes, I rented a meeting room in the hotel. Dr. Finkle and his associate are waiting with Molly."

Fitzgerald and Isabella hurried directly there. Before Paul could make introductions, Fitzgerald recognized the elderly man and extended his hand. "Dr. Finkle, we know your work. Thank you for meeting with us. You are not required to donate to the Benevolent Foundation."

Dr. Finkle appeared stunned. He took the proffered hand. "Fitzgerald and Isabella, I am honored to meet you. Your foundation is worthy. I will follow through on the offer."

"Thank you, sir. The honor of meeting is ours. I had intended to ask for a private meeting with you after our United Nations address."

Still acting disoriented, the scientist directed their attention to his associate, a small late-forties woman reflecting a determined, perhaps even severe, demeanor. "This is Dr. Laura Holdridge. She's a future Nobel laureate for her work preventing genetic deformity. Many people are intelligent. *Laura* is a genius."

"I have a teenage son with Down Syndrome. Part of my research is directed toward repairing genetic damage before the very early fetal stages of development," Laura explained. She hesitated. "Would you allow us to be absolutely certain of your identity?" She then showed a kit for taking saliva samples.

Isabella looked at Fitzgerald who nodded silently. Each of them opened their mouths for Dr. Holdridge to collect samples. When she had finished, Dr. Finkle started to ask questions about their origins. The extraterrestrials disavowed any expertise in genetics, but they answered honestly about what they knew.

Dr. Finkle summed up, "Your creators pieced you together based on the pirated human genome from many sources of DNA and even created some sequences from amino acids?"

To Fitzgerald's confirming nod, the scientist exclaimed, "Extraordinary! Simply extraordinary!"

"Making us was a joint project," Isabella explained. "At the UN, Fitzgerald will reveal that there are other sentient civilizations. Some are more mammalian than the Benevolents. They offered advice and even provided some gene sequences."

Paul and Molly watched and listened. Paul, with a graduate degree in biology, understood much of what they discussed. Molly simply appreciated the complexity of genetics. Fitzgerald turned to them to say, "You are our closest friends. We owe you more than we could ever repay. Would you do us another great service by allowing us to speak with Drs. Finkle and Holdridge in private?"

The entire situation with the extraterrestrials and Dr. Finkle confounded Paul. But he responded, "Of course. Um...do you need anything else?"

"Would you please meet us tomorrow for breakfast and then accompany us to the United Nations? That is the biggest day for us. Your presence will reassure us."

"Yes, certainly." Paul and Molly rose to leave. Isabella got up to give Molly a little hug but didn't speak.

Outside the conference room, Paul started, "Molly, I—"

"You and I are just too different." Molly started to walk away.

"Wait!"

But Molly didn't.

Paul went outside and walked the streets of New York for hours.

Chapter 13

•••

A shuttle service conveyed all of them together to the United Nations Headquarters the following morning. Deep in concentration, Fitzgerald stared out the van's window at the passing streets without speaking. Paul and Molly remained polite to all, albeit obviously distracted. Isabella observed each of them with her engineer's sense of analysis. No joy permeated the group.

A United Nations representative met them at a drive-up entrance. "Please follow me," he instructed. They briefly met the secretary general, Tibor Iscaderian. Next the UN representative ushered them to a small waiting room near the General Assembly. "You are scheduled to speak at 9:30," he told Fitzgerald and Isabella. Then he pointed at a TV and spoke to Paul and Molly, "The news media will carry the address live. You can watch from here."

The group of four remained tense. "You'll do well," Paul

attempted encouragement. Fitzgerald nodded acknowledgment without speaking. They waited in silence. The UN representative returned to lead Fitzgerald and Isabella to their seats, leaving Paul and Molly alone.

"Molly, about the other night..."

"Forget about it!"

Paul pleaded, "I can't. Please talk to me."

"Why should I? I'm sorry for your loss, Paul. But you rejected me in favor of a memory of...Beth."

"You don't understand."

Molly stood up and reacted in anger. "Oh, then enlighten me!"

• • •

Fitzgerald stepped to the microphone in front of the General Assembly of the United Nations and smiled broadly. "Mr. Secretary Iscaderian, President Johnson, and all of you who represent and lead your nations, Isabella and I thank you for this opportunity."

He paused during light applause. Fitzgerald continued, "To those watching around the world we bring greetings from another sentient species far away." He then took time to speak a few sentences in each of the sixteen other languages in which he was fluent. Eighty percent of the world's population heard him speak in a tongue they understood.

"Today you will hear a short speech. And after first speaking in English we will go to a private chamber here at the United Nations building and re-deliver the same speech in each of the languages in which I am capable."

• • •

"Beth insisted we have a sexual relationship, even though it was uncomfortable for her. That was her expression of love and commitment directly from her heart."

"What you did for Beth and what I now know she did for you is amazing. But how do you expect me to compete with that?" Molly demanded.

"I don't expect you to compete." Paul also stood up.

"Why can't we just have a good time together?"

Paul's voice rose. "We *were* having a good time together."

"Sex is part of having a good time together," Molly returned even louder.

"Maybe I want more from sex than just having a good time!" Paul shouted.

• • •

Fitzgerald began officiously, "We have an offer to make to the human species. You are not alone in the universe. We invite you to join a partnership with fourteen other sentient species and civilizations. We are mutually connected by goodwill and radio waves. Our partners exchange ideas, science, philosophy, literature, and arts. The exchange of knowledge has made the individual lives of each species immeasurably better.

"However, the partnered species have a requirement for your membership. Humans must learn to cooperate with each other to deal with the issues which threaten your species' future. The partners do not wish to make humans part of our family and then observe you destroying yourselves and your planet. You must begin to think of not just the good of those currently living, but also the good of future generations of humans."

Fitzgerald paused a few seconds to let those words hang in the air. "Now let me tell you some hard truths. There will be no mass exodus of your species from this planet. No species has invented an interstellar drive to transport you across many light years to distant worlds. Nobody has created anti-gravity capability. Channeling and controlling affordable energy is a universal challenge. Physics has limitations.

"Without cooperation among yourselves, your civilization will eventually disintegrate and likely ruin this planet. Pollution, proliferation of nuclear weapons, overpopulation, careless genetic engineering, drug-resistant microbes, crop failures due to chemical-resistant pests, irresponsible use of Earth's resources, and perhaps other challenges will terminate your future. To join the partnership, you must begin to deal seriously with these issues.

"However, through partnership with the fourteen species you can explore the universe, perhaps more than one universe. You can learn about technology and bioengineering to make Earth a wonderful place for all your descendants to live. The fourteen sentient species can help you to eliminate war, disease, hunger, and poverty. Human life spans can extend to hundreds of years.

"The planet Earth itself is not important to the partners. You, a unique sentient species and the potential you possess, are all that the other civilizations care about. Unfortunately, the partnering species have discovered the universe littered with debris of civilizations that destroyed themselves and frequently their own planets. Civilizations inevitably decay into chaos unless they develop a sense of the common good."

• • •

"Maybe you want more than I can give!" Molly shouted back. "I offered you what I could. I'm not Beth."

"A relationship is built on friendship and trust. Can't you trust me?"

"My mother put her trust in men. Man after man. Every single one of them betrayed her trust. They rejected her when she became inconvenient to them."

Paul spoke in a monotone. "Do you think that I would do that to you?"

Once engaged, Molly didn't know how to back off. "You're a man, aren't you?"

• • •

Fitzgerald paused again. The audience twittered nervously. He changed to a friendly tone as if confiding in his listeners. "I love watching human science fiction movies. Several of the partnering species watch your movies. Humans have such wonderful imaginations. One movie I saw was called *The Day the Earth Stood Still*. An alien visitor arrives on Earth and threatens to destroy humankind unless they change their ways. Let me assure you that the Benevolents who created Isabella and me are *not* going to destroy you. Most human languages have some form of an English idiom called 'a carrot and a stick.' If you don't know the story, it refers to getting a stubborn animal to move. Today we have offered the carrot." Fitzgerald became serious again. "You, yourselves, are providing your own stick."

To everybody's surprise, Isabella rose from her seat and joined Fitzgerald at the podium. He stepped aside to let her speak. "Although we are not exactly like you, Fitzgerald and I are nearly all human. We cannot leave your planet. Your future is our future now. We ask you to let us help you to make a future together."

Fitzgerald spoke again, "We would like to visit your countries to talk about issues. We do not represent the United States. However, we do not have the knowledge or understanding to organize visits with those who might welcome us. The American State Department has offered to help for the time being. They will be reimbursed just as we reimbursed NASA for their hospitality."

● ● ●

Molly spoke more quietly, "Paul, I hope you find what you're looking for. What you need. You and I are just too different," she said for the second time in less than 24 hours.

"Now I know what rejection feels like."

"Maybe that's the one thing we share in common."

The door opened. The United Nations representative brought Fitzgerald and Isabella back into the waiting room. "Now you understand our mission. What did you think of the speech?" Fitzgerald asked.

"You did great. I knew you would do well," Paul replied. Molly murmured a few vague accolades.

Fitzgerald looked back and forth at Paul and Molly, who stood about ten feet apart with their arms crossed. "You didn't even listen to my speech!" For the first time, the humans heard anger in him. "How could you not listen?" Neither Paul nor Molly could look at him. "You—"

"Stop, Fitzgerald!" They all turned to see Isabella speaking. "You have too much energy from the circumstances. Can't you see that our friends are in distress?"

"Our mission—"

She cut him off. "Sometimes you think only of our mission."

"Whatever they suffer can't be more important to them than the future of their species."

Isabella calmly reasoned with her mate. "To them it is. We have learned that humans are nearly always more concerned with their individual futures than the common good or with their identity group rather than their species. That's why we are here. We can't blame Paul and Molly for being human."

Fitzgerald listened as she continued, "You and I are a mated pair. I love that our human-like bodies allow us an enjoyment of sexual intimacy that our creators don't know. But we have the same history and are much alike. We are the only ones of our kind and thereby the only ones for each other.

"But mating and sexual relations are more complicated for these creatures. Paul and Molly, although both human, are more different from each other than you and I are. And they have very different histories. Fear and desire compete within them in a way we don't understand."

Fitzgerald contemplated Isabella's words a moment then looked again at Paul and Molly. "Isabella is correct. She is becoming a good scientist of humans. I apologize for my

123

words and emotions." His former impish side started to re-emerge. He smiled and teased them, "This was perhaps the most important speech in the history of humankind. And you missed it."

"Yes...we...did," agreed Paul with an embarrassed smile.

"I'm sorry," Molly added.

"Forget about it now. You can hear the speech later." Fitzgerald waited a few seconds as the humans expressed assurances and promises. "Isabella and I are planning a worldwide tour to represent the offer we made in our speech. Would you each accompany us as friends and advisers? We trust you."

Paul and Molly didn't look at each other. "I would go," Paul said.

"Yes, I'll join you," Molly said. "But I have one question: what did you talk about with Dr. Finkle in private?"

Fitzgerald spoke, "Molly and Paul, our mission will become more difficult than it has already been. The Benevolents had instructed us to meet and encourage Drs. Finkle and Holdridge. The science of genetics will probably be necessary to solve some of Earth's problems such as eliminating diseases like malaria, fighting pests without chemicals, producing more crops, and even controlling climate. But many humans are fearful of genetic engineering. We didn't know how you might react. You will need to trust us."

Molly hesitated and then decided. "Okay."

"Okay with me too," Paul added.

Chapter 14

• • •

"I'm sorry, but I could not reschedule you." Paul had become Fitzgerald and Isabella's defacto schedule manager. In the week after Fitzgerald's speech, many UN representatives and dignitaries had requested and received private meetings. Then Paul got a call from Washington.

"When the United States Congress gives you a time and opportunity to speak, you don't argue," Paul explained. "And the National Education Association convention had already slotted you. They rearranged their entire program to fit your availability."

Fitzgerald looked at Isabella. She spoke for them both, "Neither of us likes this, but we'll need to split up. Fitzgerald will address Congress. I'll take Molly with me to the convention."

• • •

Paul guided Fitzgerald to the US Congress. To their surprise, not only the representatives and senators attended,

125

but also the president, his cabinet, key military leaders, and Supreme Court justices. Most TV networks provided live national coverage.

Fitzgerald began by reiterating the offer he had made to the United Nations. "But the process will not be easy," he emphasized. "Compromise and cooperation will be necessary. Sacrifices will be required by every human. This not only applies to within your country, but with other peoples of the world."

From somewhere within the assembly a man shouted, "America first!"

"Yes!" Fitzgerald responded with enthusiasm. "You have exactly identified the problem. All the nations are concerned with themselves first, oftentimes at the expense of the others. Some call that a 'zero sum game.' But in the end, all will lose. Thank you, sir, for making that point."

Fitzgerald continued, "Please allow me to be candid in the context of urgency. One looming problem is that this government borrows and spends tremendous amounts of money. Don't you realize that this will eventually result in economic hardship on future generations? And most of you are more interested in being reelected than you are in solving this and other problems."

A different voice objected, "I represent the will of my constituents."

"Ah, but sometimes your constituents are misinformed and divided by political rhetoric. Your political system needs to work toward actually solving problems. Otherwise future generations may decide that the representative democracy of your system is not the best choice of government."

Whoa! thought Paul. *That's like a guest preacher telling a church that God is dead.*

Fitzgerald finished the speech by talking about the ultimate benefits to mankind.

The customary mingling after a speech to Congress felt restrained. Politicians wanted to hitch themselves to Fitzgerald and Isabella's star. But they had vested interest in maintaining the status quo.

"That was pretty direct language," Paul said to Fitzgerald afterwards.

"Maybe some fear of political change will motivate them to actually cooperate."

"You answered the congressman who interrupted brilliantly," said Paul. "How did you think so fast?"

"I didn't. Part of my ambassador training was years of practice responding to different ideas and confrontation. You may see me use that response again."

• • •

Isabella stepped to the podium at the National Education Convention. "I deeply admire and respect you who are educators. You are the key to our future. The greatest tragedy is the loss of human potential."

A heavy round of applause interrupted her as the delegates rose to their feet in affirmation. Isabella continued after they resumed sitting. "Fitzgerald and I are privileged to support the Benevolent Foundation to help young people get the education they would not otherwise!"

More applause forced Isabella to pause. She started again. "Please allow me to introduce Molly Powell to tell you about the foundation's plans."

Molly took Isabella's place behind the podium. "With a single mother who had few job skills, I was an at-risk child. But the education system gave me a chance. Many of you are doing an amazing job. We have no intention of replacing you. Rather, the Benevolent Foundation will discover programs that are working and get behind those efforts. We will give priority to programs which include emphases on cooperating with others for the common good." Molly paused for a solid round of applause. "So far," she announced, "the Benevolent Foundation has received $186 million from those who believe in education like you do. We are hoping to raise ten billion dollars for education." This time the answering applause was thunderous.

The National Education Association had arranged for Isabella to meet a group of school children from the Washington, DC, area. Some of the children would likely be beneficiaries of the foundation's efforts. Molly used her cell phone's video camera to record Isabella's interaction with the kids. The girls especially crowded around Isabella. Her being an alien was of secondary interest. "Are you really a spaceship pilot?" one little girl questioned.

"Yes, I am. And I'm an engineer."

A little boy asked, "Have robots taken over many worlds?"

"Not yet."

Another asked, "Can you take the spacecraft back to space?"

"No, our spacecraft is only capable of landing. Taking off would require big rockets and a lot of fuel."

"Where did the spaceship come from?"

"The spaceship came from a planet named Benevolent. They sent it into your solar system in pieces through a giant machine. Then I assembled them into the vehicle that brought Fitzgerald and me to Earth. I had to call home a few times for extra instructions."

"You can call home?" asked another little girl. "Will you say 'Hi' to them for me?"

"You can tell them yourself. Just look at the camera and say, 'Hello from Earth.'" The girl glanced at the camera and back at Isabella in uncertainty. "Let's all tell them 'Hello from Earth,' together," Isabella suggested. "Everybody look at the camera now and speak on 'go.' Three, two, one, go."

"Hello from Earth," all the children repeated.

After them, Isabella added with an oddly hiss-filled voice, "Sneznar 9724."

"Will they really hear us?"

"If Ms. Molly puts this on the air, they will."

"Will they answer back?"

"No, they will not answer now. But when Earth joins the partnership, they will communicate freely."

"What does Sneznar mean?"

"That's my name on Benevolent. The computers that monitor Earth's broadcasts will prioritize your greeting when they identify my voice."

● ● ●

The US State Department had provided a diplomatic jet to convey Fitzgerald and Isabella to meetings in Los Angeles. Paul rode beside Fitzgerald near the rear as they went over the upcoming schedule of events.

Paul handed Fitzgerald a printout of the meetings. "First is the Conference on Climate Change. Many humans feel like global warming is one of the most critical issues on Earth. But others dismiss the danger."

Fitzgerald examined the printout. "Will both sides be present at the conference?"

"No, this will likely be a coalition of environmentalists."

"Global warming wasn't one of the most critical threats the Benevolents identified to Isabella and me. And we don't know much about the opposing arguments. Could you and Molly write us an objective summary of the facts? And include both sides of the issue?"

● ● ●

Isabella and Molly sat together near the front of the plane. Isabella practically gushed, "Weren't those children cute? I just love them."

"They loved you too. Especially the little girls. They need good role models maybe even more than they need education. Are there many children on Benevolent?"

"Not so many. Living to 300 to 400 of your years and allowed only two offspring per mated couple, Benevolents consider the young especially precious." Isabella sighed. She still thought about the kids she had met. "Parents share their young with others, though. Getting what you call a 'babysitter' is never a problem there."

Molly interrupted her thoughts. "Will the Benevolents really get the 'Hello' the kids sent?"

"Yes, five to ten minutes after you broadcast it. Our probe near the path of Earth's solar orbit will relay the signal. They don't answer because clever humans would easily trace the signal and find the probe. Some could possibly disable it."

"Why did you add the password?"

"The probe can't relay every signal emanating from Earth. There are millions. The probe's computer will prioritize that message."

"Can anyone use that code?"

"No, the computers know my voice. And the number sequence changes."

"That means you could send a special broadcast to Benevolent any time you want."

"Yes, I can."

"I just had an idea. What if we were to create the first interplanetary TV program? It could be a travelogue of your and Fitzgerald's worldwide tour. You would send a program from each stop on the tour."

Isabella smiled broadly. "The Benevolents would love that! They are intensely curious about everything human. They have a lot of resources invested to send us here. And they would likely forward your broadcast to the other species."

"I'll bet my network would buy and broadcast the series. The money could be used to pay the State Department back for their help in the tour."

"Molly, I don't know what we would do without you. Would you agree to be a business manager for Fitzgerald and me?"

"Sure. Now let me call DSC. Let's see if this phone works."

The phone on the jet did work. "George, I've got another idea for you." She outlined her idea for the travelogue. "The episodes would be ten to fifteen minutes each and could serve as a human-interest segment."

"That sounds like dynamite, sweetheart. What cost are we talking per unit?"

"They were thinking two million."

"Do you remember who you're working for? See if you can get the aliens to do each unit for a mil."

"I think they'll accept one-point-five."

"Okay. But for that much we'll want the segments to appeal to men as well as women. So use makeup this time. But your appearance in the exclusive without makeup last time was brilliant. That made the internment look like a hardship. The viewers loved it. And don't forget you'll still be getting that million-dollar bonus."

● ● ●

While Molly and Isabella plotted in the jet's front, Fitzgerald approached a confusing issue with Paul. "I see on television two men in a square of ropes fighting. Many are hurt. Some men must be killed. Why do humans allow killing on television?"

"You mean professional wrestling? They aren't really fighting. The men are only playacting."

"They pretend?"

"Yes, it's an act. They rehearse beforehand and probably go out to dinner together afterwards."

"I also see groups of men fighting on a place of grass.

Many appear to be hurt. They are playacting?"

"I think you mean football. Do they use a non-round ball about this big?" Paul held his hands apart.

"Yes, sometimes they throw and catch it. The others try to stop them."

"No, they're not acting. Men are really hurt. Occasionally men are killed."

"They still go out to dinner afterwards, though?"

"I don't think so."

● ● ●

"How are you and Paul getting along?" Isabella asked Molly.

"Oh, we work well together. He's very smart and competent."

"That's not what I meant. Neither of you is mated. Fitzgerald and I thought maybe you would be good for each other."

"Not really." Molly told Isabella all about the day they spent together in New York and the confrontation afterwards. "We're just too different," she concluded.

"Maybe that's not the only difficulty. You are an attractive, healthy female and have not been mated to any other well beyond the age most human females find a mate."

Molly told Isabella some of her mother's experiences with men. "I'm afraid to get into any serious relationship that could cause me as much grief as my mother suffered."

Isabella responded, "Those men treated your mother terribly. I can't imagine being a little girl and experiencing that with her. But Paul is not like those men."

"I know."

• • •

"I wonder what Isabella and Molly are talking about so intently," Fitzgerald thought out loud while looking toward where the women sat.

"They do seem to get along well," Paul said.

"Isabella has never had a female human friend." Fitzgerald sat contemplating. "I'm glad Isabella has Molly to show her how to be a human woman. She received the genes but no example."

"Don't the Benevolents have male and female?"

"Yes, but the differences are not so great as for humans." Paul glanced toward the front of the jet and saw Molly and Isabella deep in conversation. Fitzgerald saw him watching them. "Isabella has many questions for Molly about being a female person," Fitzgerald said.

"Like what?" Paul asked. "She seems to be doing a pretty good job of it so far."

"Yes, she is. I think she's adapting very well to Earth. But some things are still a mystery to her. Why do women wear shoes that contort their feet and are nearly impossible to walk in? Why do they use paints on their fingers and toes to make it look like their nails are bleeding? Why do they pay so much money to smell like fruit? And we have noticed in many of the movies we've watched that the women seem to be able to persuade men to do nearly anything they want them to do. What is this power they have, and how have they learned to use it so effectively?"

Paul laughed. "Boy, I'd like to know the answers to those questions too."

•••

Molly continued the conversation while accepting a box lunch served by the flight attendant. "Do the Benevolents have males and females?"

"Yes, male and female is universal among all the sentient species." Isabella opened her box lunch. "Scientists believe the Great Creator may have created the species that way to ensure genetic diversity. This aids species development and reduces harmful abnormalities."

Molly tried to make her voice sound casual. "Then how do the Benevolents choose a mate?"

"Their society is more communal than Earth. Everybody spends most of their time in groups. So when an individual reaches an age of independence from parents, all of their family and friends assist in the search for a mate by recommending candidates. The choice is less emotional, more based on qualifications, than among humans."

"Do you mean compatibility?" Molly asked while ignoring her lunch.

"Sometimes. Those less bold tend to seek someone like themselves. That provides an easier life together. Individuals who have more ambition seek a mate different from themselves based on complementary skill sets. More difficult to partner, but more capabilities as a team. Eventually each mate-seeker has a list of acceptable candidates of the opposite sex, which they prioritize. Then the seekers approach their candidates, who have their own lists, in order of priority. A mutually acceptable partnership is eventually identified."

Molly protested, "That doesn't sound very romantic."

"Romance is connected to sex or the possibility of sex in human culture. The Benevolents' act of reproduction process isn't individually pleasurable. The female lays an egg that the male fertilizes, like many of Earth's non-sentient species. Both Benevolent parents take joy caring for the resulting larva. I mean baby. But Benevolent relationships are intensely satisfying and pleasurable. After a partner is identified, the couple secretly goes away alone. They say a pledge of acceptance and commitment to each other and to the Great Creator."

"Why do they go away alone?" Molly wanted to know.

"Aren't you going to eat your lunch?" asked Isabella. Molly opened her box. After sampling her fruit cup, Isabella answered Molly's question. "Because of the communal nature of the Benevolents, aloneness makes their mating more special. Then without interruptions the couple can spend time in close physical proximity. Each one's body learns to recognize the other through traces of DNA inhaled with air. Once the body starts to recognize its partner, hormones are produced that give an overwhelming sense of peace and joy, sometimes for hours. Once that happens, the pair is mated for life without any concept of divorce. When the couple returns to family and friends mated, everybody celebrates."

"That's amazing."

"Yes, the mated relationship is wonderful. All the remainder of their lives, mated couples' bodies recognize each other and produce the hormones after a period of proximity alone. This pleasure is something special they can share only with each other. You could say a mated pair becomes addicted to each other. Mating is also productive to raise offspring and accomplish much in life. Fitzgerald and I have human bodies that don't produce the hormones. But we are learning how human cuddling and intercourse can produce some of the same results."

Chapter 15

•••

"Genetic Cheating" the newspaper's headlines accused. The Russian informant had finally come to terms with the International Olympic Committee. The informant claimed that the Russian Sports Federation created super-athletes through gene splicing.

"Technically, that's not against the rules," an IOC spokesman reported. "We would make genetic enhancement against the rules, but we have no current way to test for it. However, this would explain the unprecedented success the Russians had at the last summer Olympics. The future of the Olympic games could be in jeopardy unless we find a way to address this problem."

•••

At the conference on global warming, the foursome sat in the front row through hours of dire predictions. Images of polar bears in peril, ocean waves eroding coastlines, polar icecaps melting, and famines in Africa stirred their fellow conferees to urgency. Many eyes continually glanced toward the alien dignitaries. All in attendance hoped for an endorsement of their cause.

Paul, assisted by Molly, had prepared opposing argument summary sheets concerning global warming. Fitzgerald and Isabella studied them during any lull in the proceedings and made a few notes. Late in the day the conference organizers rearranged the schedule to allow their famous guests to speak.

Fitzgerald and Isabella stood together behind the microphone. "We congratulate you for your commitment to conservation of resources and preserving Earth for future generations. We also want to protect the environment for future generations." Thunderous applause interrupted Fitzgerald.

Isabella spoke next, "Statistical studies of temperatures prove that Earth is warmer than when the recordkeeping began. Science clearly shows that increasing levels of carbon dioxide in your atmosphere reduce irradiation of heat into space and contribute to global warming. To deny these things is simply to deny reality." The audience erupted with affirmation. Most believed she shared their belief.

Cheers drowned out the applause until Fitzgerald held up his arms asking the crowd for permission to continue. "But the amount that carbon dioxide emission due to burning hydrocarbon fuels is contributing to Earth's warming is uncertain. And science also shows that Earth has been warming and the oceans rising for thousands of years. Only fifteen thousand years ago, ice covered much of your northern hemisphere and the oceans were 300 feet lower. Most of the warming occurred before humans began burning huge quantities of fuel stored in the earth. Now think of the two largest countries on earth, Canada and Russia. Much of their land is frozen. Global warming could make these places, and the large landmass of Greenland as well, more hospitable to human life. One very simple answer would be to move the people from the threatened areas to places that are becoming more hospitable. But your political system would not allow that."

The audience sat stunned. A few boos began. Others shouted challenges. "What do you know?" and "Whose side are you on?"

Fitzgerald spoke above the shouts. "Furthermore, your human standard of living is currently dependent on cheap energy. We applaud using alternate energy sources such as solar and wind to reduce the burning of fossil fuels, especially to lower pollution levels. But curtailment sufficient to affect global warming would cripple your economies, especially those of developing nations."

Boos and shouts then filled the auditorium. Fitzgerald answered the shouts with his own shout into the microphone. *"Do you want a plausible solution now?"*

This quietened the crowd. Paul and Molly looked at each other. They had not proposed any solutions. Isabella addressed the audience. "The Great Creator has given to you a means to adjust your planet's average surface temperature. That is the carbon dioxide in your atmosphere as you have already discovered. Other species have controlled their planet's mean temperature by adding or removing carbon dioxide or other compounds. Simply storing the carbon dioxide won't work long term because that also takes the oxygen you need out of the atmosphere. For each pound of carbon removed by sequestration of CO_2, four pounds of oxygen are removed from Earth's atmosphere.

"But you can reduce carbon dioxide by using phytoplankton organisms, a form of algae, which absorb carbon plus heat and release oxygen. The organisms then die and sink to the bottom. This is how much of your carbon-based fuel was created over millions of years. New bioengineered forms of phytoplankton could accelerate putting the carbon back and lowering the earth's temperature."

The audience spontaneously broke into a myriad of groups of two or more as participants discussed and argued the implications. Fitzgerald and Isabella hurried out a side door followed by Paul and Molly.

• • •

"Tumult at Conference on Climate Change" proclaimed newspaper articles the following morning. A morning talk show host began his broadcast, "Benevolent's ambassadors yesterday proposed introducing a new life form to the world's oceans. Controversy has rocked the world of environmentalists, many of whom oppose any form of genetic modification. Others see a viable solution to the threat of global warming."

The newscaster then explained the function of the potential new life form and concluded with a question, "But is creating such an organism even possible? Today we have Dr. Laura Holdridge from Future Tech, a bioengineering firm. She is representing Dr. Ben Finkle, who is experiencing some health concerns." Laura's upper body appeared in a box on the screen. "Dr. Holdridge, is creating such an organism possible using genetic engineering?"

Laura, unaccustomed to public scrutiny, remained rigid and stared directly into the camera lens. "Probably yes, certainly yes with help from those who created Fitzgerald and Isabella. But precautions would need to be taken to maintain control of the organism."

"What sort of precautions?"

"Lifespan and breeding rate balanced with predators. But genetic engineering might not even be necessary. Humans made chihuahua dogs from wolves by selective breeding. Eventually, we could breed existing organisms to perform the task. Genetic modification could speed the process, though."

• • •

The foursome watched the interview from a hotel room. "And I thought that I could create controversy," Molly laughed. "You two can turn the world upside down."

"As I told Paul," Fitzgerald responded, "we don't see global warming as threatening your species. But we took this opportunity to demonstrate how to deal with a controversial concern. You honestly accumulate the facts on both sides. Then you look for creative solutions or compromises. The issue is really whether the opposing parties are ready to work together toward a solution."

Paul answered a knock on the hotel room door. The publisher Molly located for Fitzgerald and Isabella's book had provided a substantial advance and arranged for a ghostwriter to meet them in Los Angeles. She had already listened to and organized the major interviews they had given and would use those to fill most of the book. She followed Paul into the room and greeted Fitzgerald and Isabella before getting down to business. "Do you have the unreleased photos?" the writer asked.

Isabella showed them on her computer. "Would you help us to select twenty?" The writer did.

"Now what I'll need is for you and Fitzgerald to talk into a recorder about the pictures," she instructed. "Describe what the readers will be examining."

Later, after several hours of talking to and recording the extraterrestrials, the ghostwriter promised, "I can give the publisher 60,000 words to go with your pictures in four weeks. We might need to Skype together a few more times to fill in some details. But I think your book could be on sale in about five months. Meanwhile you have the publisher's advance."

"I'll review your submission first on behalf of Fitzgerald and Isabella," said Molly.

"Of course."

• • •

At breakfast the next morning, Fitzgerald said, "Molly, Isabella told me that she asked you to be our business manager. We've already seen how good you are with money. Thank you."

"You're welcome, Fitzgerald."

"Some people, mostly women, gave me phone numbers. A few put them in my pocket without telling me. I think maybe they want to make donations to the Benevolent Foundation."

"Could I see the numbers, please?" Molly answered. Examining the paper slips she found only women's names, sometimes only the first name. Molly looked at Isabella, who sat expressionless. She had no idea of the numbers' meaning. "I'll take care of these for you, and any more you get like them," Molly promised.

"Thank you. You are a wonderful business manager." Fitzgerald and Isabella left together to get ready for the day's activities.

Paul had watched their interchange with amusement. "Aren't you going to tell him what the numbers are really for?"

"They're confused enough about human sexual mores. And I promised Isabella to take care of business for her."

● ● ●

Paul had rented a conference room at the hotel for Fitzgerald and Isabella to meet influential Californian leaders and give interviews to local media. He generally waited at a table outside the room to ensure their privacy. Isabella came out and saw Paul working at his laptop. She sat down beside him. "Thank you, Paul, for helping us to arrange our meetings and keep track of the schedule."

"You are very welcome. This has been my privilege. And you're bringing us an important message."

Isabella acknowledged his words and then got to her real

purpose for sitting down. "Paul, how are you and Molly getting along?"

Her words surprised Paul. "Well...she's speaking to me again. I thought for a while she never would. Thank you for intervening after the argument at the UN. What you said about humans is true."

"Both you and Molly are our friends. We care about each of you." Isabella paused. "Paul, I don't know about you and Molly together. And I know that you are still sad about your former mated one, Beth. Could I tell you what I think?"

"Of course."

"You need to find someone completely different from Beth. Otherwise, the female will always be compared to your lost love. That's all I should say. Thank you for listening to me."

"Thank you." As Isabella walked away, Paul thought, *Nobody could be more different from Beth than Molly. Too bad that I blew my chances with her. I should have...I don't know what I should have done.*

• • •

"This is Molly Powell beginning a new segment for DSC Network. For the first time ever, the program will be deliberately broadcast to not only American viewers and the world, but to another civilization. At the United Nations, Fitzgerald and Isabella proposed a worldwide tour to explain the offer they made to mankind. I, on behalf of DSC, will accompany Fitzgerald and Isabella on their tour and report to viewers on both Earth and Benevolent about their experiences.

"Currently Fitzgerald and Isabella are in Los Angeles on

the west coast of the USA. What is Los Angeles famous for? Hollywood, of course. Today Fitzgerald and Isabella performed a cameo role in the new movie *Star Trek: Emancipation*, being filmed at a studio for Paramount Pictures. Let's ask them what they thought of human movie making." Molly turned to interview Fitzgerald and Isabella, each wearing Star Trek costumes. "What roles did they give you?"

Fitzgerald answered first. "I played an unnamed human crew member on the Enterprise who was killed by a Klingon."

"Let's see." A clip showed Fitzgerald exchanging phaser shots alongside the movie's stars with a group of actors depicting aggressive Klingons. Fitzgerald disappeared in a patch of light when one of the Klingon shots connected. An outtake showed Fitzgerald inadvertently glance at the camera, forcing the scene to be re-filmed. "I see you looking at the camera," Molly chided him.

"Yes, the movie director said that if I did that again, he would only let me play a dead body."

"How about you, Isabella?" Molly continued.

"I was an alien female in a bar approached by one of the human crewmen. He left when I blinked my inner eyelids." The clip showed Isabella made up to look sultry. Her now-famous eyelid trick drove the human away.

"So how did you enjoy the movie-making experience?"

"I love science fiction," Fitzgerald explained. "It is so funny! Humans are so imaginative. The Star Wars series is my favorite. I love their theme of self-sacrifice for others."

"What movies do you like, Isabella?"

"I like the ones when people start singing and dancing.

I'm hoping that I see that happen someday in real life. I've wondered how they all know the same song and dance."

"Fitzgerald and Isabella, since this program is to be broadcast to Benevolent, do you have anything special you would like to say to those watching there?"

Fitzgerald and Isabella looked at the camera. Fitzgerald spoke first. "You have made a great investment of time and resources for this mission to a sentient species. On behalf of all earthlings, which Isabella and I are now, we thank you."

"We love you and miss you," said Isabella. "Sneznar 1369."

• • •

Afterwards Paul explained the business of movie making to Fitzgerald. "The most important actors you met today are all very wealthy."

Fitzgerald looked surprised. "But not as wealthy as real astronauts, right?"

"I think the actors are much wealthier."

"Why do actors who are pretending to travel in outer space make more money than astronauts who actually travel in outer space?"

To this Paul had no simple answer. So Fitzgerald tried a different issue. "But I'm confused about human weapons. What is that small weapon depicted in so many human movies?"

"Which one?"

"Humans hold them in their hands and point them. The weapon makes a noise, then the enemy falls."

"I think you mean a handgun or a pistol."

"That weapon is amazing. The enemy can be shooting with bigger weapons that do much damage, then the hero points the weapon and stops them. This weapon is more science fiction, correct?"

"No, that weapon is real. The fiction is that it is shown more powerful than the other weapons. Would you like to fire a real handgun?"

"At people? No, I wouldn't want to damage anyone."

"You would only fire at a target."

"I could do that?"

"Let me take you to a firing range."

Chapter 16

● ● ●

"You should start by giving us the technology we need to solve our problems," a Canadian member of Parliament demanded.

Paul had been unsure how Fitzgerald would react to the open style of debate favored by Commonwealth parliamentary governments. But Fitzgerald thrived in the give-and-take environment.

Fitzgerald's voice carried a tone of sincere appeal. "You already have plenty of technology to grow food. Then why are people starving to death on Earth while others shorten their lifespans with overeating? New technology isn't Earth's greatest need. The real need is a heightened sense of the common good of mankind and the willingness to work together toward real solutions. If Benevolent gives you technology without these, some will benefit and others will be left behind. Some groups are even likely to use the technology to gain advantage over others."

Another member of Parliament spoke up. "During your speech at the UN, you mentioned irresponsible use of Earth's resources. What do you mean by that?"

Fitzgerald looked down at notes prepared for him by Molly with help from Paul. "Pardon me a second, please, while I look at my notes. I haven't been on Earth very long. And there are many examples," he quipped. The Canadian legislators laughed with him.

"Ah, here." Fitzgerald held up a piece of paper. "Let me answer by way of example. How's the cod fishing in the ocean near Newfoundland?" He paused as the Canadians fidgeted, then continued citing from the paper. "In the 1960s, up to 800,000 tons of cod were harvested a year. In 1992, zero. Although fishermen had been making marvelous catches on the Grand Banks for 500 years, new technology allowed unprecedented hauls. And even after the fish started dramatically declining, each fisherman hurried to get the last fish before the others could. Together the fishermen ruined the fishery for themselves. Unless they change, humans could do the same with all of Earth."

Fitzgerald smiled. "This example also applies to the previous question about technology. Used improperly, new technology can cause problems, not solve them. In this case, were it not for the new technology, a lot of cod would still be available in Canadian waters. Fishermen would still have a livelihood."

• • •

"Fitzgerald's message about people working together for

the common good is code language for communism. History has proven that communism doesn't work. Why then do we subsidize the so-called 'aliens' traveling the world to promote a communist agenda?" Bill Samuel loudly demanded on his program in response to Molly's popular segments. "The cultures that have emphasized individualistic capitalism have ultimately prevailed over those that didn't. We need political leaders with the courage to stand up against those who oppose the ideals that have made America the greatest nation in the history of the world."

• • •

Fitzgerald and Isabella found Ottawa to be a beautiful city. In early April, most Canadian trees remained dormant. They marveled at the bare limbs. "Are they like this always?"

Paul answered, "No, they're green in the summer. But when the chlorophyll in them dies, the natural color comes through. They're very colorful—yellows, golds, and reds. You'll see them in the fall about six months from now."

Molly, being from upstate New York, relished the cold. Her interplanetary broadcast began with, "Don't you love the chilly air? We're here in Ottawa with Fitzgerald and Isabella. As you can see, Ottawa is experiencing a late snowfall." The camera panned to the right to show Fitzgerald and Isabella busily making a snow creature of undetermined nature. Molly turned her back on them as the camera refocused on her. "Yesterday Fitzgerald and Isabella debated with members of the Canadian Parliament. Several lawmakers expressed a reluctance to cooperate with other nations on the issue of global warming.

One said, 'Canada could benefit from a somewhat warmer climate.' Not all Canadians agree, however."

The camera showed Isabella sneaking up behind Molly with a snowball bigger than her head. "Some Canadians.... *aaah!*" Isabella had broken the snowball over Molly's head, sending crystals of ice down her collar.

"Excuse me, please." Molly laid down the microphone and chased Isabella back toward the snow creature where she engaged both Isabella and Fitzgerald in a snow fight. Paul, serving as the cameraman, laid the camera on the ground still recording. The picture showed him joining the fracas against Fitzgerald and Isabella. The microphone picked up a monkey-sounding laugh.

After a few minutes, Molly gathered Fitzgerald and Isabella for an interview. Paul picked up the camera to frame the three. "You've just witnessed the first interplanetary battle," Molly said while catching her breath. She turned to Fitzgerald and Isabella. "Is this your first experience with snow? Your inner eyelids give you quite an advantage in a snow fight."

Isabella answered for them, "Yes, ice precipitation is quite rare on Benevolent. Only on the highest mountains occasionally. Benevolent has mostly a dry tropical climate."

"Do Benevolents play games like this?"

"Oh, yes! They are very playful with each other. And athletic competitions are most popular."

"What sort of competitions?"

"Running, jumping, flying, snark chasing."

"Benevolents can fly?"

"They can. Except that as one gets older and gains weight

the flying is more difficult even with the gravity only two-thirds of Earth. Flying is mostly a game for children. As children, Fitzgerald and I felt left out because we could not fly."

● ● ●

"Welcome to Buenos Aires," a male TV interviewer from an Argentine network greeted. "I understand you've been on a whirlwind tour of Latin America."

"Yes. Thank you for your welcome," Fitzgerald responded.

"Where have you been?"

"We wish that we could stop at every capital. But on this trip, we have been to Mexico City, Cartagena, Brasilia, and now your lovely city, Buenos Aires."

"Fitzgerald learned Portuguese in two days before going to Brazil," Isabella interjected.

"What about you?" the interviewer asked.

"I am learning some Spanish, but Fitzgerald is the linguist. I'm an engineer."

"The travelogues created by your traveling companion, Molly Powell, are very popular here in Argentina. What will the episode on Argentina be about?"

Fitzgerald resumed speaking. "Well, with Molly we never know. In Mexico City she did a segment of us shopping in the market and eating food from street vendors. In Colombia, she filmed us exploring a tremendous fort from colonial days and riding in a local bus. I think in Argentina she will take us to a soccer match."

The man smiled in appreciation before asking, "I've noticed that Molly usually includes some interviews conducted by local newsmen. Will she use part of this interview?"

"Almost certainly. Your program will be broadcast to most of the world and several other planets."

The interviewer leaned forward in anticipation. "Then could I ask you a rather serious question?"

"We will answer if we can." Fitzgerald made a bring-it-on gesture with one hand.

"How do you propose addressing problems such as the increasing number of drug-resistant microbes called 'superbugs'? Physicians are running out of effective drugs for some infections."

Fitzgerald looked at Isabella. "You are correct," she said. "Microorganisms, because they have a simple structure and reproduce asexually, evolve very quickly. Microbes evolve about 40 million times faster than more complex life forms like mammals. New strains constantly emerge able to survive the drugs being used to suppress them. Insects and weeds that attack food crops also develop resistance to chemicals. In these cases, genetic mutations are allowing the pests to change. Already humans are using genetic modification to fight the insects and weeds. Ultimately, humans will probably need to use genetics to fight the superbugs."

"You mean like creating an anti-superbug?"

"Maybe, yes."

"You've mentioned genetics. You've said that Benevolents created you from various DNA parts. Most people in Argentina believe they were created by God. Does that make you feel... artificial, maybe even illegitimate?"

Fitzgerald resumed the answers. "Congratulations on

asking a question many others are likely wondering. We are all created. Don't most believe that the Great Creator uses people to build a great cathedral? I believe the Great Creator used the Benevolents to make us. We know that we are part of the Great Creator's universe just like any other being. And related to the superbug, the Great Creator might even use humans to make an anti-superbug.

"But the manner of our creation has an advantage. Isabella and I know clearly the purpose of our creation. And that purpose is good. Humans would be better off if all knew a good purpose for their being. We believe that a worthwhile purpose is to serve the Great Creator by helping others."

• • •

Paul joined Molly, Fitzgerald, and Isabella, who were watching BBC news in a London hotel room. "Tomorrow the visitors who are making such a stir around the world will be entertained by the royal family at Buckingham Palace," the news anchor reported. "This meeting is anticipated to be more congenial than today's meeting with members of Parliament and Prime Minister Brown. Controversy occurred when several MPs demanded assurances that British sovereignty would be respected."

A clip showed Fitzgerald speaking. "Our purpose is not to erase national boundaries. They carry great cultural and historical significance to the inhabitants. But Isabella and I cannot guarantee anybody anything specific. Neither can the Benevolents. Humans must work those things out themselves. The one guarantee we can give is that mankind is headed toward catastrophe unless we work together. The catastrophe may not occur in this generation, or even the next generation, but it will come. We are asking you to make changes that will benefit your descendants more than yourselves."

The BBC broadcast continued by interviewing several skeptical Parliament members.

"Blah, blah, blah," Molly expressed her opinion. "I've been a part of this news machine. They must cover all sides or possibly lose viewers who have strong ideas."

Paul spoke to Fitzgerald and Isabella, "How about a break? Would you like to see London at night?"

"How would we get away from the reporters outside?" Isabella asked.

"The stairwell leads to a back door. Hotel guests can open the outside door with their room cards."

"Wouldn't people recognize us?"

"Try these on." Paul opened a bag. He had purchased two wigs. In a few seconds, Fitzgerald and Isabella featured afro hairstyles. Paul also had umbrellas. "The weather is rainy. These can also hide part of your face."

Molly could hardly contain her glee as she showed Fitzgerald and Isabella how to use the umbrellas. "What about me?" she asked.

To her Paul gave a stocking cap. "Stuff your hair under this." When she had done so, he added a pair of ugly stage glasses. "In the dark, nobody is likely to know you."

"What about you?" she wanted to know.

"My face isn't as well-known as you three." He put on a pair of sunglasses. They all looked at themselves in the mirror.

"We'll pass," Paul predicted.

"Sometimes it's the quiet ones who are the most unpredictable," Molly said to Fitzgerald and Isabella.

To Londoners, the quartet was invisible as they visited the most famous London sights: Trafalgar Square, Piccadilly Circus, Big Ben, Westminster Abby, Harrods Department Store. Riding the well-lit underground trains to Oxford Street, a few people looked closely at Fitzgerald and Isabella. But if they recognized them, they made no sign. "Let's eat in here," Paul proposed when they passed a local restaurant. Molly, Fitzgerald, and Isabella took a back table with Fitzgerald and Isabella faced toward the wall while Paul ordered some food at the counter. He joined them with orders of fish and chips and meat pies. Then he returned to the front to pick up a pitcher of beer and four large mugs.

"We'll see if you like British food," Molly commented. "Not many people in the world do."

But Fitzgerald and Isabella relished all human foods. They consumed everything.

Using the train, the group crossed the Thames River. On the other side, they rode the London Eye Ferris wheel. Paul and Molly riding together could see Fitzgerald wrapping one arm around Isabella's shoulders to warm her and using the other arm to point out interesting viewpoints.

"This is nice, what you organized for Fitzgerald and Isabella," Molly said

"They needed a chance to be non-celebrities for a few hours." Paul and Molly finished the ride in an uneasy silence.

Molly's international and interplanetary broadcast from

England emphasized the meeting Fitzgerald and Isabella had with the royal family. She showed interior scenes of Buckingham Palace and included Fitzgerald making an error by trying to shake hands with the Buckingham Palace guards. But she made no mention of their nighttime ramble. *No sense in alerting reporters that we might do that again,* she thought.

● ● ●

The African children shrieked with joy as Isabella joined their line of dancers. To the beating drums, she tried to copy their steps. After the dance finished, the children mobbed around her, touching her skin and trying to feel her straight hair. Molly taped it all.

"That is unusual diplomatic behavior," the American ambassador to Nigeria observed in a whisper to Fitzgerald. "I'm not sure the president approves."

The Nigerian president sat nearby under a parasol with a dour look. His formal welcome carefully planned for the world's cameras had been disrupted. "Maybe not," Fitzgerald whispered back. "But look who did approve." Thousands of ordinary Nigerians jamming the stadium cheered and shouted.

"They don't necessarily make the decisions here," the ambassador returned.

The cultural program finished, the president, wearing a long robe with billowing sleeves, led the way to a banquet hall. After several long speeches welcoming Fitzgerald and Isabella to Africa, a long line of servers entered pushing carts laden with exquisite European foods to rival the best even in Paris. After the president's plate had been filled, all the other dignitaries approached the carts.

"What do you personally prefer to eat?" Fitzgerald asked one of the servers.

The server, a thin young man with dark skin and closely cropped hair, bowed slightly. He pointed to two carts at the end. A few older Nigerians congregated there selecting the foods they liked. Fitzgerald, followed by Isabella, joined the line to receive a mashed root that looked like potatoes covered by an oily red sauce with bits of meat.

"Oh, you like Nigerian food?" commented the vice president, next to whom they found seats.

"We wanted to try it. What is this made from?"

"It is pounded yam and a sauce made of palm oil, tomatoes, and spices. The meat is goat." Fitzgerald took a spoonful of the sauce and felt his mouth burning. He calmly reached for his glass of water. "Nigerians use a lot of pepe," the vice president continued.

"By 'pepe' you mean hot peppers?"

"Yes. Can you taste it?"

"It is very strong." Fitzgerald wiped tears from his eyes. "Isabella, try the yam with just a little sauce."

After the meal, the president stood and made a long speech reviewing the abuses of various European oppressors and placed particular emphasis on the American slave trade. "As a result, our countrymen are poor. They need financial help from western countries. But we only receive the little they do not need." Eventually he asked Fitzgerald to respond.

After a few complimentary words to the president and other dignitaries, Fitzgerald said, "I enjoyed the yam tonight. The sauce is tastier than any other food I have eaten on Earth."

Most of the Nigerians laughed heartily. All knew the spiciness of their food to outsiders.

Fitzgerald changed his tone. "Everyone needs to change. We cannot allow outside powers to take advantage of Africa anymore." The group responded with enthusiastic applause. "But Africans need to change as well. Corruption is part of your culture. Corruption undermines the competition that makes economies more efficient. You want aid from western countries? Rich countries must be convinced that corruption will not channel their aid to enrich only a few. Also, your countries could progress more quickly toward economic parity by voluntarily having fewer children or alternatively adopting neglected children. Parents with many children cannot always nourish them well or educate them for important well-paying jobs. We must fundamentally change our ways of living for our children five, ten, twenty generations from now."

The African crowd sat politely silent. *More of the same from the west,* most thought.

● ● ●

"Welcome to Australia, mates," the tour driver greeted as he loaded their carry bags.

"We are mates," Isabella indicated herself and Fitzgerald. "They are not," she pointed to Paul and Molly.

The driver stood perplexed. "They use the word 'mate' differently here," Molly explained. "That's a friendly term usually between men."

"Yeeah," the driver added. "My mates are my drinking buddies."

"I'll never get this right," Isabella complained.

"Well mates, I could use a brew or two," Paul said to Fitzgerald, Isabella, and Molly.

"Now you're talking Aussie." The driver grinned.

An hour later, the driver stopped by a group of large kangaroos. "I wouldn't get too close, mate," he warned Fitzgerald. Ever adventurous, Fitzgerald stepped a few steps closer as Molly filmed for the Down Under travelogue. A large male "roo" balanced on its tail and used both hind feet to knock Fitzgerald sprawling.

"They look so friendly," he complained after scrambling back to his feet. "I caught a kangaroo," he added to Isabella.

"That one caught you, mate," she answered.

Chapter 17

• • •

Fitzgerald surveyed the Colosseum in Rome. "And men fought here? Was it like professional wrestling? Did they practice together and have dinner together afterwards?"

"Men did fight here, sometimes against other men, sometimes against animals," Paul affirmed. "But they fought for real, usually until one was dead."

"How long ago was this?"

"About two thousand years. The Roman civilization eventually collapsed. But a different civilization recovered."

Fitzgerald commented, "Then Rome must have been a regional, technically un-advanced civilization, I think. Am I correct in my Earth history that they had no internal combustion engines, no electricity or electronics, no automation, and no genetic engineering? And nearly all the people were slaves or peasants. Is that correct?"

"That would be true," Paul admitted.

"Unfortunately, the discoveries that the Benevolents and others have made indicate that when a world-wide technological civilization fails, it never returns to its zenith. This is because they have squandered the easily available energy resources created by their planet over millions of years and likely destroyed their environment. When a post-technical civilization does emerge, it will be like ancient Rome, not current-day Earth. And nearly all of the people will be slaves or peasants." Rarely had Paul or Molly seen Fitzgerald so somber.

"Why don't you say something pleasant rather than being so dire?" Isabella reprimanded her mate. "You won't convince mankind talking like that."

"You are right, Isabella. I was just talking to my friend, Paul. I do feel the weight of our mission. I'll behave in front of the cameras. You should keep reminding me to be fun and positive."

Isabella turned to Molly. "Do you need any more pictures for the broadcast?"

"No, I have plenty of film of you and Fitzgerald looking at old ruins."

"Then what shall we do now?"

New human foods always cheered up the extraterrestrials. "Let's try some genuine Italian ravioli." To herself Molly suspected, *Fitzgerald and Isabella aren't yet telling Earth the full story.*

• • •

"The Vatican's car will pick you up for your appointment

with the pope in half an hour," said Paul the next morning. "They're documenting everything and will forward a recording of you with the pope to Molly."

"Aren't you both coming with us?" asked Isabella.

"You're the ones they want to see. They didn't really invite us," Molly explained. "And I still have a lot of work to do editing the broadcasts from Paris and Madrid. I don't know about Paul."

Paul nodded in agreement. "I saw the Vatican on a trip several years ago. And I've got a lot to iron out about your upcoming itinerary. I really need to stay here and catch up on some work."

Fitzgerald and Isabella left the hotel with the Vatican representative while Paul and Molly worked in their respective rooms. About noon, Molly felt hungry and decided to try the hotel's restaurant. Walking by Paul's door she thought, *I wonder if he's still working. I don't want to be rude.* She tapped on his door.

Paul seemed surprised to see Molly when he answered the door. "I was going downstairs for some lunch, if you'd like to join me. No big deal."

"Aaah, sure. No big deal. Let me save my work." Molly waited in the hall while Paul secured his laptop. In less than a minute, he closed the door and followed Molly to the elevator.

Seated in the restaurant they made small talk until the waiter took their orders. Paul ordered a linguini after Molly had selected fettuccine. An awkward silence followed.

"Listen, Paul, I need to apologize for the sexist comment I made," Molly began.

Paul was tempted to quip, "Which one?" But rather than deliver that cheap shot, he shrugged lightly and acted clueless.

"You know, the one about men being untrustworthy. After what you did for Beth, you didn't deserve that."

Paul certainly did remember her comment, but responded kindly, "Oh, you mean at the UN. Hey, I didn't think through how you would interpret my intentions on our ramble around New York. I don't blame you for being upset. My head was messed up from Beth. Still is, I think."

"Probably I felt more embarrassed than anything." Another awkward silence followed. Molly toyed with her soft drink, not looking at Paul. "I wish my mother could have met a man like you, just one. But she didn't. And I've not trusted men since. I've never had one serious relationship. They scare me because I know how relationships can ultimately hurt."

"Well, I've never had a romantic relationship. I always expect an unattainable standard of trust and emotional intimacy. Beth and I were best friends from grade school on. I truly loved her, still do. After her death, I vowed never to be so heartbroken again. But our relationship was never very romantic. It just was."

Molly laughed out loud. "We make quite a pair, don't we? I don't know how to have a serious relationship. You don't know how to have a romance."

Paul grinned back. "That pretty much sums it up."

Their food came. Neither said anything for a few minutes as they ate.

"Beth was so pretty. I saw her picture on your desk at NASA." Molly hesitated. "Pretty girls make me jealous. They can control any situation."

"You mean manipulate any situation. Beth could be selfish, and she did know how to get what she wanted." Paul spoke his next words carefully. "You're not like that."

"Oh, I know what I want and I usually get it!"

"But you're straightforward. You're honest." Molly sat still, waiting for Paul to finish. "Full disclosure, Molly. Isabella talked with me. She said that I should find a woman completely different from Beth. A woman who would make me feel differently than Beth ever did."

"Do I make you feel differently than Beth did?"

"Oh, yeah." Paul sighed deeply and rubbed his face. Molly could see him trembling slightly from fear and uncertainty. His voice quivered as he spoke. "Molly, would you be willing to try at having a relationship with me? I don't know exactly what it would look like." He held his breath.

"Isabella told me that I shouldn't be afraid to trust you. I'm willing to try a romantic friendship."

Paul exhaled. "Then let's start by understanding each other. Intercourse is off the table until I figure myself out and feel secure with you. Is that okay?"

"Agreed. And I ask that you always be straight with me. If you start losing interest in me, I want to know right away. Don't use me and then just leave when you're tired of me."

"Well, if you want straight, I think you're the best woman I've ever met and absolutely drop-dead gorgeous. I sure would welcome another kiss like the one you gave me in the carriage."

"Let's forget about work this afternoon and go exploring, just you and me. I think we might find a few kisses for both of us."

"Waiter! Could we have the check, please?" Paul almost shouted.

• • •

At the Vatican, Fitzgerald and Molly admired the Sistine Chapel and, led by a priest, climbed the dome overlooking the city. Afterwards, a priest ushered them to meet the pope. "His Holiness will see you now," a male receptionist announced. Entering a private chamber, both bowed slightly in respect as the elderly man rose to meet them.

The pope spoke in English so that Isabella would not be left out of the conversation. "I understand that you and those who sent you believe in a Divine Creator."

"Yes sir. We do," Fitzgerald answered. "Our scientists have also identified the beginning of the universe in what your scientists call 'The Big Bang.' To us, that speaks of a Great Creator. I believe that The Big Bang was first recognized by a Catholic Priest, Georges Lemaitre."

The pope nodded in surprised acknowledgment. "And I have heard that you are an admirer of Jesus Christ. Is that true?"

Fitzgerald repeated, "Yes sir. We respect the principles he taught about loving your neighbor as yourself and even loving those who would be your enemies. Those sound like the Great Creator we believe in. Your church has stood for those principles since Jesus' lifetime."

"We also believe that Jesus died for human sins."

"I greatly admire Jesus' sacrifice for others. And I understand that his death is the unifying principle for all of

170

Jesus' earthly followers. I do not understand all the variations of human theology of how the Great Creator deals with humans. But nothing I believe is contradictory to what you said about Jesus."

The pope appeared pleased and said to Isabella, "And what about you, young lady?"

"I believe that the Great Creator would have us all work together to help each person to realize the potential they are given."

"And the two of you are married?"

"Yes sir," Isabella answered. "To the Benevolents, mating is a solemn lifelong commitment. Fitzgerald is my mate and I am his."

"Congratulations. We also believe in the importance of marriage."

Fitzgerald spoke respectfully, "Your Holiness, could I be so bold as to mention another issue?"

"Please do."

"Christians anticipate the return of Christ to found a new kingdom. Unfortunately, some are so expectant that they fail to plan for those who may live after them. But Jesus has been absent for two thousand years. What if he takes…"

The pope held up his hand for Fitzgerald to stop. "Yes, the scriptures even indicate that in the first years after Jesus' departure some stopped working and just waited. Jesus may come soon. But in case he doesn't, current-day Christians should plan for the welfare of future generations."

"One last thing, please? Would you be willing to bestow a blessing on us?"

And the pope did.

• • •

When Paul and Molly grabbed two seats together in the State Department's jet traveling to Budapest, Fitzgerald and Isabella knew that something had changed between them. This was the first time the human male and female had sat closely on the worldwide tour. Everybody on the flight wondered about the laughter coming from their row.

• • •

"Our people suffered under communism for nearly five decades. Why should we retreat from the gains we've made since 1991?" the Hungarian president confronted Fitzgerald on camera.

"We are not asking you to retreat. Communism came out of an untenable situation. A few lived like or actually were kings. Most others suffered a miserable existence. Communism tried to overlay ignorance and bad character onto an unrealistically idealistic plan. Your people suffered the results."

Fitzgerald realized the political implications of his next words and spoke carefully. "We believe the greatest loss to mankind is the failure to allow individuals to achieve their potential for the good of all. Not all individuals, including on Benevolent, have the same potential or motivation. Any successful system needs to reward individual initiative and sacrifice.

"Conflicts still exist on Benevolent. The beings there have found that they need individuality to function well as a society.

Individuals still think differently and frequently act in self-interest. The Benevolents still need police or referees. But the most successful systems also reward those with the character to think not only of themselves but of others. Ultimately, this accelerates the well-being of all.

"Change is difficult. Making the decision to change is the most difficult because the decision implies past values or beliefs to be wrong. Nobody wants to acknowledge errors of their own or predecessors. However, mankind's ancestors, despite errors, have brought us to the point that humans can make a great leap forward. We ask humans to develop the ability, the willingness, to deal with the issues that threaten your species' future. Some of these I mentioned at the UN. Others you will identify for yourselves. You should do this not necessarily for yourselves, but for many future generations."

Chapter 18

• • •

"Reports of cooperation and acts of kindness are pouring in from around the globe," the BBC News anchor reported. "In one recent example, traditional enemies Pakistan and India have opened their borders so that their citizens can exchange gifts. The message of goodwill and seeking the common good brought by the extraterrestrials Fitzgerald and Isabella Benevolent seems to be having effect. Optimism of a new wave of prosperity created by alien technology has pushed the US Dow Jones Industrial up 64% in the last two months. Other financial indexes are not far behind."

Molly used the remote to turn off the hotel room TV. "Can you believe this? The whole world is changing," she said to Paul. "I saw a report yesterday about American drug companies making their pharmaceuticals free for international relief organizations."

"I feel like I'm living in a dream," Paul returned. "This could literally be a new day for mankind."

Molly put her arms around his waist and looked into his eyes. "This is a new day for me as well. For the first time, I'm excited about the future."

Paul kissed her and then squeezed her tight. "I feel the same way. And I hope you and I will see this future together."

A knock at the door interrupted them. Paul opened the door to admit Fitzgerald and Isabella. He missed the questioning look Molly received from Isabella. "Where do we go next?" Fitzgerald asked.

"Back to New York. The United Nations is convening a special assembly to deal with the opportunities before humanity. Secretary Iscaderian has asked for you and Isabella to deliver an address that outlines the priority issues mankind must face."

"When do we leave?"

• • •

A week later Fitzgerald stood before the UN General Assembly for the second time. After the obligatory acknowledgments he began, "Imagine a world with minimal crime, no infectious diseases, bio-engineered fuel sources, communication and sharing amongst a galactic network of civilizations, climate control, much longer human life spans, human knowledge and skills that aren't lost within a short life span, crops that don't require pesticides or chemical fertilizers, and peace among nations. Imagine a world in which each person can realize his or her own potential and contribute that potential toward the good of all.

"The path to achieving this world will be difficult. Mankind

176

has many challenges. On the surface are problems such as pollution, armed conflicts with increasing probability of someone using nuclear weapons, the danger of irresponsible genetic engineering, unsustainable use of Earth's resources, the growing resistance of pathogens and parasites to chemical control, and the heavy debt load carried by many nations. In the past, the only operable answer was to delay facing the inevitable consequences. Or as the English language idiom says, 'kick the can down the road.'

"In our discussions around the world, we have met many who have a vested interest in keeping the problems alive by not solving them. Governments hold onto power by convincing their people of certain aggrievements and bringing out their most primitive instincts. People make money by representing a special interest. There is no benefit to such governments or people to solve a problem. Therefore, only the ordinary humans can resolve these problems by demanding that their leaders move beyond maintaining the status quo.

"Now there is a new hope. A partnership of sentient species wishes to help you and have mankind join them. Our presence here," Fitzgerald gestured toward Isabella, "is the proof of their commitment to the success of mankind. But the offer is contingent on mankind's willingness, on their ability, to work together for the common good. Providing you with additional technology without you first developing the ability to cooperate will only exacerbate your problems."

Fitzgerald stood silently scanning the audience for a full minute. A nervous rustle began among his listeners. "You have many different belief and value systems. Each people has a unique history. Customs are part of your identity. To achieve success, you must establish a system that values individuals who work toward the common good rather than keep an issue unsolved for personal gain. You must create a new history together. You must find identity in what you share as human beings beyond your specific group.

"In the earliest days of man, Earth was raw and wild. The few humans competed with wild beasts for life. Survival of the fittest bred aggression and importance of self into your species. As the number of humans increased, they competed with other humans for the best resources. The competition led to group identity and tribalism. Those qualities that allowed individuals and groups to survive now make working for the common good difficult. Mankind needs to create a new set of guidelines by which you can live and cooperate. The first principle must be the importance and value of all. Do this for your children and their descendants for hundreds of generations—10,000 years and more of prosperity for all. Take a chance on the future."

Isabella joined Fitzgerald at the podium. "Thank you for allowing Fitzgerald and me to be among you. We will die on Earth. Your future is our future." They nodded to the secretary general and sat down.

In the waiting room, Paul and Molly, unlike the previous occasion, had listened attentively to Fitzgerald's speech. "What do you think will happen now?" Molly asked Paul.

"The secretary general has proposed subcommittees to deal with the most critical issues."

DSC Network's evening news anchor, Steve Wilson, reported, "Discussions at the United Nations have been intense during the last week. Our reporter Molly Powell has an in-depth report. Any progress for us, Molly?"

"Steve, Fitzgerald and Isabella have tirelessly shuttled between various subcommittees trying to broker some compromise solutions. The subcommittee on climate control is deadlocked between cold weather nations who would welcome global warming versus nations threatened by rising oceans and droughts. African nations have refused to submit to mandatory population controls proposed by Europe.

"Arab nations have insisted that for the common good of mankind Israel give up the lands they have controlled since the 1947 partition of Palestine according to the Balfour Resolution. Israel refuses to comply, citing Old Testament assurances of God and referring to the Holocaust in World War II.

"China opposes curtailment of their widespread burning of low-grade coal, which is affecting world-wide air quality. They accurately point out that industrialized nations such as the United States and Britain used inexpensive coal extensively during their economic development."

"Is there any good news, Molly?"

"Today the General Assembly voted overwhelmingly to abolish nuclear weapons. But after the North Koreans refused to comply, the other nuclear powers withdrew their assent. Nobody wants to leave North Korea as the sole remaining nuclear power."

"What about the Security Council?"

"That's another problem, Steve. Some members of the Security Council are insisting that all decisions must be approved by them. Any one member of the Security Council could veto any resolution. This in effect makes the deliberations of the subcommittees meaningless."

"Molly, this sounds like business as usual among the world's nations."

"I'm afraid that's right, Steve."

Steve continued, "In other news, the world's financial markets took a beating losing another 12% today. The US Dow Jones Index has lost nearly all the euphoric gains of the previous months. The other indexes have followed suit."

• • •

Fitzgerald and Isabella sat watching the news with Paul and Molly. Fitzgerald looked listless and defeated. "We knew this would be hard," Isabella told him.

"Yes, we did," he admitted. "But I did not realize how impossible the task would be. I can't believe how many apocalyptic groups are actually eager for the earth to be destroyed or to bring on a dystopian future. To a starving man, only supper matters. Most humans aren't starving, but they retain the mindset of immediacy like the earliest humans."

"Remember," Isabella urged, "that humans have been brought up for their entire lives to think a certain way. And their self-importance and tribal identity have been bred into them. As you explained, those things used to be necessary for their survival. Changing mindsets will take generations."

"I know you are right. But I need to be reminded often."

"Your personal approval ratings are still at 90% with the public," Molly volunteered. "And your book is making sales records. Do you remember when your release from the quarantine quarters was in doubt?"

They did remember.

Molly continued, "We went right to the people then. Their grassroots support enabled you to be released. Why don't we try that again?"

"The problem is that 100% of Arabs want Israel to relinquish the land. Nearly 100% of Africans oppose any measures to encourage population control. The United Nations representatives are generally supporting what their people think. I don't want to be perceived as taking sides. And humans hate to be told what to do by an outsider," Fitzgerald answered.

Molly didn't give up. "Maybe you could propose some specific compromises. One of the reasons Africans oppose population control is that they're dependent on offspring to care for them in their old age. If the Europeans guaranteed some sort of old-age protections, the Africans might be more receptive to voluntary limits on family size."

"Alright, let's try that one."

• • •

Paul brought the morning paper into Fitzgerald and Isabella's hotel room. There they and Molly enjoyed a room-service breakfast before going to the United Nations for another day of frustration. "Hey, you've made the Europeans and Africans agree," Paul said.

"Really?" Fitzgerald asked, surprised and hopeful.

"Yes. They both agree that your proposal about population control and old-age subsidies is impossible." The newspaper had printed some examples of the comments:

"Ridiculous idea."

"Having children is a God-given right."

"A communist proposal."

"Racist to the core."

"Let Fitzgerald guarantee the old-age subsidies."

Fitzgerald visibly slumped. Paul consoled, "It was worth a try. And the proposal still might bear fruit, if they come up with their own better idea. For what it's worth, I agreed with Molly when she suggested trying this proposal."

Molly looked at Paul with appreciation.

"Okay, now I've got an idea," Paul continued. "We all need a vacation. The internment, the world tour, and now these UN confrontations have worn us all out."

"How would we take a vacation?" Isabella asked.

"Leave that to me."

Chapter 19

• • •

Three days later Paul told Fitzgerald, Isabella, and Molly, "Tomorrow morning we'll leave at 3:00 a.m. for a vacation."

"Why so early?" Isabella wanted to know.

"We don't want reporters to follow us. No offense, Molly."

Molly smiled. "None taken. And I don't blame you."

"Where are we going?" Isabella persisted.

"Somewhere very different with few people. Put your personal items and laptops in this backpack and pack everything else you have in your suitcases. We'll be leaving the suitcases behind." Paul provided three backpacks plus one for himself.

At 2:30 the next morning, Molly heard a gentle tapping on her hotel room door. "Molly, this is Paul. Are you ready?"

Molly opened the door. "Sure, I'm ready." In spite of herself, Molly giggled. "Won't you tell me what's up?"

"This operation is top secret." Paul leaned in to give her a quick smack on the lips. "Don't you like surprises?"

"Of course I do. But do we need to bring anything special?"

"Just your personal things. I've got some new clothes for you and our friends. Anything else we need can be bought where we're going. Just leave everybody's big suitcases in their rooms. I've arranged for the hotel to collect and store them."

"Are you going to make sure Fitzgerald and Isabella are awake?"

"How about you do that? Then all of you sneak down the stairway and out the back entrance. Don't forget to wear your disguises. I'll pull up a small car to pick you up."

"Aren't you afraid of being recognized yourself?"

"Not hardly. You, Fitzgerald, and Isabella are the stars on TV. Nobody is likely to remember me."

"This is fun, Paul."

At precisely 3:00, Molly stood with Fitzgerald and Isabella in a shadow on a side street next to the hotel. An economy car pulled up. Molly jumped into the front and Fitzgerald and Isabella got into the back seat. "A clean getaway!" Paul shouted and accelerated onto Fifth Avenue.

They all had caught Paul's spirit of clandestine mischief. Everyone talked at once speculating on the reporters' surprise to find them missing. "They'll think we've beamed up," suggested Fitzgerald.

Isabella spoke above the clamor, "No! They'll think humans have abducted the aliens."

"Won't they miss Fitzgerald and Isabella at the United Nations?" Molly asked.

Paul answered, "I phoned in that they would be in seclusion for high-level meetings with top dignitaries at a secure location. All of them will be wondering who other than themselves Fitzgerald and Isabella will be meeting."

Their merriment continued as Paul drove to a private terminal at New York's JFK airport. He dropped them off while he went to return the rental car. Inside the small waiting room, they found someone they knew. "Dr. Holdridge?" Fitzgerald reacted.

"Call me Laura, please. This is my son, Jeff." A fifteen-year-old boy with Down Syndrome looked at them in a friendly manner. Laura herself appeared more relaxed and friendly than the previous time they had met her.

"What are you doing here?"

"When Paul asked Dr. Finkle for transport, we thought we would come along for the ride. Jeff and I are going to take a cruise ship leaving from Anchorage."

Molly's mouth gaped open in surprise "Are we going to Alaska?"

"Didn't Paul tell you?"

"No, he's kept this operation hush-hush."

"I don't blame him. The reporters would have followed you thicker than Alaskan mosquitos."

At that moment Paul returned carrying his own backpack and pulling a large roller suitcase. Molly could not restrain herself. "I've always wanted to go to Alaska!"

"My parents took my brother and me there three times when I was a kid. Where else can we go without many people and where you don't need to show passports?" said Paul. "Plus you won't need to wear the disguises except when we go into a town." He noticed their other traveling companions.

"Dr. Holdridge! I didn't know you would be coming. Is this your son?"

Laura affirmed that and then said to the pilots, "We're ready."

On board Ben Finkle's Learjet, Paul opened the suitcase to reveal outdoor clothes and hiking boots for each of them. Jeff watched with interest as Paul passed out the things. He smiled and laughed when Paul handed him a new fishing rod. *Paul must have purchased that for us, but he didn't want Jeff to be left out,* Molly thought.

• • •

The flight to Alaska would take seven hours. Fitzgerald, obviously fatigued from the rigors of meetings at the UN, fell asleep. Isabella spent much of the time talking and laughing with Jeff. The pilots invited both of them to the cockpit and let Jeff sit in the co-pilot's seat. "Jeff is a sweet boy," Molly said to Laura.

"Yes, he is. And he really likes Isabella. Usually he's a bit shy." Laura hesitated. "I worry about what will happen to Jeff when I'm gone. I'm an only child and my parents are elderly."

"What about his father's family?"

"I don't have any idea where Jeff's father is. He left us when Jeff was diagnosed with Down Syndrome."

Molly sympathized, "My father left my mother and me."

"But you were a tremendous blessing to your mother, I'll bet. Jeff is to me."

"Didn't Victor Hugo say, 'To love another person is to see the face of God?' "

"Yes, you're right, and I can see the truth in his statement. Still, I kick myself for being smart enough to get a PhD in applied genetics and dumb enough to marry..." Laura caught herself and broke off.

A somewhat painful silence followed. Paul spoke to change the mood. "What got you interested in genetics, Laura?"

"I always loved science. In high school, I wrote a paper for English class about women scientists. I found that Rosalind Franklin said, 'In my view, all that is necessary for faith is the belief that by doing our best we shall succeed in our aims: the improvement of mankind.' That inspired me. The story of how she was cheated pulled me into genetics in her honor."

Molly looked lost. "Who is Rosalind Franklin?"

Paul sighed at his failure to change the mood and reluctantly summarized, "She was a young Jewish woman scientist in the early 1950s. Rosalind photographed the DNA helix and theorized the structure. A male colleague took her data and ideas without her knowledge and gave them to men who published her work without acknowledgment. They later received a Nobel prize."

Molly visibly bristled with female umbrage. "Didn't Rosalind object?"

"She tried. But she died of ovarian cancer before her major contribution to mankind was eventually recognized." Paul attempted to alter the potentially anti-male mood again. "What have you found from the DNA samples you took from Fitzgerald and Isabella?"

Laura looked embarrassed. "We didn't mean to doubt you by taking their saliva. But we just had to make certain. And we were also curious to see what we could find."

"No problem. We understand," Paul said.

She acknowledged his comment with a shrug. "Their DNA is remarkably human and at the same time very unusual."

"I can hardly imagine."

"We managed to replicate the DNA for testing and are trying to identify sequences, but without a larger population, we can't correlate with human characteristics. And then there's that twenty-fourth chromosome pair. We don't know what that's for. Have your friends given any indication about its purpose?"

Paul waved to get Isabella's attention. She looked up from a thumb wrestling game Jeff had taught her. "Isabella," he asked, "do you know that you have one more chromosome pair than humans?"

"Yes. I have a little biological knowledge."

"Do you know what that extra chromosome contains?"

"Fitzgerald and I are not geneticists. But I think it relates to possible genetic damage during long space travel and our resistance to human diseases." Isabella resumed entertaining Jeff.

Paul returned to Laura, "Have you tried to inject DNA from that chromosome into a test subject?"

"You mean a reproductive cell, from a test subject." Seeing Paul's confusion, she explained, "We can modify reproductive cells with sets of unpaired chromosomes. But once the chromosomes combine in the zygote and start multiplying by mitosis, we have no way to modify them. If doing so was legal in the US, we could correct genetic abnormalities like cystic fibrosis before pregnancy, but not afterwards. Certainly, we can't treat anything like..." Laura looked toward at her son. "But testing on any human subjects, even single reproductive cells, is fraught with ethical concerns. So no. We haven't tried the twenty-fourth chromosome even in the laboratory."

"You mention cystic fibrosis. My wife died of that."

"I'm sorry. With the CRISPR gene splicing technology we have now, we could have prevented that affliction by modifying chromosome twenty-one in her mother or father's reproductive cell. But there are serious ethical challenges. A lot of people are opposed to genetic modifications even in the case of such devastating diseases. We've also made progress isolating the gene sequences that would identify propensity among humans of behavioral tendencies. The process is to collect DNA analysis and personality traits on a large pool of subjects. Computers can then statistically correlate tendencies with the genetic markers. Some people are genetically more likely to take up smoking, for example, or suffer antisocial personality disorder, called ASPD. Those studies result in probabilities, not certainties. We haven't done any experimentation, only analysis."

"Antisocial personality disorder is like psychopathy, right?" Paul asked. "When individuals have a lack of empathy or concern for others."

"Yes, psychopathy is one of many forms of ASPD. But all forms can be characterized by disregard for others and frequently impulsive and aggressive behavior that leads to conflict with the law and strained relationships. Those so afflicted are also prone to substance abuse and addiction. Genetic markers can indicate a tendency toward ASPD. Like victims of cystic fibrosis, they could possibly have been helped before conception and mitosis."

Molly had sat listening. She couldn't understand the genetic technicalities like Paul. But she clearly realized, *Laura's heroine, Rosalind, wanted to improve mankind. She believes they can alter human behavior genetically. I wonder if Fitzgerald also talked about that with Dr. Finkle.*

• • •

The Learjet touched down at the Anchorage airport and taxied to a private terminal. Laura said goodbye to all and took a cab to the cruise ship embarkation point. Jeff hated to leave Isabella.

"Wait here," Paul told his group. "I'll be back in about an hour." He too caught a cab.

An hour later, *Beep, beep*, summoned them to the parking lot.

"What is this?" Fitzgerald asked about a large vehicle sitting before them.

"Paul has rented an RV!" Molly squealed.

"What is an RV?"

"That means recreational vehicle. It's like an apartment on wheels. Bring your backpacks." Molly hugged Paul around the neck. "This will be so much fun."

Chapter 20

●●●

"Eeeeee..." Isabella shrieked. The fishing line cut diagonally through the water.

Fitzgerald stood beside her staring at the point where the line entered the water. "Keep the line tight," he coached. "Remember, pull the rod tip up and then reel in line as you lower it. Tire the fish out."

Isabella grimaced with effort. "The fish is so strong."

"You've nearly got him." In a minute, Fitzgerald splashed knee deep into the water, heedless of getting shoes and pant legs wet. That hardly mattered. His feet and legs had been wet since morning. This time, though, he also got his shirtsleeves wet grappling with the exhausted fish until he straightened up, holding a beautiful salmon. Keeping a careful hold on the fish, he waded to the shore to carry Isabella her catch. After admiring the last fish of the day, they put it back in the water and watched it slowly swim away to spawn.

Molly stood on the gravel bank of a milky-blue river just above the tidal zone of an estuary. Dark green Douglas firs lined the river's banks. The water splashed over rocks forming deep pools where salmon waited before moving further upstream. She took a deep breath of alpine-scented air and remarked, "I could do this all day."

Paul answered, "You mean fish?"

"No, I mean watch them fish."

"Actually, you have been watching them fish all day. And you've caught a few too."

Molly smiled. "I caught the biggest one."

"Yes, you did. And you'll get the privilege of cleaning it for supper."

"My mother and I moved around a lot and mostly lived in the city. I don't know how to clean fish. Would you do mine for me, please?"

Paul looked at Molly. She had never used the helpless female gimmick before. He had to admit, she managed it effectively, though. "Okay, I'll clean your fish. And I'll show Fitzgerald how to clean Isabella's."

"Then I'll head back to the campsite with Isabella. I can build up the campfire and make fried potatoes to go with the fish."

But Isabella preferred to observe the fish cleaning. So Molly started walking back to a state campground, which had been sited to the proximity of productive fishing. At a cleaning station by the river provided by the campground, Paul demonstrated on Molly's salmon. Seagulls swooped down to grab up scraps. Then he watched as Fitzgerald and Isabella each cleaned the fish they had caught. Those three fish had been kept from more than a dozen caught that day. Each of them carried a fish to their campsite.

"You should take a hot shower, or you'll catch a cold," Molly told Fitzgerald on their return.

Fitzgerald returned a blank look. "We don't catch colds," Isabella explained. She then pushed her mate toward the campground's community shower. "Take a shower and put on clean clothes anyway. You smell of fish."

Inside the RV, Molly fried potatoes. Paul wrapped each fish in heavy aluminum foil and punched in a couple of holes for steam to escape. Always the inquisitive one, Isabella wanted to know, "Why do you wrap the fish in metal?"

"You will see." After raking out some coals from the campfire, Paul placed the wrapped fish on top of them. Then he piled more coals on top. "By the time Fitzgerald is back, we'll have supper cooked."

In a few minutes, Fitzgerald did return. Paul pulled the packages of fish from the fire and carried them to a picnic table. There he peeled back the aluminum foil on one of the packages to reveal a beautifully steamed salmon. "The foil prevents burning and will keep the other fish warm while we eat the first one."

Isabella watched amazed. "I never saw anyone cook in a wood fire before."

"This is how our 'primitive' ancestors cooked food."

"Where did they get the metal wrap?"

Paul laughed. "They used other methods. Sometimes they wrapped the food in leaves. They boiled food in ceramic pots.

Or they used a stick to hold the food over the fire."

Unlike Isabella, Fitzgerald was simply hungry. "Can we eat it now?"

Fortunately, Molly arrived with the potatoes. "Although the British call these 'chips' we usually call them 'french fries.'"

When dark came at about 11:00, the foursome cleaned up the campsite and entered the RV to escape the mosquitos. A chilly rain typical of Alaska started. Fitzgerald and Isabella went into the RV's bedroom Paul had assigned to them. Molly crawled into the sleeping space above the driving cab she had been given. Paul started to convert the RV's small dining area into a bed for himself.

"I'm cold up here," Molly whispered.

"Do you want me to turn on the propane heater?"

"I was thinking you could warm me up." Seeing Paul's sudden look of uncertainty, she added, "Paul, I'm not asking for sex. I'd just like to be near you. And I *am* cold."

Paul glanced at the door where Fitzgerald and Isabella rested and then back at Molly. "I'm cold too."

"Then come on up."

Three seconds later, he was beside her along with his sleeping bag. They lay alongside each other and soon each could feel the other's warmth.

"What are we going to do tomorrow?" Molly whispered.

"Maybe we could try berry picking. We should be able to find plenty of wild blueberries, salmonberries, and my favorite—thimbleberries. They're a lot like raspberries."

"That would be fun." They whispered together until they both fell asleep. Molly's last conscience thought was, *This is really nice.*

．．．

About 3:00 a.m., Paul felt Molly nudge him. "I hear something outside." Awakened, he could discern something moving around the campsite. The garbage can rattled.

Paul slipped out of his bag and went to the window. He felt Molly beside him. A dark shape stood by the picnic table. "Wake up Fitzgerald and Isabella. They'll want to see this."

Molly tapped on their door. From inside, a sleepy voice responded, "Yes."

"Please come out. Paul has something to show you."

After they had all gathered at the window, Paul turned on the RV's outside lights. Everybody saw a black bear sniffing around the campsite. Her two cubs wrestled on the ground.

Isabella whispered, "What is that?"

"That's a bear. Remember we saw one at the zoo," Paul explained. "They're looking for food. That's why we cleaned up the campsite so well."

"To deny them food?"

"To encourage them to find food in the wild."

Fitzgerald turned the doorknob. Paul stopped him. "No, no, don't go out there." He pointed at the cubs. "Those are her babies. She would hurt you if she thought you endangered them."

"What if she didn't have babies?" Fitzgerald asked.

"Then she would probably run away from you."

In a few minutes, the bear wandered into the darkness, followed by her cubs. They all went back to bed.

．．．

In the morning, Molly woke first. She enjoyed lying beside Paul and feeling his breathing for a while. Then she slipped out and busied herself in the tiny kitchen.

The smell of pancakes and bacon cooking greeted the others as they woke. "My mother and I made pancakes on her days off work," Molly explained as she served them on the RV's small dining table. "That's probably my best memory of childhood."

Everybody poured on a fruit syrup and complimented her on her cooking. Naturally, Isabella wanted to try cooking. "You turn pancakes over when the bubbles come up," Molly instructed her. Isabella soon proudly served Molly pancakes.

After breakfast, Paul piloted the RV down one of Alaska's highways. Molly rode in the passenger seat while Fitzgerald and Isabella stared at the scenery through a picture window. They marveled at snow-covered mountains, rolling tundra, and alpine forests. "Look! Look! Look at those animals. See the ones with the huge horns?" Fitzgerald shouted.

Paul slowed while a herd of caribou ran stiff-legged roughly parallel to the road. "Those are caribou. And their horns are called antlers," Molly told them.

"How do they hold their heads up all day with that antler weight?" Isabella asked.

"I've wondered that myself," Paul commented. "And wait until you see a moose."

A few miles later Paul stopped in a turnout where several foot paths branched into the brush. Molly distributed plastic bags saved from grocery shopping. "These are to collect berries for tomorrow morning's pancakes."

Paul and Molly soon became separated from their friends as ripe berries drew the couples in opposite directions. "We'd better split up and go looking for them," Paul suggested.

Fitzgerald and Isabella had found that larger and more plentiful berries could be picked farther from the road where fewer people had been. As they penetrated deeper and deeper into the bush, Fitzgerald suddenly stopped. "Look, Isabella. There is a caribou antler." The antler, rather than being attached to a live animal, protruded from a mound of dirt and turf.

Fitzgerald, followed by Isabella, advanced farther to see more closely. *Woof.* A low grunting sound made them look thirty yards to their left. They saw a huge shaggy brown animal stand erect and stare at them through tiny eyes. On its hind legs, the grizzly stood eight feet tall.

"That's a bear," Isabella whispered. "Stay away if it has babies."

But instead of running away, the animal dropped to its four paws and started stalking toward them. They could hear a deep rumbling coming from its chest. *Mnnn, mnnn, mnnn.*

"Stop! Don't run!" ordered Molly's voice. She stepped around Fitzgerald and Isabella and faced the bear. "Now walk slowly away," she told them. Molly had once read about talking down a grizzly. "We are leaving, Mr. Bear. We don't want trouble, Mr. Bear," she tried.

Her voice puzzled the bear for a bit. It stopped and sniffed carefully in her direction. Then it continued stalking closer. Molly continued talking as she edged backwards. "Please don't eat me, Mr. Bear."

Suddenly at twenty yards the bear charged. "Run! Run!" Molly screamed and turned to run herself. She could hear Fitzgerald and Isabella's feet hitting the ground ahead of her.

Molly managed only three steps before the bear crashed into her and knocked her sprawling. The bear's momentum carried it another five yards beyond her. As the bear turned to pounce, another figure jumped between them. Paul doused the bear's eyes with pepper spray. "Run, Molly!"

Molly had rolled after hitting the ground and had already come up running. Paul sprinted down the trail after her. Behind them they could hear the bear roaring and thrashing about. Even with the fear of a bear, they couldn't keep up with Fitzgerald and Isabella.

Neither of them stopped until they had reached the RV. There they found Fitzgerald and Isabella standing just outside the RV door looking ashen but otherwise unaffected. Paul and Molly's chests heaved from exertion and excitement. Molly sat down on the ground in relief.

Nobody spoke for a minute. "That was a different type of bear, right?" Fitzgerald asked.

Paul stood leaned over, gasping for air with his hands on his knees. "Yes, that was a grizzly."

"And it would have hurt us even without babies?"

"The bear could have killed all of us easily. I should have warned you about them. I've never seen one this close to the road."

"How did you stop it?"

Paul showed them the pepper spray. "Good thing I purchased this at the last grocery store. The bear will be fine in a few hours."

"Thank you both for saving us," Fitzgerald concluded.

Not knowing what else to say, Isabella tried to cheer them up. "Look, we still have the berries."

Chapter 21

●●●

Later that night around a campfire, the bear incident seemed long ago. Paul had stopped at a roadside store to buy a case of beer, which helped their mood. The others teased Molly about talking to the bear. "Please don't eat me, Mr. Bear," Fitzgerald mimicked her.

Molly enjoyed the jesting and added, "What if it had answered, 'Why not? Are you tough?'" Everybody laughed.

Next they teased Isabella for saving the berries. "Do you think I wanted to go back and ask the bear for them?" she retorted.

After their laughter died down, Paul acknowledged, "In truth, Molly talking to the bear bought us a little time. Without those seconds, things might have ended differently."

Fitzgerald told about the caribou antler coming from the ground. Paul responded, "Ah, that explains the bear's actions. They preserve a kill to eat later by covering it up. The bear was probably sleeping nearby and woke up to think you were stealing its food."

"Were grizzly bears common in the early days of mankind?" Fitzgerald had become more serious.

"Oh, yes. And many other dangerous animals. But these bears are rare today."

"Now I better understand why humans became so tough." Fitzgerald sighed. The others could tell he was thinking about his mission for the first time in days. His eyes looked past them as he seemed to be speaking to himself, "But now that toughness will cause the humans to destroy themselves."

Nobody spoke, waiting for Fitzgerald's thoughts. "You could change the bear," he suddenly said.

"What do you mean by, 'change the bear'?" Molly asked.

"Humans could alter the bear's DNA to make it less dangerous."

"But then it wouldn't be a bear anymore."

"Who is to say what a bear is? Humans altered the ancient auroch's DNA by selective breeding to make cattle. Now there are many cattle and the original auroch is extinct. If bears were altered, they could live among you. Their species would thrive like cattle," Fitzgerald reasoned.

Oh my God! Molly thought. *Maybe this is why Fitzgerald and Isabella talked to Dr. Finkle privately. Is it possible they're thinking about modifying human DNA?*

● ● ●

Laura and Jeff waited for them when Paul dropped off the others at the Anchorage airport to return the RV. "Did you have a good time in Alaska?" Laura asked.

"Oh, yes," Isabella answered for all of them. "Alaska is beautiful. We saw rivers, glaciers, mountains, and wild animals."

Jeff obviously felt happy to see his friend Isabella again. "We saw a whale, seals, walruses, and sea otters," he shared.

"That's wonderful. We saw a grizzly bear," Isabella returned.

"Did you get close to it?" the boy asked.

"Pretty close," Molly answered for all of them. "Was the cruise fun?"

"It was perfect for us," Laura answered. "They provided everything in a safe environment. And the captain even invited Jeff to visit the bridge."

Paul arrived back at the airport in a taxi. He had purchased several newspapers and news magazines at Fitzgerald's request. They all boarded the Learjet Dr. Finkle had sent.

Inside the jet, Isabella resumed visiting with Jeff. Molly chatted with Laura. Fitzgerald excused himself to read the news reports. As Paul watched, his friend's spirit seemed to droop. "Can I join you?" he asked. Fitzgerald waved toward an empty seat without speaking.

Paul picked up a paper. He read reports that during their seven days in Alaska the UN had descended into turmoil. In previous decades of posturing and arguing, the UN had settled into relatively peaceful antagonisms. Now faced with the impetus to do something, the delegates had descended into vicious vitriol. Several physical altercations had broken out in the subcommittees.

"This doesn't look good," Paul commented.

"I should never have left."

"Sorry to disagree, Fitzgerald. But you could not have made a difference in this. Some of these conflicts have been going on for centuries. Change will be very difficult. And human nature is to be contentious."

Fitzgerald sat back in acquiescence. "Even the bear listened to Molly."

"Only for a few seconds. Then you saw what happened. The world listened to you for a while..." Paul left the remainder unsaid.

"I will continue to try, though. We must succeed." Fitzgerald returned to studying the news reports.

Paul reached for another section of newspaper. A section headline announced, "Cancer increasing exponentially in Asia." The article reported that various types of cancer in Asia had become much more prevalent than statistically predictable. The writer called the outbreak an epidemic.

He carried the paper to show to Molly and Laura. "This is the first time I've seen this," said Laura. "We didn't follow any news while on the cruise."

"The best part of vacation is getting away from the news," Molly assured her.

Laura looked at her. "Aren't you a reporter?"

Molly shrugged. "I know bad news better than anyone. But I tell myself that accurate bad news is better than inaccurate good news."

When Paul became serious, he tended to revert to honorifics. "Dr. Holdridge, isn't cancer linked to genetics?"

"Yes, much of my work is related to identifying heritable

gene sequences that increase the propensity to various cancers. When a family has a history of a certain type of cancer, we may be able to eliminate that in the next generation."

"But at NASA we were told that one of the possible dangers of prolonged space flight is that cosmic radiation could damage DNA in astronauts, leading to cancers."

"That's a separate issue. Many cancers are caused by genetic damage perhaps beginning with a single cell. The damage can occur by chemicals or by radiation. The damaged cell can start to multiply uncontrollably resulting in a cancerous growth. Oncovirus or papillomavirus, called HPV, can also damage DNA leading to cancer. A lot of teenage girls are immunized against HPV to prevent cervical cancer."

"And viruses multiply by forcing cells to reproduce them," Paul contributed.

"That's right. But viruses can be either deadly or useful. We can attach a useful gene to a retrovirus. After a chromosome is cut by a restriction enzyme from certain bacteria, the virus can transfer the useful gene to DNA. We use that for beneficial genetic modification of various plants, including a lot of foodstuffs."

"All this sounds scary to me. Can we please change the subject?" Molly requested.

"You're scared of a virus after facing a bear?" Paul told Laura about Molly and the grizzly bear.

"That happened so fast, I didn't have a chance to be scared," said Molly.

"Your legs were sure scared. I couldn't catch you running down that path," Paul teased her.

"I knew that I didn't need to outrun the bear. All I had to do was outrun you."

Laura laughed, then became pensive. "I wish that Jeff's father and I could have been like you two."

"Oh, we aren't..." Paul and Molly both started.

"Well, you should be." Laura finished the conversation.

• • •

In New York, Paul had them all return to their disguises. He used the same subterfuge to spirit them back to the hotel and into rooms where their bags containing regular clothes waited. Watching televised news broadcasts, Fitzgerald found the news had become even worse. The constituencies of feuding UN delegates acted out their frustration and enmity. Dozens of riots had erupted around the world. Nations had started mobilizing their armed forces to protect those of like persuasion.

"Thanks for a wonderful vacation, Paul. You were right. We all did need it," Fitzgerald said while looking at the TV screen. He sighed and used the room phone to call the hotel front desk. "This is Fitzgerald Benevolent. Would you notify the media that we will give a press conference tonight at 8:00 p.m.?"

After hanging up, he turned to face Isabella along with Paul and Molly. "I might as well get started."

Reporters gladly responded to Fitzgerald's announcement. They needed something fresh in the daily barrage of negative reports from the UN. News media filled the hotel's main ballroom.

At precisely 8:00 p.m., Fitzgerald stepped before a battery of microphones. Isabella stood on the riser with him. Before he could even speak, one question shouted by many set the tone. "Where have you and Isabella been?"

"We have been trying to pull in some we wished to join us. And we have been avoiding confrontation with those who could be harmful."

Molly stifled a laugh and whispered to Paul, "He's talking about eating the fish and running from the bear."

"I know." Paul held his nose to avoid laughing out loud. "At least we know our friend has retained some of his mischievousness."

Another shout, "Are you aware of the controversies that have prevented progress at the UN?"

"Yes, we are." Fitzgerald rattled off some of the reports he had read on the flight back from Anchorage.

"What are you going to do?"

"Isabella and I can only continue trying to help humans to work together to address their common challenges. But the changes must be made by humans themselves."

"Are you aware that some are saying that mankind was better off before you came?"

Fitzgerald became sterner than anyone had seen him previously. "That is because you were simply passing your problems to the next generation without seriously addressing them. Now you are trying to deal with your problems. Nobody said this would be easy."

Suddenly dozens of reporters looked down at their cell phones where a tweet had been received. "War has broken out!" one shouted out for all in the ballroom to hear.

Fitzgerald waited while nearly every reporter checked media sources. One shouted, "The Associated Press is reporting that heavy fighting has broken out all around Israel's borders. Were you aware of this?"

"Of course not. I have been standing here before you. Isabella and I..."

Another shouted, "Are you willing to take responsibility for instigating this war?"

Chapter 22

• • •

"The so-called 'Fitzgerald and Isabella Benevolent' are not helping to solve Earth's problems. They are causing Earth's problems with their communist agenda!" Bill Samuel asserted. "Think back before their arrival. Ask yourself, 'Were stock markets falling like proverbial stones?' Investor portfolios have lost one-point-six trillion dollars in the last month alone. Unemployment is already increasing as businesses lay off workers in fear of a major recession or maybe even a depression. So ask yourself, 'How safe is my job?' Inflation is at a twelve-year high as people rush to buy necessities."

Paul and Molly stood watching the broadcast in their hotel room along with Fitzgerald and Isabella. "I guess Bill's forgotten the surge in stock prices and record hiring binge the last few months," said Paul.

"He just doesn't care," Molly responded. "This is ratings week. He's trying to attract viewers that result in advertising dollars. That's the television business."

They watched Bill angrily staring directly into the camera. His jaw twitched and short breaths came quickly as he prepared for the next tirade. "Ask yourself, 'As divided as the UN has been in the past, have there ever been fist fights between delegates before? Were there four separate wars going on before?' I thought the so-called 'aliens' promised peace and prosperity for all."

Isabella looked at Fitzgerald. He looked haggard. She tried to reassure him. "This isn't our fault. Humans have always been fighting. Most people are too smart to believe this man." Fitzgerald didn't answer.

Back on the TV screen, Bill had changed his demeanor. His voice took a reasonable and thoughtful tone as he seemed to muse to himself, "Even if these troublemakers are from outer space, and we have only NASA's self-serving reports and some eye tricks to go on, why would they come here? If an alien species were preparing to invade Earth, what better way to begin than by destroying Earth's economy? Wouldn't an invasion be easier if humans were divided against themselves and killing each other?" Bill finished with, "Didn't I warn against releasing them from custody?"

Fitzgerald spoke to Paul and Molly, "You know that's not true about an invasion, don't you?"

Molly chose that unfortunate moment to try a joke. "Do we?" she said in an exaggerated voice reminiscent of a cheap 1950s sci-fi movie. Fitzgerald's expression of horror revealed her mistake. "I'm sorry, Fitzgerald. That was just a bad joke. You know that I think Bill Samuel is a total ass."

Paul had also heard Fitzgerald's question and seen his

expression. *This is getting to him,* he thought. *It would get to anybody, and especially someone not used to Earth's contentious culture. He feels responsible for humankind.*

• • •

Crowds of angry demonstrators blocked streets around the New York hotel where Fitzgerald and Isabella stayed. Signs proclaimed, "Prepare for invasion," "I'll fight," "This is our planet," and "Reverse the release."

Another more restrained group stood together demanding, "Confiscate the alien spacecraft. Take the technology to solve our problems."

Protecting the hotel's entrance, New York police stood shoulder to shoulder, two deep, and dressed in riot gear. Men crowded the line occasionally engaging in a pushing match with the police. Insults derided the police as "anti-humanity." Now and then thrown objects hit the police.

Paul answered the hotel phone and talked for a few minutes. "That was the mayor's office," he told the others. "He's asking that you leave New York."

"We haven't done anything wrong," protested Isabella.

"The mayor says that the city can't afford the overtime pay to protect you. And the state governor has refused to call in the National Guard. But I think that the real reason the mayor wants you gone is that the demonstrations are disrupting business."

"They are thinking about today's business when the future of your species is at stake?" Fitzgerald asked. Paul only shrugged.

Fitzgerald continued speaking in exasperation, "That's how humans came to the point that they need our help."

Isabella responded more practically, "How would we leave?" She pointed to the crowds outside the hotel.

"The mayor has promised to clear a path out. A police van and escort will take you to a helipad on top of a nearby building. They want to do it today because the crowds are growing larger and more violent. I'll need to arrange a pickup by the State Department."

"Where will we go?"

"I don't know that yet."

Paul busied himself making phone calls. An hour later he came back to them. "A State Department helicopter is on its way. They're coordinating with the city police. You'll need to meet the police escort in the hotel lobby at 3:30. That's just over an hour from now."

"How about us?" Molly asked Paul and indicated herself and him.

"Please don't leave us, Molly," Isabella begged. Fitzgerald nodded in agreement.

"The State Department said there would be room for two with baggage, four with what they can hold in their laps. If you want Molly and me, we'll go with you."

Molly smiled back at Isabella. "I guess it's a good thing Paul bought us those backpacks for Alaska."

"You should all take your disguises in case you need them later," Paul added.

● ● ●

"Stand right here until I signal you, then run to the police van that will come to the front door," the police captain instructed in the lobby.

The foursome stood ready each wearing backpacks, but they could see little beyond the uniformed backs of the police officers. Molly heard a loudspeaker outside instructing the crowds to disperse. Curses and shouts of defiance came from angry voices. Suddenly, a roaring sound and screams erupted. Men maddened with fear and fury surged against the police, striking at the officers with their fists and previously concealed weapons. The police officers fought back with department-issued batons. Above their heads, Molly could see streams of water knocking down anyone in the street.

"Get ready!" the police captain said. The police line parted. Through the gap, she could see policemen dragging prone men and a few women out of the hotel's driveway. The water cannons had shifted their aim to push the crowds back. Several men in the mob brought out concealed pistols and fired toward the police. A van passed through the police line gap and pulled up to the front door. The police van's door slid open. "Now go!" the captain shouted.

Somebody's foot caught Molly's heel, causing her to stumble. Fitzgerald and Isabella didn't notice and reached the van door quickly. Paul started to turn back to help Molly. But she bounced up and joined Isabella climbing into the van. Above their heads she heard rifle shots as police marksmen sought out those using the pistols against them. The captain followed and closed the van door.

The van sped away led by three motorcycles. Inside, no one spoke. In their mutual shock, they didn't even look at each other. They could feel the van speeding through the streets of New York with siren and lights. Soon the van stopped in front of a tall building. A female police sergeant opened the sliding door. "Come this way, please."

She guided them through the magnificent lobby of a bank building. There they startled well-dressed men and women. Some stood still and gaped in surprise. Several others turned to run from the commotion. Another policeman held open the door to an elevator. The police sergeant calmly led them into the elevator where she quickly punched the button to the sixty-fifth floor.

The quiet in the elevator seemed surreal compared to the commotion they had escaped. Molly could hear an instrumental version of a Beatles tune through the Muzak. "You should carry your backpacks now. Hold them in your laps on the helicopter," suggested the policewoman.

On the roof, a State Department helicopter waited. Molly had always imagined a rooftop helicopter escape under whirring blades. But this helicopter remained inactive until they were all seated and strapped in before revving its engine. The police sergeant waited on the roof until they had lifted off.

• • •

"The New York massacre," Bill Samuel had dubbed the confrontation between police and demonstrators. Paul and Molly watched a TV at a facility where the State Department had taken them. Footage showed water cannons clearing a path for the police van that had ultimately carried the foursome away. Bill's voice spoke over the tape, "Police bullets killed two civilians. Dozens were treated for serious injuries."

Following Bill's program, DSC Network's traditional news broadcast began. Steve Wilson, looking a little chagrined from the previous diatribe, reported, "One policeman suffered a life-threatening gunshot wound. Six policemen were hospitalized and an undetermined number treated for injuries. Police only returned fire after demonstrators shot at them. Marksmen killed two protestors as they fired on the police. Police arrested eighty-six protesters. Eight more have been hospitalized from injuries suffered during the riot."

"That's a little more balanced news report," Paul suggested.

"I would hope so," Molly answered. "Steve is pretty objective and factual."

"The location of Fitzgerald and Isabella Benevolent is uncertain tonight," Steve went on. "Rumor is that they are at a secure federal facility in the Catskill Mountains. Our own reporter, Molly Powell, may have been sequestered with them. Molly, if you are listening, we hope you are well.

"In other news, the number of reported cancer cases in parts of Asia is escalating. Several high-ranking officials from North Korea have sought treatment in Seoul, Tokyo, and Beijing. The South Korean government is asking for international aid due to overcrowded treatment centers." Footage showed crowds of South Koreans outside of hospitals.

"The Centers for Disease Control and Prevention headquarters in Atlanta, in cooperation with the World Health Organization, has dispatched investigators to attempt to determine the source of the unprecedented outbreak."

The network showed a reporter standing with a doctor

215

in Atlanta. "Cancer is generally not contagious in the types reported," the doctor explained. "We haven't yet determined what the pathogen is or how it's spreading."

"Would you call this a pandemic?"

"Yes, I'm afraid so."

"Would this outbreak have been discovered sooner if the current administration in Washington had not forced major cuts to the federal funding for the CDC?"

"It is true that we didn't have enough staff to thoroughly investigate the earliest reports."

Steve reappeared on the DSC broadcast. "In an unusual move, the CDC has consulted with Future Tech, a biogenetic laboratory in North Carolina. The company was founded by Nobel Prize-winning scientist Dr. Ben Finkle. Because of age and declining health, Dr. Finkle has sent his protégé Dr. Laura Holdridge to Seoul. They are hoping that the emerging field of genomic diagnosis can identify the pathogen." A picture of Laura filled the screen.

"Which bed do you want?" Paul asked Molly and waved toward two twin beds. The government facility's receptionist had assumed the guests to be two couples and assigned Paul and Molly a room together. They had been too distracted and disoriented to protest.

"You can choose," she replied. "What do you think Fitzgerald and Isabella are doing?"

Paul placed his backpack beside one of the beds. "I'll bet they're too shocked to do anything. I'm pretty much in survival mode myself."

"Me too." Molly's cell phone rang. Caller ID identified George Baker from DSC. "Hello."

"Molly? Where are you?"

"I don't actually know. We..."

"Are you with the aliens?"

"Maybe."

"I thought so. So how about another interview? You know. Let them tell their side."

The thought of conducting an interview after what had recently transpired surprised Molly so much that she became befuddled. "Well, I suppose..."

"You have your laptop, right? You could Skype the interview to us."

"Skype?"

"The initial picture quality would be marginal, but you won't believe what our graphics guys can do to clean it up. You could ask the questions the public wants to know. You could counteract Bill Samuel."

George really knows how to make a sale, Molly realized. "Maybe, George. I'll have to get back to you."

"Not too long, sweetheart. This is hot right now."

"Who was that?" Paul asked.

"My network. They want another interview with Fitzgerald and Isabella."

"I'll bet they do."

Chapter 23

●●●

"My network wants to let you answer the accusations against you," Molly told Fitzgerald and Isabella at breakfast the next morning.

"Would you allow us to make a broadcast?" Paul asked the State Department representative who sat listening.

"The State Department is only providing temporary asylum to officially recognized diplomats and their..." the representative struggled for words to describe Paul and Molly. "Uh...assistants. Other diplomats have an embassy where their country has sovereignty. The State Department takes no official position in your next actions."

"We have no camera. How would you take the pictures?" Fitzgerald asked.

Molly pointed at her laptop. "The computer will take a picture and upload it through the internet."

"Would it be broadcast live?"

"No, the network would record it and then enhance the picture."

"I don't know about this, Molly," Paul said. "I've got a bad feeling."

"This is the only way for them to get the truth out," Molly argued.

"Why not use Fitzgerald and Isabella's blog?"

"That doesn't come from their mouths. It would seem staged. As an interviewer, I can stand in for a skeptical public. Remember how our program from the quarantine quarters made such a difference?"

"Those circumstances were different," Paul persisted. "We had control of a live broadcast."

Molly turned directly to Fitzgerald and Isabella. "Don't you want to tell your side? To tell everybody the truth?"

Fitzgerald looked uncertain. "Our tutors taught us to simply tell the truth. 'The truth will convince people,' they said." He looked at Isabella. She in turn looked at Molly then back at Fitzgerald and nodded. "We will do as you suggest, Molly." Paul looked chagrined, but made no further comment.

• • •

"Look at this spot," Molly said as she set the computer before Fitzgerald and Isabella. "I'll sit behind the computer and ask the questions. They'll hear my voice but not see my face." The couple from Benevolent nodded. "I'm going to ask the hard, direct questions that the public would ask."

"Are you getting this in New York?" she asked the network.

"Gotcha, Molly," a voice came back.

"This is Molly Powell of DSC Network News reporting from an undisclosed location. I'm with Fitzgerald and Isabella, the diplomats from the planet Benevolent. Thank you for appearing tonight to answer various allegations. First, are you aware of the turmoil your arrival on Earth has created?"

"Yes, we are and regret this deeply," Fitzgerald answered. "But we are not the cause of the problems humans face. We have only come to help mankind face their problems so that the future will be better for other generations. The Benevolent species wants to be your friends."

"Then why won't you give us the technology to solve these problems right now?" Molly asked.

"Because mankind's basic challenge is not one of technology. The most important issue is mankind's inability to work together for the common good and to consider the long-term effects of their actions." Fitzgerald continued to give several examples.

"Some have advocated confiscating the spacecraft you arrived in. It must have advanced technology inside."

Fitzgerald looked at Isabella, who answered, "We are saving advanced technology until humans are ready to use it. Some technology could do harm if applied improperly. Some groups could even use the technology to gain advantage over others."

Molly started slipping into her familiar role as an antagonist reporter. "What keeps us from simply opening the vehicle and taking its secrets?"

Isabella answered forcibly, "Have you ever seen magnesium burn like a firework? Any unauthorized entry of our craft will trigger a fire inside. All the technology will be destroyed. We would not have it to help you later."

Molly redirected her questions to Fitzgerald. "Are you responsible for the economic volatility that has so many people fearful for their livelihood?"

"When we arrived, your financial speculators caused a great surge in business. Your economic system is now readjusting to premature optimism. And the failure of the world's leaders to cooperate is causing great tension and uncertainty. Working together can ultimately create peace and prosperity."

"What about the hostilities and even wars that have broken out since you intervened on Earth?"

"Wars are not necessary when cooperation is present. The issues between those fighting existed before our arrival. Some for a thousand years or more. This is an opportunity to resolve them for future generations."

"Are aliens about to invade Earth?"

Isabella spoke up, "No, this is silly. Physics would prevent that." She outlined a few technical reasons an invasion would be impossible and fruitless. "And," Isabella continued, "Fitzgerald and I were genetically engineered to live in Earth's environment. The inhabitants of Benevolent would die here."

Molly forgot herself in the excitement of conducting a confrontational interview. Without thinking she blurted her own suspicion, "You mentioned genetics. Is it true that you've investigated the possible genetic modification of mankind?"

Fitzgerald sat stunned. He realized that the computer transmitted everything. "We've never said anything about genetically altering humans."

"But didn't you consult with Dr. Ben Finkle about genetic tendencies among humans?"

Fitzgerald stalled while trying to think. "We talked to Dr. Finkle about many things like eradicating diseases or creating easy-to-grow foods. His work on determining gene sequences that affect human behavior is already publicly known."

"What about psychopaths? Do you think mankind would be better off if likely psychopaths had prior genetic modification?"

Isabella spoke up, "Molly why are you asking this? Your own doctors will say that psychopaths hurt themselves and others. They care only for themselves and can cause great harm to society."

"And so you would change them?"

"We will change no one. Humans have to change themselves."

• • •

"What the hell have you done?" Paul's anger surprised Molly. She had never seen him so angry.

"I'm an investigative reporter. I ask hard questions."

"But you were supposed to ask questions the public wanted answered. The public hasn't had any questions about altering humans. They will now, though!" he returned.

Molly realized the truth of Paul's words. But backing down wasn't part of her nature. "Maybe I had some questions of my own!"

"Then why didn't you ask your questions privately?" When Molly didn't answer, Paul walked away.

She turned to Fitzgerald and Isabella. Fitzgerald appeared crushed. Isabella had tears in her eyes. "Isabella, I..." Molly's words trailed off as they followed Paul away.

Back in their room, Molly turned on the TV in time to see DSC break into their usual programing with a news bulletin. Steve Wilson appeared grim at the anchor desk. "Breaking news from our investigative reporter Molly Powell." The network played the last minute of Molly's interview starting with her first question about genetics. A caption started flashing on the screen, "Aliens Propose Genetic Alteration of Humans."

Oh, my God. What have I done?

• • •

"Didn't I tell you so?" Bill Samuel gloated into the camera. He replayed DSC's broadcast of Molly's last questions to Fitzgerald and Isabella over and over. "Even if they don't send spaceships to conquer us, they'll create alien-human hybrids to populate the earth." He sat a minute in smug satisfaction.

"Oh, and here's something else to consider. Isn't Dr. Laura Holdridge part of Dr. Finkle's firm, Future Tech? Do you think it's just a coincidence that she's in Asia investigating the unprecedented outbreak of cancers? Could that have something to do with the alien invasion? Did we ever have a contagious cancer epidemic before the aliens came here?"

• • •

Paul had watched the DSC bulletin along with Fitzgerald and Isabella in their room. None of them had any words to say. Then they watched Bill Samuel's rant. In disgust, Paul switched to the alternate networks. Each of them had hastily pieced together a story using the DSC and Bill Samuel clips.

He settled on a talk panel of commentators discussing the entire situation.

"Consider that," one older man wearing a bow tie postulated, "maybe Earth would be better off with fewer psychopaths among us. They make everybody defensive to protect themselves and their families. What if somehow the psychopaths developed a sense of altruism? Our entire society might become more cooperative."

The other commentators vehemently argued him down. "Then we wouldn't still be fully human," one insisted.

"Isn't that a form of denying free will?" another questioned.

A woman became so irate that she rose from her chair to demand, "What next? Will they alter some people to give them advantage over others?"

"Isn't that what the Russians are already doing with athletes?" the bow-tie man retorted.

Paul knew that linking Fitzgerald and Isabella to the Russians would not help their cause in most people's minds. He switched the channel again. There a daytime talk show discussed Molly herself. "DSC doubled her salary and promised a million-dollar bonus when she got connected to the aliens," one host confided.

"That was a bargain for DSC," her guest responded. "Their ratings are through the roof."

Paul, Fitzgerald, and Isabella all exchanged looks.

● ● ●

Later the trio went to eat supper in the small dining room

at the government facility. Molly came in from sitting most of the afternoon under a tree outside. She approached the table. "Listen, you guys. I screwed up. I just—"

"Have you seen the broadcasts?" Paul interrupted.

"Yes, but I didn't know the network would edit out the truthful things Fitzgerald and Isabella said. They—"

"Did you see Bill Samuel?"

"Yes, he's a total asshole. I can't stand—"

"Is it true that DSC doubled your salary and gave you a million-dollar bonus after the quarantine quarters special?" Paul asked.

"Yes, I suppose so," Molly answered. "But I didn't ask for the money. I haven't seen the money. I've been with you the whole time."

"Why didn't you tell us?"

"The money wasn't important!" Molly stopped and considered the implications. *What would I think if I uncovered a conflict of interest like that?*

She started again, "I'll admit that looks bad. But honestly, I—"

"Was our relationship part of the plan?"

"You mean you and me? No!"

"Molly, I think maybe you should go," Paul stated without overt emotion.

"Go?"

"Yes, go back to New York or wherever you want."

"Listen, we're all acting on emotion here in a stressful situation." Molly looked to Fitzgerald and Isabella for support.

Fitzgerald looked away. "We thought you were our friend," Isabella said.

The State Department representative had been listening and approached the table. "Ms. Powell, if you're no longer part of the diplomats' group, I'll have to ask you to leave this facility. One of our security guards will give you a ride into town."

Chapter 24

• • •

"You used me," Molly said between clenched teeth two days later.

"Of course I did," George Baker answered from behind his desk at DSC's headquarters in New York. "Everybody in this business uses everybody else." He leaned back in his chair. "But I also made you a star like I did Bill Samuel. You're somebody now."

He contemplated Molly standing in front of him. "You're not bad-looking either. The camera loves your big features and long legs. How would you like a news talk show after this is over? After a makeover, you could pull in both male and female viewers. You could play up the battle of the sexes angle. Controversy between men and women. You might even get ratings close to Bill's. Since I brought him in, he's boosted our overall ratings into first place."

Maybe for the first time in her life, Molly was speechless.

"But that's for later." George leaned forward again. "Right

now, we need to wrap up this alien business. Would you like to be in on the kill? I remember when you did the investigative field reports you always liked to be there when an arrest was made. Your presence could double our ratings."

Molly controlled herself. "What do you mean?"

"I've got this guy inside the president's office. He gives us a few leaks. We lean stories their way." George laughed to himself. "Your alien friends' approval ratings are near zilch right now. My guy says that the president will order the State Department to revoke their diplomatic status. Then they can be arrested and interrogated. We can force them to open the spacecraft."

"Arrested? What for?"

"The Feds will find something. Maybe suspicion of planting that cancer epidemic in Asia. You just need to decide whether you're in or out."

"I'm in," Molly forced herself to say. "When should I be ready?"

"That's my girl. My source says the immunity will be revoked two days from now. The FBI will then seal off that facility somewhere in the Catskills until the arrest warrants are processed. They'll be sitting ducks after that."

"So I should meet the camera crew here early day after tomorrow? Then we can be in position in plenty of time." After confirmation from George, Molly started to leave.

"Where are you going?" George asked.

"I'm going to get that makeover and a new dress. See you in two days."

"You've got a future in this business, sweetie."

• • •

Molly leaned against the elevator wall after leaving George's office. She comforted herself thinking, *George, I'm coming after you when all this is over.* Then, *What do I need to do next?* All she had was the stuff in her backpack: driver's license, passport, credit cards, laptop, cell phone, a few personal items, and her disguise. And she had the rental car she had been forced to hire to get to New York. *First, I need some money.*

On the New York streets, she withdrew $500, the maximum allowable, from an ATM on each of three different credit cards. Molly saw a woman staring at her. *She thinks she recognizes me, but she's not sure.* Molly ducked into a restroom and put on her stocking cap and ugly glasses. Next she bought a disposable cell phone. *I doubt if Paul will answer my call otherwise.* The sun had set by the time Molly crossed the George Washington Bridge across the Hudson River into New Jersey. She called Paul's cell phone number using the disposable phone.

"Hello."

"Paul, this is Molly. Please don't hang up. You must hear this."

"Okay." Skepticism filled Paul's voice.

She told him what she had learned. Then she added, "You know this president believes in 'enhanced interrogation' techniques." Silence came from Paul. "Are you still there, Paul?"

"What do you want us to do?"

"Don't say anything to the State Department representative. You three be ready to go about 3:00 a.m. tomorrow morning. I'm coming to get you."

"What then?" Paul asked.

"I have no idea."

"Okay, leave that part to me," Paul promised. "And Molly... all of us are pretty bummed without you around."

"We'll have a lot to talk about later."

• • •

Paul put away the phone. He tapped on Fitzgerald and Isabella's door and invited them for a walk outside. There he quietly told them about Molly's warning. "I thought they couldn't arrest us because of our diplomatic immunity," said Fitzgerald.

"They can revoke your diplomatic status and immunity. But you have no country to return to. Then they can arrest you."

"What would that mean?"

"Not good."

"Why did you bring us outside to talk?" Isabella asked.

"Because of possible bugs."

"How would the insects tell?"

"Bugs is slang for secret listening devices. They may be able to listen to us in our rooms." Isabella's eyes widened.

Fitzgerald remained cautious. "Can we trust Molly?"

"She faced a grizzly bear to protect you." Paul shook his head. "Molly is an impulsive and headstrong woman. She made a serious mistake. But she won't deliberately double-cross us."

"But you thought..."

"I was surprised and hurt. Molly and I..." Paul didn't know how to finish.

Male and female humans, Isabella thought. *I'll never figure them out.*

• • •

"I'm here," Molly phoned Paul. "Just walk out the gate and down the road a bit. The guards shouldn't be able to stop you if Fitzgerald and Isabella still have their diplomatic status. And don't forget your backpacks."

"We're on our way."

Followed by Fitzgerald and Isabella, Paul sauntered down the driveway in the wee morning hours. At the facility gate, the lone guard on duty challenged them. "Where are you going?"

Paul gave the guard a mock salute. "They're diplomats. They can go where they choose."

While the bewildered guard phoned his sleeping superiors for instructions, the trio stepped around the barrier, walked a short way, and joined Molly in her rental car. "I'm very sorry..." she began.

Isabella hugged her neck. "Molly, we are so happy to see you. Paul said that we could trust you."

"Maybe we should go," Paul interrupted the reunion.

Molly sped away. "This is just like in the movies," Fitzgerald observed with some delight.

"Then you two lie down like in the movies. There's no sense in taking a chance of your being recognized." To Paul she said, "Okay, Big Boy. What's your plan?"

"Have you got any cash?" he asked her.

"We have money in the bank," Fitzgerald offered.

"The authorities are certain to be monitoring your account. They would quickly locate you if you tried to access it."

Molly answered Paul, "I withdrew $1,500 from ATMs in New York."

"That was good thinking. Then I need to buy some disposable cell phones."

"Here ya go." Molly handed him the one she had purchased.

"Did you use this one to call my cell phone?"

"Yes, why?"

"Then the computers can link this number to my phone. Save it, though. We might find a use for it later. Right now, I'll need another phone not linked to any of us. That's what criminals call a 'burner.' Will you stop here for me to get a new one?" Paul indicated an all-night discount store. He and Molly entered the store separately to buy items the foursome needed with the cash Molly had brought.

Back in the car, Paul dialed from memory on one of the two new disposable phones. "Pick up. Pick up. Ah, Mrs. Sawyer, this is Paul Sanders. Sorry for the midnight call."

After some quick pleasantries, Paul asked, "Becky, could you put Tom on the extension, please? I have a big favor to ask of both of you." With Tom added to the call, Paul asked, "Would you let somebody stay at your mountain cabin for a couple of weeks?"

Paul heard Tom's gruff older voice coming back, "We've been following you on the news. Is the somebody—"

"Yes, it is." Paul interrupted. "What you've heard on the news is all crap. The somebodies are alright and safe. You can trust me."

Becky broke in, "If there's anyone in the world we do trust, it's you, Paul. Send them to us."

"Thanks! I'll call you back in a few hours with details. Please don't tell anyone and don't phone me."

Paul ended the call. "Who was that?" Molly wanted to know.

"That was Beth's parents. Now head for Pennsylvania."

"Where are we going?" Isabella asked from the back seat.

"You? You're going to Oregon." He started explaining his plan to everyone.

•••

In Allentown, Paul directed Molly to the bus station. Using some of Molly's cash, Paul purchased two bus tickets to Eugene, Oregon. Molly worked on Fitzgerald and Isabella in the car. When Paul returned, he hardly recognized them himself. Molly had used the wig disguises and some makeup from the discount store to hide their well-known faces.

"Here are your tickets and a map so that you can follow your progress across the country. You'll need to change buses several times. The ticket gives the times and destinations. The trip will take three days. Stay in the bus stations and try not to give yourselves away by talking."

"Why would talking give ourselves away?" asked Fitzgerald with a distinctly African American accent.

"You forgot that he is a linguist," Isabella explained.

"Yes...I...did. You two continue to amaze me." Paul smiled. "But listen to me. Don't talk to people unless you have to. An older couple, Tom and Becky Sawyer, will meet you at the bus station in Eugene. They'll take care of you for a while. Give them this picture to prove who you are." Paul took a photo of Beth from his wallet and handed it to Isabella.

"This is like witness protection in a movie I saw," Fitzgerald commented.

"Right, except the government will try to find you rather than hide you."

"Here's some money to buy food and anything you need on the trip." Molly stuffed $500 into Fitzgerald's pocket. She gave the second new cell phone to Isabella. "Don't use this phone to call anyone but Paul. And then only in an emergency." She gave them the number of Paul's new disposable. And he took their number.

"Try not to mention your names or ours whenever we talk," Paul told them.

"Why not?"

"Computers will be filtering for the name. They could discover this burner phone number and track it."

The final boarding call for the first bus segment west came over a loudspeaker. "Thanks for saving us again, Molly. We love you both," cried Isabella. Fitzgerald had a few tears too. They hugged Molly and Paul before climbing onto the bus.

Paul and Molly waved at their friends as the bus pulled away, leaving them in an empty parking lot.

They turned to face each other. "Now what do we do?" Molly asked.

"What we'll do is buy them some time by creating a diversion in the New York area."

Chapter 25

•••

"Molly, we need to talk about what happened."

She kept her eyes on the highway leading back to New York. "What's to talk about? I screwed up big time and you didn't give me a chance to apologize. You booted me out like you would a dead skunk."

Paul sat quietly for a few minutes. "What you said is true. I thought you had betrayed us. I had never experienced betrayal before and couldn't handle it. I made a mistake sending you away."

Molly continued driving and thinking, *You've got a decision to make here, girl. Are you going to make up or nurse a grudge?* "What did you mean when you said that all of you were bummed after I left?"

"I can only say that Fitzgerald and Isabella acted like the world had ended. As for me, I felt like a big part of me was missing."

"Did you feel that way when Beth died?" Molly glanced away from the road at Paul.

"No, this was different. When Beth died I mostly felt heartbroken for her and her parents. This time I felt heartbroken for myself."

"Do you want to know how I felt?"

Paul braced for a rebuke. "Go ahead."

"I felt like I'd blown the best opportunity I ever had. I felt alone again."

"I'm sorry, Molly."

"I know you are. Do you know I'm sorry?"

"Yes, I really do."

She continued, "I've been a pain in the ass all my career. I need to get control over myself."

"I think you're about perfect the way you are."

Molly stared at the road. "You do?"

Paul looked at Molly. "Well yeah. And I think this situation will get tougher. We'll be needing your feistiness. We just need to make sure you're pointed in the right direction."

Molly laughed at his comment. "All of us were under a lot of stress then. Could we just hit reset and start over?"

"I'd love that. Thank you."

"Okay then, plan-maker, what do we do next?"

Paul thought out loud, "We'll need more money. A lot of money."

"DSC owes me a million dollars, remember?"

"I hadn't thought of that. It could come in handy."

Paul started to talk through some ideas with Molly.

The following day, Molly reported to George Baker at DSC as promised. She had her hair piled on her head, a short, tight dress, spike heels, and bright red lipstick.

"Wow!" George surveyed her up and down somewhat lewdly. "Can I call 'em or what?"

Molly smirked back, sat down, and crossed her legs. "When does the takedown begin?"

"Aaah...there's been a hitch. The two aliens and their boy walked away last night. We'll need to postpone." George looked disgusted. "Where were you last night?"

Molly used her two hands to gesture at herself and gave a look that said, *You idiot.*

"Oh yeah. I remember."

"Do the Feds have any idea how they got away?"

"The boy got a couple of calls from a disposable phone bought in the city. The Feds are working on the theory someone sympathetic at the UN used it. They're monitoring that number. If that phone calls somebody else, they should be able to nail the caller and use them to find the aliens."

"Okay then, I'm due a few days off," Molly said. "Afterwards, I'll be ready for that career move you suggested. But George, I've got a little problem. You see, I owe some people money. You promised me a million-dollar bonus. I need that money right now."

"Drugs? Hush money? You got some negatives out there to buy? No problem. Everybody in this business has some secrets."

Molly thought, *If you only knew my secrets.*

George called accounting. "Issue a bonus check for a million dollars to Molly Powell. She'll be right down to get it." George listened to a question from accounting. Yeah, withhold taxes like you would on any paycheck."

• • •

"Would you call the bank and tell them that I'm coming in to cash a big check?" Molly asked DSC's CFO down in accounting.

"They'll need to call us back to confirm," he responded.

"Whatever."

• • •

"Cashing a check this large is unusual, Ms. Powell," cautioned the bank manager.

"Maybe. But you've got the check, seen my driver's license and passport, and received confirmation from DSC. Plus you probably recognize me from TV. Put the money in these suitcases, please. I'll pull a car up to the front door and open the trunk."

Thirty minutes later Molly pulled away from the curb with a trunk full of money. A few blocks away, she pulled to the curb where a somewhat scruffy, unshaven man with two backpacks opened the passenger door and joined her. She re-entered the New York traffic.

"I've got the money!" Molly shrieked. Paul responded by pounding the dashboard in joy. "And I've got news! They think maybe someone at the UN helped. I'm not suspected in your escape. But they are onto that disposable cell phone I used to call you."

"What about the phone I used to call the Sawyers?"

"No mention. That number must be safe."

"Great work, Molly! I love you!" Paul realized what he had uttered. His cheeks burned and he stared out the window a minute self-consciously. Molly pretended not to have heard.

Paul recovered. "Let's make them think Fitzgerald and Isabella and I have somehow gotten to New York and are trying to elude them."

"How will we do that?"

"I'll start using my credit cards and cell phone around the city like we're running. You can take the first disposable phone near the UN and call my cell phone again on it. That'll confirm to them that we have an accomplice there." For the first time Paul noticed Molly's appearance. "Uh...you look stunning."

"Surprising what you can find at a thrift store in New York."

"You're too conspicuous, though. How about changing and we'll celebrate with a nice dinner?" Paul suggested. "You're buying because you've got the money. Do you still have your disguise?"

"Sure do. Later maybe I can dye and curl my hair too. What else will we do in New York?"

"We'll start converting some of your cash into prepaid credit cards. Sometimes they're easier to use when you're on the lam."

"Have you spent a lot of time 'on the lam'?" Molly teased him.

"No. But I've always wanted to see how far I could get."

• • •

The next morning Paul called Fitzgerald and Isabella on their undiscovered phones. For a second, he thought something had gone wrong when an African American seemed to answer. Then he remembered Fitzgerald's abilities. "Are you enjoying your trip?" Paul asked.

The extraterrestrials rejoiced to hear his voice. "We are crossing a place called Iowa right now. Riding the bus is fun. But we wish we could meet and talk to the people."

Paul handed the phone to Molly who said, "We just wanted to make certain you're doing okay." Fitzgerald and Isabella assured her they were. "We shouldn't talk long. We'll check on you again tomorrow."

Afterwards, Paul called the Sawyers to give a report on Fitzgerald and Isabella's progress. "The news media reports that a big manhunt is on for them and for you in New York," warned Tom.

"Yes, there is. Please trust me."

"We do."

• • •

Despite the seriousness of the circumstances, Paul and Molly had a wonderful time darting around New York together and laying down false leads. Because nobody suspected Molly, she could rent a nice hotel room under her own name with her own credit card. Each night, Paul snuck in and slept on the couch. They both rested soundly from exhaustion. Each day, Molly phoned George Baker at DSC ostensibly to find out if an arrest was imminent. But really she called to find out the Fed's strategies.

On the fourth day, Paul announced, "The odds will catch up with us soon. Fitzgerald and Isabella should arrive safely in Oregon today. We can skip town now."

Molly had obviously relished her roles as spy and decoy. "Where to next?"

"How about driving me in your rental car to New Jersey? We'll need a different vehicle."

In New Jersey, Paul checked a local paper's classified ads and made a call. An hour later he inspected a nearly new minivan for sale by owner. "I'll take it, if you'll take payment in cash. I've got a little money I'd rather not report to the IRS," he confided in the owner. "I could maybe throw in an extra thousand."

The owner had expected to be dickered down three thousand. Rather, he was being offered an extra thousand. "No problem," he responded, glad to be the beneficiary of someone else's larceny. "What name should I put on the title?"

"You just sign it; I'll fill it out and take care of the registration."

Even better, the owner thought as Paul counted out $32,000.

• • •

"You don't have any intention of registering the vehicle, do you?" Molly asked after the minivan's previous owner went back into his house.

"No way. That would tell the police what you and I will be driving. I'll follow you back to New York to drop off your rental car. Later we can make them think we've escaped. Where would you like to go?"

"How about New Orleans?"

"You got it! We can give them another false trail on the way."

While Molly turned in her rental car in New York, Paul transferred the money and their few belongings to the vehicle they had purchased. He then laid down the seats to create a sleeping area in the rear. "Behold a mini-RV!" he proclaimed on her return. "If you're willing, we can pick up an air mattress and some sleeping bags. Then we can sleep in the back whenever we need to."

Molly had been caught up in the surreptitious adventure. Her face radiated excitement. "Lead on." As the sun set, they headed south on I-95 with Paul driving.

"Paul, I can't believe the way you've pulled this off. You are really some kind of guy."

"I'm a bit surprised myself. I've always been sort of a play-it-safe person. But I've got to admit that these last few months have been the best of my life. And you've been a big part of that." *More than a part*, he thought. *Now what are you going to do? How would she respond*

244

to any overture you make? Remember, you blew this before. He gripped the steering wheel tighter.

Molly responded, "We've been through a lot together." They rode in silence for a few miles, then she ventured, "Did you really mean it when you said that you felt heartbroken for yourself when we had that fight?"

"Yes, I did. To tell you the truth, Molly, I don't think I could stand being separated from you again." *Time to take a chance. Just tell her how you feel.* "I know that I'm not the most romantic guy, but I think you're wonderful. And...and...I'm in love with you like I've never experienced before."

"Actually, this whole adventure has been pretty romantic in a non-sexual sense. And I think I'm in love myself for the first time in my life." Molly gathered her own courage. "Do you feel like we have a relationship now like you and Beth did?"

"We absolutely have a relationship and stronger than I ever had with Beth. Just seeing you makes me feel passionate like I never did for her."

"You feel passion for me?" A long moment passed. "Then what are we going to do?"

Go for the whole thing, Paul. Take a chance. Go for the whole thing. "Molly, your mother's experiences gave you plenty of reasons to be leery about men and their commitments. But tonight, I'll give you the final challenge. Would you marry me?"

Chapter 26

• • •

Fitzgerald and Isabella watched eagerly out the bus window as it pulled into the Eugene terminal. They couldn't see anyone matching Paul's description of Tom and Becky Sawyer. On the positive side, no police vehicles waited either. With some trepidation, they descended the bus's steps.

"Are you Paul's friends? We're Tom and Becky Sawyer."

They turned to see a lively looking, late-middle-aged couple smiling hesitantly at them. The man was tall, thin, gray headed, and carried himself with confidence. He held out his hand to Fitzgerald. They shook. His wife, shorter and a bit more heavyset, approached Isabella less formally. "Welcome to Oregon," she said, hugging Isabella's neck.

"We're supposed to give you this to show you we are from Paul." Isabella gave her Paul's photo of Beth.

Becky looked at the photo. "This is our daughter."

"We know. She was your only child. We are sorry she died."

"Can you ride another couple of hours?" Tom asked. He took Isabella's backpack away from her to carry it to their SUV. "We can take you directly to our cabin in the mountains. You'll have privacy there. Why don't you keep those disguises on until we get home?"

"Yes, we can ride. Thank you for meeting and helping us," Fitzgerald answered.

• • •

Neither couple knew what to expect. Quiet ruled the car as Tom started the drive toward the cabin he and Becky owned on the western slope of the Cascade Range. The cabin bordered on and was nearly surrounded by lush national forest. Fitzgerald noticed Tom glancing at them frequently in the rearview mirror.

What is going to happen to us? wondered Isabella.

These are the most famous people in the world, thought Becky.

Where did I go wrong? pondered Fitzgerald.

Honest-to-God aliens are in my car, realized Tom.

Becky made the first move. She turned in her seat and looked at Fitzgerald and Isabella. "You've had a long trip from Pennsylvania."

"Yes. But in space we lived in a vehicle not much larger than this car for nearly two years," answered Isabella. Fitzgerald saw Tom's eyes get bigger.

That silenced Becky. But Fitzgerald, recognizing Becky's attempt at goodwill, added, "We enjoyed seeing America from the bus window. The countryside is beautiful."

Thus encouraged, Becky tried again. "What was your favorite part?"

"I liked the Ohio and Mississippi Rivers," said Isabella. "So much beautiful flowing water. The place we came from is more dry."

Fitzgerald liked the Rocky Mountains. "They are so still and powerful."

"Did you have mountains on...Benevolent?" Becky asked.

"Yes, but they are mostly piles of loose rocks. Your mountains are steep and sharp at the top."

"That's because the glaciers carved our mountains," Tom responded.

"Glaciers? I know that word," said Fitzgerald. "A river of slow-moving ice. They were here?"

"Yes, in the mountains. They melted about ten thousand years ago. Still are melting some places."

Soon everybody was talking about the earth. Tom and Becky loved nature and enjoyed telling about Earth's wonders. "We saw a grizzly bear," Isabella volunteered. Pressed for details, she explained, "Paul and Molly took us on a secret trip to Alaska. We lived in an RV and didn't need to wear disguises." She then told about Molly and Paul saving them from the bear.

"Is that the Molly Powell we see on TV?" Becky asked.

When Isabella confirmed that she was, Becky said, "We told Paul to find another girl after Beth died. He is such a nice young man. Do you think he and Molly feel romantic toward each other?"

"I don't know." Isabella rolled her eyes. "They don't know themselves. These human mating rituals are too complex for me to understand."

At this, Tom started laughing out loud. He laughed so hard, Becky reached over to help him hold the steering wheel straight. As he settled down, Tom said, "Where are my manners? Are you two hungry? I'll bet you didn't find much to eat at the bus stops."

When Fitzgerald confirmed that truth, Tom turned off the highway to a local buffet restaurant he and Becky frequently patronized on their trips to and from their cabin. Inside, Becky told them, "Just take whatever you want from the buffet line." Once seated, Fitzgerald told about himself and Isabella eating the flowers when dining with the president. Tom's boisterous laugh made people in the restaurant turn their heads.

After a big dinner, Tom invited Fitzgerald to ride in the front seat with him. There he gave the younger man an unvarnished understanding of human politics. Then Fitzgerald told Tom about the frustration of trying to work with self-serving UN delegates. In the back seat, Becky talked about Paul and Beth. Isabella told about Paul and Molly. Then she shared with Becky about all the difficulties she and Fitzgerald had experienced that year. Becky duly listened and sympathized.

● ● ●

"This used to be Beth's room," Becky explained as she showed Fitzgerald and Isabella around the log cabin. "You are married, right?"

"We are mated. Like human marriage. Probably stronger," Isabella confirmed.

"Then you can sleep in here together. Before Paul married Becky, we made him sleep on the couch. Tom and I are in that bedroom. We've been married forty-one years." Becky collected towels and sheets for them. Together she and Isabella made up the bed.

In the basement, Tom turned on the hot water heater and showed Fitzgerald the circuit breakers, well, and backup generator. *Isabella would understand this better than I do*, Fitzgerald thought. But he recognized a male ritual and listened attentively.

Becky started helping Isabella remove some of the dark makeup Molly had applied as a disguise. "You're such a pretty girl. You need to let that show."

Ah, 'pretty' is a human female attribute of self-value, Isabella thought. *Becky means well,* she realized. "I'm pretty?"

"Doesn't Fitzgerald tell you?"

"He is my mated one."

Fitzgerald had just returned from the basement. "Young man, don't you ever tell your wife she's pretty?"

The diplomat in Fitzgerald rose to the occasion. "She *is* pretty. But her many other talents outshine her beauty."

Tom laughed again. "I love this kid!" He slapped Fitzgerald on the back.

To Tom, Isabella explained, "Fitzgerald and I share a mated bond that goes beyond love." To her mated one, Isabella threw a towel and said, "Wash off the makeup and then shave your face. Let Becky and Tom see how handsome you are."

●●●

The next morning dawned clear and bright in the Oregon backcountry. Fitzgerald joined Tom watching satellite news. "DSC has learned that searchers are convinced that extraterrestrials Fitzgerald and Isabella are still somewhere in the New York area. They may have been aided by an accomplice, perhaps a contact at the UN. They are wanted for questioning in several matters, in particular the outbreak of cancers continuing to spread through Asia. Dr. Laura Holdridge of Future Tech, a bioengineering firm, returned yesterday." A clip showed Laura hurrying through an airport. Several reporters cornered her and shoved microphones in her face. "What did you learn, Doctor Holdridge?"

"We haven't learned anything yet. We only..." A sneeze interrupted her words. "Sorry, I caught a cold somewhere. As I was saying, we only collected samples in Asia. We'll need to examine them carefully in the laboratory."

Tom turned to Fitzgerald. "You aren't..."

"No sir! You know as much about the cancer epidemic as we do."

"I didn't think so. People are just using you as a scapegoat for their own idiocy."

"Scapegoat?"

"That means somebody innocent to take the blame."

Becky interrupted them. "Would anybody like breakfast?"

"I can make pancakes," Isabella offered.

"How did you learn to make pancakes?"

"Molly taught me."

"The kitchen is yours, honey."

• • •

After breakfast, Tom showed Fitzgerald around the cabin property. He owned fifty acres surrounded on three sides by Willamette National Forest. Around the cabin stood mostly pine and Douglas fir trees with a few big-leaf maples. A winding driveway from the state road led through the trees to a gravel parking area in front of the cabin. "My grandfather bought this land more than eighty years ago. When my father was a boy, they built the cabin together using logs from the property," Tom explained. Seeing Fitzgerald admiring some nearby peaks, he offered to take him for a hike in the nearby mountains. Of course, Isabella wanted to go too. "Sure," Tom agreed. "But both of you will need to wear these orange vests."

"I thought we should try to be inconspicuous," said Fitzgerald.

"This is hunting season. We wouldn't want anyone to mistake you for a deer."

"What about bears?"

"Black bears only. No grizzlies here."

Tom found his unusual guests more than able to keep up with him. He waited by a stream for three hours while they assailed a nearby peak. Tom didn't mind. Maple trees nearby had turned a bright yellow. He loved sitting with only the gurgling water and soft wind for companions. Laughter drew his attention to see two young people jostling each other on the path as they competed to be the first to return. Fitzgerald won in the final sprint.

"We saw a caribou," Isabella gasped, out of breath from the run. "He," she indicated her mate, "tried to outrun it. But it beat him."

"The caribou had four legs," Fitzgerald protested, his chest heaving.

Tom marveled at their vigor. "That was probably an elk. That's what the hunters are looking for, or for mule deer."

"The hunters must be fast to catch them."

"They shoot them with a rifle."

"Oh!"

Chapter 27

• • •

Molly sat stunned. *Get married?* She had never wanted or expected to get married. Didn't really consider marriage an option for herself. She looked back at Paul, who glanced her way anxiously as he continued to drive. *You'll never find a better man. It's decision time.*

"Yes! I will marry you," Molly spoke with determination and then watched Paul slump a little in relief. "But I have to say that getting married scares the hell out of me."

"I understand." Paul's voice revealed that he had choked up.

"Okay," Molly continued, "I've already said 'yes' because you're the best man I'll ever meet. And despite my resolution to keep a distance between myself and men, I do love you. Now you tell me what our marriage is supposed to look like."

Paul smiled and tried a joke. "This won't be a romantic knee-bent moment to remember, will it?"

"Honestly, I need realism right now more than romantic gestures. But we *will* remember the moment."

"Molly, to me marriage should be passion and friendship mixed together. A good marriage combines two people with different strengths into a partnership. A married couple loves and trusts one another even during hurt or disagreement." Paul took a deep breath. "Being married means I can never send you away again, like I did last week."

He didn't say, 'I'll never leave you,' Molly realized. *That's not because he might leave. But leaving his wife isn't even in his comprehension. This is forever for him. He can't think or act any other way.*

"Can I add something?" she asked.

"Of course."

"Let's try to do what Fitzgerald and Isabella have been talking about. We can work together for our common good. And we can try to think of the other person first even when that means making sacrifices."

"That sounds like a good description of genuine love. I think they base their 'mating' concept on that."

Molly described to Paul what Isabella had told her about mating on Benevolent. She concluded with, "Mating is for life. If you want to be mated like the Benevolents, we'll need to first say a pledge to each other and to God."

"I'm willing." Paul noticed a rest area on the interstate, pulled in, and parked. He looked into Molly's eyes. "What sort of pledge?"

"Isabella didn't specify that. Whatever is meaningful to us, I suppose."

Paul sat in a daze. "I wouldn't know where to begin."

"Then I'll go first. Paul, I pledge to accept you as my lifelong mate. I give my solemn word that I will consider your welfare as more important than my own. I'll love you unconditionally and do everything I can to make you successful. I'll work to make our relationship full of fun, passion, trust, and teamwork. This commitment before God is until I die."

"Wow! That's a bit more than 'for better, for worse, for richer, for poorer, in sickness and health, until death do us part', isn't it?" Paul tried to form his thoughts into something articulate and meaningful like Molly's pledge but struggled for words. "Could you write your words down, please?"

Molly produced a pen and paper from her backpack. Together she and Paul recreated her pledge.

Paul took a deep breath. "I'm not so eloquent, but I'll promise the same for you." He read Molly's words and added, "To start considering your welfare, I know that from your mother's experience, you're suspicious of marriage. So you don't have to officially marry me, if you're not comfortable doing so. I'll be mated to you regardless."

This was a bigger shock to Molly than Paul's original proposal to get married. *He would prefer to be married, though. And Mom would want me to marry the right man.* "No, Paul. I want us to make our relationship official by getting legally married as part of being mated. I'll legally marry you as soon as we can show IDs." *I never expected to hear myself say that.* "But do you still want to wait until our marriage is legal to..."

"I think we've waited long enough."

"Good, because according to Isabella, a form of intimacy is what finalizes the pledge."

• • •

"Name please," the interstate hotel clerk asked.

"Smith. John Smith."

The desk clerk smirked. "Do you have a credit card, Mr. Smith?"

"We'll pay cash."

"I'll still need a credit card for incidentals." He recorded the pre-paid card Paul offered. "You and...Mrs. Smith will be in room 254. The elevator is to your left."

Upstairs, Paul fumbled nervously with the key card. He pushed open the door for Molly.

"I don't think so, Big Boy. I've never been carried across a threshold. This is my chance."

Paul joyfully complied.

• • •

The next morning Molly stretched and asked, "Now wasn't that fun?"

"You're not kidding." Paul snuggled closer to Molly. "How did that make *you* feel, in addition to having fun?"

"Loved...secure..." Molly struggled for words. "Being part of more than just me." Molly thought a few seconds more. "And worth waiting for."

"Me too. Would you like to go out for breakfast?

"That's a great idea."

• • •

Paul stopped by the front desk after breakfast and a trip to a local grocery. The same desk clerk was on duty. "We'd like to stay two more nights, please."

"You and 'Mrs. Smith'?"

"We need some rest."

"I'll bet you do."

If you only knew, Paul thought.

Paul and Molly indeed enjoyed an intimate passion previously unimaginable to either of them. But both had also been physically and emotionally drained by the previous week. They slept a lot then ordered pizza and other delivery foods. And they turned the air conditioner to its lowest setting to cuddle while watching old movies on TV. By the third day they began to feel more like venturing out again. "How would you like a ring?" Paul unexpectedly asked.

"What sort of ring?"

"A diamond. An engagement ring. We can get wedding bands after the legalities."

Molly had never imagined herself wearing a ring announcing her attachment to a man. She took a couple of minutes getting used to the idea. *Why not go all in?* she thought. "Yeah, I think I would."

"I would enjoy seeing you wearing it," said Paul.

"Would I get to help pick it out?"

Paul grinned. "You should. You're paying for it."

Molly playfully pushed him. "I'll find a way to collect."

●●●

"Will you please keep your eyes on the road?" Paul teased Molly as she drove southwards.

"I can't help looking!" Her eyes glanced at the ring on her left hand. "It's so beautiful."

"I expected that jewelry store clerk to faint when I counted out sixty-two hundred-dollar bills."

"She probably thinks you're a drug dealer or something."

"She took the money, though."

Molly grew more serious. "What do you think the Feds are doing?"

"They're looking for Fitzgerald and Isabella and almost certainly me too. And they'll probably be wanting to talk to you by now. When they can't find you, they'll suspect we're together. I don't know if they're looking outside of New York City yet."

"Why did you send Fitzgerald and Isabella to the Sawyers rather than your own parents?"

"The Feds are certain to check with my parents when they come looking for me. The Sawyers, probably not. And to be honest, my parents are so by-the-rules oriented that they might turn in Fitzgerald and Isabella."

"Tom and Becky Sawyer?" Molly questioned. "Was Mark Twain their father?"

Paul laughed. "I asked them about that once. Tom

said that his parents had a sense of humor. They loved it when he started dating a girl named Rebecca. They dubbed her Becky and it stuck."

Molly looked over at Paul. "That beard coming in looks good on you. I like your hair a little shaggy too."

"You look good as a curly-headed brunette."

Molly glanced at her ring again. "This is kind of like a honeymoon for us. Is there anywhere you'd like to go while we're on the run?"

"Do you think Isabella would call this a 'mated-moon'?" Dave teased.

"Maybe," Molly answered. "I interpret being mated as a stronger commitment than legal marriage. We should have a mated-moon. So anywhere special on the way to New Orleans?"

"We could stop in DC and visit the Smithsonian. Then we could take the Blue Ridge Parkway. The trees should be getting their fall color. How about you?"

"Charleston. I love Charleston. And I know a seafood restaurant there that you'll love."

"Molly, you make me very happy."

"I love you, Paul."

• • •

That night in a roadside hotel in the environs of Washington, DC, Paul and Molly watched the news expecting to find reports about the search for themselves. But the news had another bombshell to reveal. "A high-ranking official from North Korea seeking

261

cancer treatment in Manila today revealed the extent of the cancer epidemic in that reclusive country," reported Steve Wilson at the DSC desk. "Health workers there started noticing the surge in cancer cases over a year ago. The government kept the news private rather than face the humiliation of asking aid from western sources. The official claims that over 50% of their citizens had been diagnosed with some form of cancer before the medical facilities became swamped with patients."

"Wow, that is serious," Paul commented.

"This certainly exonerates Fitzgerald and Isabella from any blame," Molly pointed out. "They haven't been on Earth a year."

"Since when have facts influenced some people?"

Molly clenched her teeth. "You mean people like Bill Samuel?"

Somehow Molly's residual anger toward Bill made her even more attractive to Paul. "Well, he would be a prime example. But he's not the only one." Paul turned off the TV. "Speaking of Fitzgerald and Isabella, we should check in on them." He sorted through his bag looking for the disposable cell phone.

Fitzgerald answered the phone. "Hello."

Paul knew Fitzgerald would recognize his voice. "Are you enjoying where you are?"

"Oh, yes! We are in the Cascade Range mountains. Not as wild as Alaska. But just as beautiful here. The trees are changing colors. And we are trying to catch a wild elk."

"You mean hunt it?"

"No, it is a contest between Isabella and me to touch one. She got close yesterday. But she snuck up on that one. This is a game played on Benevolent. But elks are faster than snarks."

"What else are you doing?"

"I am helping Tom to build another room onto the cabin. Isabella is baking cookies with Becky. Sometimes she helps with building the room. She read some books and can do the wiring and plumbing very well so that Tom doesn't have to hire a worker."

"Can I speak with Tom?"

"Yes."

"Hello." Tom's voice sounded old compared to Fitzgerald's.

"Thank you for taking care of our friends."

"No problem. We're enjoying it. Becky thinks she's found a new daughter."

"Do you need any money for expenses?"

"No, no. They're earning their keep." Tom spoke low as he confided, "I haven't seen Becky this happy since Beth...well, you know."

Molly held up a note for Paul to see. *I want to speak to Isabella.*

"Thanks, Tom. How about putting Becky's new daughter on the phone?"

Paul handed the phone to Molly. She carried it away a few feet to talk. A squeal coming from the phone a minute later told Paul that Isabella now knew about his commitment to Molly. He took the phone back. "We need to hang up now. We'll see you in a couple of weeks."

Paul grabbed Molly and whispered in her ear, "You told Isabella?"

"Why not?" Molly asked. Paul couldn't think of any reason why not. "There could be a problem, though," she added.

"What's that?"

"Isabella says she's not feeling well, especially in the mornings."

"You don't think..."

Molly only shrugged.

Chapter 28

• • •

"Where is Tom?" Isabella asked when she and Fitzgerald returned from one of their rambles in the mountains.

"He needed to go into Eugene, honey. They needed him for something at the office," Becky answered.

"The office?"

"He's a tax accountant. You're lucky this is his slow season. After the new year begins, he'll work and work and work until the end of April."

Seeing her guests' disappointment, Becky added, "He should be back tomorrow night. He said you could work on the cabin expansion without him if you'd like."

"I think I'll save that work. He tells me things while we're working. Things about how people live and argue. I like listening to him," Fitzgerald answered. "I need to think about our mission again, though. I can catch up on the news and study more on the computer."

"I was just about to have some tea with the cookies we made. Would you like some, honey?" Becky said to Isabella.

"Yes, thank you."

While Fitzgerald busied himself online, Becky placed two cups with tea bags and a plate of cookies on the kitchen table between her and Isabella. "Did you catch an elk this morning?"

"No, they have learned to run from a long way when they see Fitzgerald."

"I used to be able to hike with Tom," Becky told the younger woman.

"What happened?"

"I just got older. My knees are giving me trouble now. I worked as a school teacher when I met Tom. Then I stayed home with Beth. After she died, I returned to school teaching for a few years. But my knees kept me from staying on my feet all day. Now I sometimes do tutoring through a community program."

"Fitzgerald and I have a foundation to help children learn. Molly started it. Then she picked some people to decide how to use the money."

Becky poured water from the kettle onto the tea bags waiting in their cups. "I saw on the news when you and Molly did that. You did a very good thing. Molly must be an interesting person. I wanted to hug her when she slapped that jerk Bill Samuel on TV."

"She felt sad after she did that, though. She expected to lose her job. Fitzgerald and I were glad when NASA asked her and Paul to take care of us." Isabella nervously nibbled on a cookie. "I told you something wrong."

"What's that, honey?"

"When you asked if Paul and Molly were romantic, I didn't know. Yesterday on the phone Molly told me that she and Paul had decided to mate. Is it wrong to tell you that?"

Becky's face lit up with joy. "That's wonderful! Maybe you did just a little wrong to tell me before they could tell me themselves. But even if it is, the wrong is very small."

"Human customs related to mating are hard for me to understand."

"Me too." Becky laughed with Isabella and commented, "Molly seems very different from Beth."

"Yes, I told Paul to find someone very different so that he wouldn't think about Beth all of the time."

"Isabella, you are a smart girl."

• • •

"Shouldn't we turn west on I-10 to get to New Orleans?" Molly asked.

"Yes, if all we wanted to do is get there," Paul answered. "But I saw on the news that the Feds are expanding their search beyond New York. I was thinking we could take a detour to start a dead-end diversion."

Molly got a devilish look in her eye. "I've got an idea. Let me drive south toward Orlando. I know that city. And it's near your home. You wipe out anything you don't want public on your cell phone. No, wait. Download anything you might need in the future to your laptop. And I'll need a couple of your credit cards. You don't have any mega limits on them, do you?"

"My cards have a limit of $3,000, and maybe half of that is already used."

"They'll be fine."

Paul pulled over to switch places. Then he laughed out loud when Molly explained her plan.

In Orlando, the couple gassed up the minivan, bought some food, and went to the toilet. "No stopping until we're out of Florida, okay?" Molly reminded Paul.

Paul suppressed his merriment. "Got it."

Molly's time investigating corruption in Orlando had taught her areas where people would be unlikely to turn in found items. As the sun started to set, she casually placed Paul's cell phone, the disposable cell phone she had used to call him, and several of his credit cards in different places where they would be found quickly. She ran to where Paul kept their vehicle running. "The bait is spread. Let's get out of town before they trace us."

Paul gunned the engine, accelerating the minivan toward the Florida Turnpike north. He stayed at the speed limit until they had reached I-75 well north of Orlando. He looked over at Molly, who still had that devilish gleam in her eye. "Maybe we're giving the Feds too much credit for quick response time. But that sure was fun."

"You never know. But you're right, it was fun. We should be able to reach Alabama with only one stop for gas."

● ● ●

"What have you found?" Isabella asked Fitzgerald.

"The authorities don't have any idea where we are. Right now, they are looking in the Orlando area, close to Kennedy Space Center where we landed."

She put her hand on his shoulder and stared at the screen. "They think we are in Orlando?"

Fitzgerald glanced up at her. "Maybe Paul and Molly—"

Isabella interrupted, "Anything else?"

"The cancer epidemic is frightening everyone. Fear is uniting mankind like I tried to do."

"So humans can respond to an immediate threat, but not a longer-range one?"

"I think you are right."

"Fitzgerald, this could be very serious. This epidemic could eventually kill all the humans. Maybe not all. But most could die and those remaining would be few, like the grizzly bears."

"Correct again. Isabella, you know science better than I do. Is there anything we can do?"

"I don't know what."

The house phone rang. "Hello," Becky answered. "That's good, Tom. And we need some things." She recited to her husband a long list of mostly groceries. "You're writing this down, right? Okay. Anything you two would like from the grocery?" she shouted to Fitzgerald and Isabella.

"More pancake mix," shouted back Fitzgerald.

After saying goodbye to Tom, Becky joined her guests in the cabin's living room where they sat somewhat solemnly. "I need to warn you that Tom is bringing Emma and Jack with him this time." Seeing her guests' looks of alarm she added, "Don't worry. They won't tell anyone about you."

• • •

Beep, beep. Tom pulled up to the cabin. He opened the door to a rear seat. An elderly golden retriever gingerly uncoiled from her place there. The dog carefully stepped to the ground and wagged with her entire body as Becky approached, followed by Fitzgerald and Isabella. "This is Emma," Becky announced. Emma moved slowly and had white hair covering most of her muzzle. "Emma, these are our guests, Fitzgerald and Isabella."

"Hello, Emma," said Isabella.

The dog recoiled in alarm and barked a couple of times. "That's odd. She usually loves new people."

"Technically, we aren't people," Fitzgerald commented.

Tom stood nearby. "She does know you're somehow different. Hold your closed hand out to let her smell you." Fitzgerald did so. The old dog tentatively approached and sniffed the hand. Her tail wagged just a smidgen. "Now rub her snout gently." In just a minute, Emma and Fitzgerald had become friends.

"Now this guy will be more difficult." For the first time, Fitzgerald and Isabella noticed a plastic box with air holes and a handle Tom had set on the ground. Inside they could see yellow eyes looking out. Tom opened the door, and a striped grey streak bounded out and disappeared around the house. "Jack will be back at suppertime," Tom promised.

"This is a canine, like a wolf?" Isabella asked while gently stroking Emma's head.

Becky laughed at the comparison of Emma to a wolf. "Yes, but much gentler than a wolf. Aren't you, girl?" she said to Emma. "And she's genetically very similar to the bear you saw."

"And that other animal is of the feline family, like a small tiger," Isabella speculated.

"That's right. And he can seem like a tiger to a mouse. He'll get used to you."

"How about you two helping me to unload the groceries?" Tom requested.

● ● ●

The fall air felt chilly. "We'll have our first freeze tonight," predicted Tom as he built a fire in the fireplace.

Emma came to lie on a rug provided for her in front of the blaze. True to Tom's word, Jack showed up for supper. He let Becky pick him up and squeeze him. He wouldn't let Fitzgerald or Isabella touch him yet, though. After skirting around them, the cat curled up next to Emma.

While Tom and Fitzgerald watched a football game on TV, Becky spoke to Isabella privately in the kitchen. "Honey, I noticed that you haven't been eating all of your breakfast like you did at first."

"My stomach feels funny. Like I ate something

inorganic. And a couple of times my stomach has thrown it back."

Becky's face reflected sympathy. "I got Tom to pick up something for you."

"Will it make me feel better?"

"Some women, yes; others, no." Obviously Isabella couldn't understand that. "Just do this for me, please. Take this stick into the bathroom and pee on it." More confusion from Isabella. "Put it in some of your urine," Becky clarified.

In a few minutes, Isabella brought the stick back. "Oh, my!" she heard Becky say.

"Am I alright?"

"That depends. Come sit with me." She led Isabella into the bedroom she and Tom shared. Together they sat on the bed. "Honey, you're pregnant."

"Pregnant?"

"That means you're going to have a baby. You're going to be a mother."

"A baby? How can I?"

"Do you and Fitzgerald have sex?"

"Yes, but—"

"There's no but, honey."

"What should I do?"

"Normally, the first thing to do is to tell the father."

"Will you tell Fitzgerald for me?"

"No, this is something you need to do yourself." Becky led Isabella back to the living room. "Tom, will you take me for a walk outside?"

"A walk? It's freezing out there. And the game is on."

"Tom!"

Tom looked at Becky's eyes, then got up and collected his coat.

Chapter 29

· · ·

Paul and Molly strolled Jackson Square in New Orleans. "The musicians are amazing, I agree. I just don't like blues music that much," Paul said.

Molly tucked her hand under Paul's arm as they walked. She had never before done that to any male. Doing so made her feel feminine somehow. She knew Paul liked it when he used his other hand to pat her fingers. Molly also knew Paul enjoyed their spirited discussions. "Maybe that's because your life has been so idyllic that you can't feel the blues."

Paul pondered that thought. Molly was darned clever at understanding people and articulating her thoughts. "I've had heartbreak," he temporized.

"Yes, you have, from Beth's death. But the blues reflect not a tragic incident, but tragic circumstances."

"Like you and your mother struggling alone?"

"Maybe."

"Molly, you are...special. I love just being with you and exchanging ideas." Paul put the arm Molly held around her shoulders to squeeze her. "How about some Cajun seafood?"

"That sounds great."

In a dark and quiet French Quarter restaurant, Paul ordered jambalaya and Molly picked a huge bowl of seafood gumbo. After each eating about half of their respective dishes, they exchanged plates. Commotion and shouting on the street drew all the patrons' attention. Cell phones started lighting up around the restaurant. "What do you think is happening?" Molly asked.

Paul noticed that all the servers had disappeared. "Let's find out."

In the restaurant's kitchen, they found all the staff clustered around somebody's cell phone streaming a news broadcast. Molly recognized Steve Wilson's voice. "The president is urging calm and has placed an immediate ban on airline flights into the US. For those who haven't heard, let's replay the dramatic announcement from just over forty-five minutes ago. The speaker will be Dr. Laura Holdridge of Future Tech, a bioengineering firm. She recently went to Asia at the request of the CDC."

Molly, with her reporter's instinct and forcefulness, wormed her way through the restaurant staff to stand near the cell phone. "Preliminary investigation of the samples I brought back from Asia has revealed a new virus very much like the common cold. All viruses typically force cells within the body to reproduce the virus. Sometimes during this process viruses can damage healthy DNA.

Many cancers are due to damaged cells reproducing without restraint. The virus we discovered appears to deliberately damage cells in a way that leads to cancer. Because I had been in the infected area, we examined my blood taken on my return. The cancer virus is present and multiplying."

A reporter shouted out, "Don't our bodies create antibodies to fight a virus?"

"Yes, they do. And more recent tests of my blood indicate that my body's immune system is winning the battle. But the virus has already done cancer-causing damage to any number of my cells."

"Can't we create a vaccine?" another shouted.

"Unlikely. Because the new virus rapidly mutates to new strains like a cold virus, any vaccine we know how to make would quickly be ineffective."

"Can't procedures recently developed turn a body's immune system against a cancer?"

"Yes, immunotherapy is a promising experimental treatment. T-cells, a type of white corpuscle, are genetically modified to attack tumors. And traditional chemotherapy and radiation treatments should still be effective as well. But what we're seeing in Asia is that a person's body can be overwhelmed by several cancers at once despite treatment. And many people aren't receiving treatment at all because the treatment centers are swamped with patients. Finally, there is evidence of reinfection among those whose cancer was treated successfully. Just like people can catch a new strain of cold."

Somebody listening with Molly said, "This means

you can catch cancer with a cold." Suddenly, nobody listening wanted to stand close to the others. The group dispersed, many holding their hands or napkins over their mouth and nose.

Molly turned to see Paul stepping out of the way of fleeing restaurant workers. "They're overreacting," he told her. "Not every cold is caused by the cancer virus. And that virus is primarily still in Asia."

"Right now, maybe. But couldn't the cancer virus spread here?" He admitted that it could, and probably would. "What should we do?" she asked.

Paul laid down some money to pay for their meal. "Let's go to Oregon."

But to Molly's surprise, instead of immediately heading for the interstate, Paul drove to a large discount store. There people already crammed aisles stocking up on perishable foodstuffs like milk, bread, and meat. "You buy food that can keep, enough for a week or more, and plenty of water. Meet me out front," he told her.

"Where are you going?"

"To gas us up."

Molly hurried around the store collecting non-perishable canned goods, crackers, cookies, and some drinks. To these she added ten one-gallon jugs of water. Not sure how much food would be needed for a week, she simply filled the cart. Waiting through the checkout line took an hour. Afterwards, Molly pushed the heavy cart to the curb outside. Paul was not there. *He'll come*, she knew.

Nearly another hour later, Paul pulled up in the minivan. He had purchased twenty-five plastic gas containers and jammed them into the minivan's rear. The reek of gasoline nearly made her sick. "Sorry I took so long. A few other people had the same idea. I'm glad we had plenty of cash to pay with." He started loading the groceries and water. "Nice work with the supplies."

Molly didn't question Paul's initiative to get the gas. The chaos in the grocery store had convinced her that they needed to be self-sufficient to get to Oregon. "Let's roll down the windows to get out some of this gas smell."

"Good idea. Let's also tighten the lids on the containers. I was in a hurry."

• • •

"You're what?" Fitzgerald wanted to know. Isabella, seated on the couch beside him, repeated what Becky had told her. "I'm going to be a father? Is that even possible?"

"Apparently our creators did a very good job making us like humans." Isabella added, "Somehow I feel more important now. Like if everything else fails and I do this one thing right, then my life is a success."

"What about our mission?" Fitzgerald persisted.

"Maybe this is part of our mission. Our creators are very smart. Surely they knew this might happen. They could easily have created us in a manner to prevent this." Isabella looked into Fitzgerald's eyes. "Do you want to have a baby with me?"

Fitzgerald sat contemplating the enormity of the situation. He visualized a somebody like himself who could see a future he would not. Somebody to entrust with the essence of who he was. Somebody with Isabella's precious essence. *Preserving Isabella is more important to me than preserving myself, he realized.*

"I do," Fitzgerald spoke aloud to himself. "Yes, I do!" he said to Isabella. "You are my mated one. Nothing is more important to me than you. But to partner with you to create a new being will be the most wonderful thing. We can extend the work of our creators and in some way the work of the Great Creator of all things."

Isabella shifted her seat to sit touching her mate. "Me and you."

Fitzgerald put his arm around her. "You and me."

Isabella put her head on his shoulder. They rested that way until a gentle tapping at the door drew their attention. The door cracked a little to reveal Becky's face. "Can we come back now? Tom is cold."

Fitzgerald and Isabella jumped to their feet like two teenagers caught necking. The door opened wider as Tom and Becky came in. "I'll bet the higher elevations are getting snow," Tom started.

Fitzgerald didn't notice. "We are going to have an offspring," he announced.

"Congratulations!" Becky responded and moved to hug Isabella.

Tom came to shake Fitzgerald's hand. "Welcome to fatherhood."

Becky, not knowing what to say, asked Isabella, "Did your mother have a difficult delivery?"

Fitzgerald answered for her, smiling. "Neither of us have a mother or a father like you know." Isabella nodded in agreement. "We were created in a beaker and grew as embryos in a tank. Our birth came when they broke the glass."

Isabella poked her mate. "They didn't literally break the glass, Fitzgerald."

"Maybe not. But we have DNA patched together from many places. None of it from actual humans. Our baby could have a tail like the snark."

Isabella laughed. "Or maybe it will have wings like the Benevolent infants."

Tom and Becky stood shocked at their guests' levity. Then recognizing the absurdity of the situation, they began to laugh as well. "I love these kids," Tom said to Becky.

● ● ●

The route from New Orleans to Eugene wasn't complicated—I-10 west, then I-5 north. When possible, Paul and Molly bypassed major cities. They dedicated themselves to the task by taking turns driving and sleeping in the passenger seat.

The couple followed the cancer virus crisis on the radio. "The president has rescinded his total ban of international travel. Millions of American citizens living abroad are trying to get home. Protests, some of which have been violent, by loved ones remaining in the United States forced the change of policy. TSA centers have been converted from screening luggage to health control of incoming passengers.

"The US Surgeon General is emphasizing that only a few cases of the cancer virus have been reported in the United States. They are being isolated by the CDC. Most colds are simply colds. Nevertheless, he urges everyone to avoid unnecessary contact with others, wash hands frequently, and get plenty of vitamin C. He has reminded everyone that once the body's natural immune system has defeated the virus, the victim may have lasting cancer effects. But the person is no longer contagious to the public.

"The World Health Organization has identified, with 99% confidence, North Korea as the source of the outbreak. The Russian Sports Federation today reversed their previous position by admitting to selling CRISPR gene modification technology to the North Korean government. The Russian spokesman reported that North Korea had promised to only use the technology to enhance its athletic success in world competitions."

"Wow! The Russians must be scared," Molly commented to Paul.

"They have reason to be. They're a lot closer to Asia than we are. At least fear is creating some cooperation among the nations. That could be too late, though, if this thing keeps spreading."

"You don't believe they can isolate the United States?"

"Not forever."

Molly changed the channel. "Please humor me," she said. "I'm just curious what that jerk Bill Samuel is saying now after he tried to put the blame on Fitzgerald and Isabella."

They found Bill on air as a guest of National Public Radio. "The United States must immediately sterilize the source of the contagion by using our nuclear arsenal, starting with North Korea," Bill insisted.

"But the cancer virus has already escaped from North Korea," the moderator reasoned. "The infection doesn't continue to flow from there."

"Sterilize the other places as well."

"You mean like Seoul, Beijing, and Tokyo?" the moderator continued.

"We must do so," Bill asserted.

"Reports are that the cancer virus may be out of control in Russia. Should we sterilize them as well? Wouldn't they sterilize back with their own nuclear arsenal?"

"We can isolate Russia—"

Molly turned off the radio. "What an idiot!"

"Unfortunately, we've learned that frightened people listen to idiots," said Paul.

"I'm frightened and I'm not listening."

"Then what do you think should be done?"

Molly sat for a minute. "I'm not normally a religious person, but I'm praying for God's help."

A thought suddenly occurred to Paul. "Maybe we already have help. Do you remember in Alaska Isabella saying that they don't catch colds?"

Chapter 30

•••

Tom, Becky, Fitzgerald, and Isabella watched the TV the next morning together. Hysteria had spread across America overnight; indeed, it had spread all over the world. Recorded footage showed grocery and other stores sold out or in some cases looted. Vehicles choked highways leading out of major cities. Skyline views of cities revealed fires burning. First response teams could not react quickly in many instances because the staff themselves had fled.

"I appeal to you for calm," the president had pleaded. Apparently, nobody listened to him. The chaos multiplied overnight.

Fitzgerald and Isabella watched Tom get up from the TV and go to a locked cabinet they had not noticed before. He unlocked the door, reached inside, and pulled out a bolt-action hunting rifle followed by a twelve-gauge pump shotgun. "Becky, get the handgun from under the bed." She returned with an old-fashioned Smith and Wesson .38 revolver.

The extraterrestrial couple watched Tom load the rifle. "Are we going hunting?" Fitzgerald ventured.

"No, son." Tom looked at them intently. "I'm afraid there are a lot of bad people. Some of them may come here trying to take our house and supplies. They would hurt us to do so. You and I have to protect Becky and Isabella."

"Are you going to kill the bad people?"

"Certainly not if I can avoid that. We'll use the guns to frighten them away."

"I fired a handgun in Los Angles. On TV, they are very powerful."

"That's only on TV, son. This is more powerful than a handgun." Tom handed Fitzgerald the shotgun. "Let's all go outside for a firearm lesson."

• • •

"Can't we pick some people up?" asked Molly. Paul passed stranded motorists walking along the highway, many holding out their thumbs hoping for a ride.

"We don't have room with all of the gas cans and supplies. Our best bet to help them is to get to Oregon and talk to Fitzgerald and Isabella."

Molly protested, "I don't understand what they can do."

"Do you remember that Fitzgerald and Isabella have a twenty-fourth chromosome pair?" Molly did. "Neither of them are biologists. But Isabella said that the twenty-fourth chromosome had something to do with cosmic-ray exposure, which damages DNA. She also said that it was the key to their immunity to human diseases. Maybe the cure is inside of them." In response to Molly's surprise he reminded, "I'm not a geneticist, but I do have a master's degree in biology."

Looking back at the people walking, Molly said, "We'd be walking too if you hadn't brought the extra gas."

"We'd be hungry and thirsty without the supplies you bought."

• • •

"Let's stay busy, son," Tom suggested. "We'll need firewood to save our propane and gas for the generator. Becky and Isabella can watch the house during daylight."

Tom led Fitzgerald to the basement where he collected his chainsaw and the equipment needed to run it. "I know where there are a couple of dead trees nearby. Technically, they're on Forest Service land where you need a permit to cut. But I don't think anybody's going to complain in the current situation." He handed Fitzgerald the chainsaw. "I'll carry the rifle in case we need it."

Four dead trees came down easily. Tom showed his young helper how to use the chainsaw to trim the branches and cut the trees into eighteen-inch lengths. "Careful you don't cut your foot off."

"Yes, then I'd have to grow another one." Fitzgerald saw Tom's look of shock and added, "Just joking. I can't really grow another foot."

Tom laughed and slapped his young disciple on the back. "You had me for a second, though."

The inexperienced woodsman let the saw bar and blade get pinched twice. Tom disconnected the engine from the pinched blade, connected a spare bar and blade, and cut a relief wedge to remove the pinched blade.

The two men enjoyed working together immensely and had nearly forgotten the circumstances. *Boom!* A shotgun blast reverberated through the woods. "That's Becky!" Tom shouted as he grabbed the rifle and started to run toward the cabin. Fitzgerald ran ahead.

At the cabin, he found Becky and Isabella staring down the driveway. Tom joined them in a couple of minutes although huffing. "Some men started up the driveway on foot," Becky explained without being asked. "I fired up in the air. They ran away. I also tried to call 911. Our line is dead."

Tom, still out of breath, gasped, "Good girl. Too bad about the phone. They might have cut the wire. Or maybe with the chaos all the phones are out." Isabella brought him some water, which he received gratefully. "I guess I'm not as young as I used to be."

They all waited for Tom to recover. "Why don't you guard the cabin?" Fitzgerald suggested. "I can carry in the firewood."

Tom nodded. "That would be good. Thanks!"

"I can help him," Isabella volunteered.

Tom dismissed her. "You're pregnant."

"You know better than that, Tom," Becky rebuked him. To Isabella she said, "Men get overprotective around pregnant women. You're young and strong. The exercise will be good for you and your baby."

Tom handed Isabella his gloves. "Don't overdo it, okay?"

Fitzgerald and Isabella worked diligently all afternoon. By sunset, a huge pile of logs had been accumulated by the house. "Well done, you two," said Tom. "Now help me stack some of these logs up in a wall, like a little fort. You'll see why later."

• • •

"Try calling Tom and Becky again," Paul suggested while driving.

Molly dialed. "Still no answer."

"Maybe the landline is out of service. Fitzgerald and Isabella aren't answering the cell phone either. We'll just have to surprise them, I guess."

"We can bypass Los Angeles to the east by going up I-15 then cutting over to I-5 south of Bakersfield," Molly proposed as she examined the road map. "Then the only big town we'll have to pass before Oregon is Sacramento. If we hurry we can go by in the early morning hours."

Paul steered onto I-15 without slowing. "I think that's a good idea. How about turning the radio back on?"

"That depresses me."

"I don't blame you. But we might hear something important."

Molly complied. "Most states have called out National Guard units," the NPR news reported. "Looting and hoarding are widespread, especially in the cities. Gun battles have broken out in some urban areas between rival groups. Citizens are advised to take shelter in their homes until order can be restored."

The announcer next attempted to shed some positivity on the situation by revealing information about the origin of the pandemic. "The World Health Organization has located a North Korean scientist near death from multiple cancers. The scientist confirmed that his government had directed him and other scientists to use the Russian genetic technology to attempt creating a biological weapon. They modified a common cold virus. The vaccine they had developed did not work when the cold-like virus evolved."

"I don't think that news is going to calm anybody down," said Paul.

"The CDC reports that discovering the origin is a key step in stopping any pandemic," the NPR announcer concluded.

Molly shook her head in dismay. "Maybe they think people will feel better knowing where the disease killing them came from."

"Look at that!" Paul pointed from the driver's seat west toward Los Angeles. Orange glows reflected off the clouds in the early evening. "Those must be fires. I'm glad we didn't go directly up I-5. We'd be right in the middle of that."

Suddenly, a section of street lights failed on the interstate. They heard sporadic popping of gunfire above the wind noise of the open windows. Molly rolled up her window. "The gas smell isn't so bad anymore."

●　●　●

Molly woke when Paul pulled to the side of the highway. She rubbed her face and peered through the windshield. A young woman carrying her baby and leading two small children approached the minvan from a stalled car. "I thought you said we shouldn't stop," Molly whispered.

Paul opened the driver's side door. "I did say that. Maybe we shouldn't. But I just couldn't pass them."

"We're out of gas. Could you please just help us get to my parents' house? The National Guard called up my husband," the girl pleaded.

"Where do your parents live?" Before she answered, Paul started discarding some empty gas cans. Then he erected the minivan's rear seat.

"A small town maybe an hour up ahead. My name is Alice Faber. These are our children."

"I'm Molly. This is Paul. How long have you been stranded?"

"Nearly all night. Could I bring the baby's stuff?"

Molly helped Alice get the children seated and buckled in while Paul collected a car seat and several bags from her car. The mother started to cry as Paul pulled back onto the highway. "I saw gangs of men roaming the streets near our house in Sacramento. Then I heard gunshots and screams. I was alone with the kids. If something had happened to me no one would be there to care for them. We had to get away."

All the children started to cry when their mother broke down. Molly turned around in the front seat. "Have the kids eaten?"

"I was in such a hurry that I didn't think to bring any food. But we could have made it to Mom and Dad in a couple of hours if sitting in traffic hadn't used most of our gas."

Molly passed back cookies, apple juice, and water plus some paper cups. "I'm sorry we don't have any milk."

Still crying, the mother crumbled a cookie and mixed it with water and a little juice to make baby food. "Could you feed him while I take care of the other two?" she asked Molly.

Molly had never cared for a baby and looked at Paul for help. His return look said, *Better you than me.*

"Sure, why not?" Molly agreed. The mother immediately passed the car seat to her, baby and all.

Taking care of her other two children composed the young mother. Soon all stopped crying. Molly found feeding the child now riding between her and Paul to be messy. *Maybe I'm getting some food inside him,* she thought.

The mother sensed Molly's inexperience. "You're doing fine. I'm certain he likes mashed cookies better than strained carrots." A juice spill distracted her for a moment. "Oops. Sorry about that." Words of frustration flowed from the distraught young woman. "The man on TV told us to stay home and practice 'social distancing.'"

"'Social distancing' is an interesting way to say, 'Stay away from everyone else,'" Molly commented.

"Apparently others stocked up first. Before the electricity went out, TV showed riots and looting in stores, depleted gas stations, and even empty ATM machines. Even if I had known, I couldn't have fought those crowds with three kids. My parents expected us last night. But I used up my cell phone battery trying to call my husband. Just put the baby on your shoulder and pat his back gently," she told Molly.

I did get some food in him, Molly thought when the baby spit up onto her blouse.

"Sorry. I should have told you to spread a napkin first. Have you heard any more about the cancer virus?" The mother continued talking without waiting for an answer. "I don't blame people for being scared. I'm terrified. I know this sounds crazy, but I've been praying that the Benevolents will help us. If they know enough about genetics to create Fitzgerald and Isabella, maybe they could create a cancer vaccine or something."

Maybe they could, realized Paul. "Why don't you use our cell phone to tell your parents that you're coming."

The mother took the phone in gratitude. "God bless you two. You're like angels."

"I'm not an angel," Molly admitted.

Paul laughed. "Maybe you're an avenging angel."

"I would accept that role."

• • •

"Have you ever been in the army? No, of course not," Tom corrected himself. "Well, what you're doing is called sentry duty. Stay hidden behind these firewood logs and in the shadows. Don't move around. Don't make noise. And above all, don't show any light. If those men try to sneak up on the house through the woods, you should be able to hear and see them before they see you. Do you understand?"

"Yes, sir," Fitzgerald answered. "This is like the movie I saw, *The Alamo*."

"We hope not, son. All the Americans there died." Tom patted his young friend reassuringly. "If you do need to fire, don't forget to release the safety. I'll be watching the driveway in the front. Every few hours, Becky or Isabella will come watch a while so you can warm up inside." Tom left the younger man with this: "Don't forget that your wife and baby are inside."

Fitzgerald gripped the shotgun in the cold as he watched the darkness over the woodpile logs. He practiced removing the safety and putting it back on through the gloves Becky had given him. His feet started getting cold. To get his mind off the discomfort, he started reviewing his mission. *Convince the Earthlings that their species is in peril. They must cooperate to solve problems for the common good.*

But he knew his mission so well that its mind-occupying power didn't last long. Instead he thought about Isabella. He thought about how she talked and laughed, her intelligence, and each part of her body. *She is so completely wonderful. My life is good just because of her.*

Then he remembered, *I'm going to be a father to Isabella's child. Part of Isabella will be in that child.* The wonder of that thought eliminated any feeling of cold.

Crack. A noise came through the dark. *Scrunch, scrunch.* A sound like stealthy footsteps came from the trees. A low voice came from the same direction. "Damn, I can't see anything."

There! Fitzgerald saw a two-second glimmer of a beam of light through the trees about forty yards away. That gave him a bearing to point the shotgun. *They are coming to hurt Isabella and her baby.* Without thinking further, he took the shotgun off safety and fired. Immediately light and smoke pierced by a column of fire from the shotgun filled the dark world.

He heard a cry of pain. A score of flashing lights came from the place he had aimed. Thuds sounded against the cabin wall behind and the firewood in front of him. Impacting bullets threw wood debris into his face. Fitzgerald used his inner eyelids to clear his eyes. He pumped the shotgun and fired again, then again, toward the flashes. Another cry of pain came, followed by crashing steps through the woods away from the cabin. The flashlight came on and bounced away, carried by a man running with another, or maybe two others, following.

Tom tore around the house and fired one rifle shot toward the now-distant light. "I didn't think I'd hit anything," he explained to Fitzgerald. "I just wanted them to know we have a rifle, too."

"What happened!" Becky's voice demanded from the door.

"Stay inside. Fitzgerald ran them off."

• • •

The next morning, Tom scouted the woods and returned carrying a machine pistol. "Look what they dropped. Too bad the 9-mm clip is half empty." He showed everybody the weapon. "You winged at least one of them with a buckshot pellet. There's blood."

Fitzgerald couldn't take a morning nap being so keyed up from the night before. Isabella tried to talk to him about what had happened in the night. But Fitzgerald wouldn't discuss anything and seemed to settle into despondency. Tom started him splitting the firewood he and Isabella had carried in the previous day. Gradually the exertion calmed him. Isabella found her mate asleep in the mid-morning sun.

Late in the afternoon a vehicle started up the driveway. Becky fired off a warning shot. The vehicle stopped. A car door opened. A voice called out, "Tom, don't shoot. It's me, Paul."

Chapter 31

• • •

"I'd like you to meet Molly Powell. Molly, this is Tom and Becky Sawyer," Paul introduced.

"Glad to meet you, Molly. And you!" Becky grabbed Paul around the neck and squeezed as hard as she could. Then she hugged Molly. Tom shook hands with Molly. Then after taking Paul's hand, Tom pulled him close for a hug that rivaled Becky's.

"Molly!" Isabella ran up to them and hugged both her and Paul. "You both look so different." She stood back to admire Molly's curly dark hair and then Paul's shaggy hair and beard.

"We needed to look different," Molly explained. "Where's Fitzgerald?"

"He is sleeping."

But the commotion had woken Fitzgerald. He also came running around the cabin and greeted Paul and Molly with no less enthusiasm than Isabella.

"Come inside. I'll make you a hot supper," Becky told

Paul and Molly. She and Tom walked ahead of the others.

"And you are mated!" Isabella spoke in a girlish squeal.

"Not legally married, yet. But mated, yes." Molly held out her left hand for Isabella to admire her ring.

"What is that?"

"A woman wearing a ring signifies a couple making a commitment to each other. She wears it as long as they're married." Molly noticed Isabella glance down at her own empty hand.

"And the ring tells other men that the woman already has a man," Paul added. Then he asked, "Have you enjoyed being here with the Sawyers?"

"Oh yes! We hiked and tried to catch an elk. Then we worked on making the cabin larger. They have a dog and a cat. We cut firewood. And Fitzgerald had a gun battle."

"A gun battle?" Paul and Molly exclaimed together.

At the mention of the shooting, Fitzgerald had hung his head in humiliation. "Are you okay?" Paul asked him.

"Shooting at real people is different from a movie. I should have talked with them. We could have worked together. But when I thought of them coming to possibly hurt Isabella and her baby, I just fired."

"Her baby?" Paul and Molly exclaimed together again.

"Yes, I am pregnant," Isabella confirmed as they entered the cabin. "I'll tell you more later. Right now, I need to help Becky fix supper."

Tom picked up the rifle. "I'll go out and watch while you catch up."

While Isabella worked with Becky, Fitzgerald told their

friends about all that had occurred, finishing with the previous night's gunfire. "I violated my own ideals," he concluded.

"Sometimes ideals have a tough time competing with reality," said Molly. "You did what you had to do to protect your family. Do you remember the black bear with her cubs? She would have hurt you to protect them. Humans also fight to protect their children. This is life on Earth, Fitzgerald."

"I think the men who came in the night are like the grizzly bear, though. They would not have reasoned with you," Paul added.

Isabella rejoined them. "Becky doesn't need me for a while."

"Do you know that Fitzgerald did the right thing last night?" Paul asked her.

She didn't reflect any concern. "Fitzgerald always does the right thing. Even if he doesn't always know so."

"He's a good man."

"I know," Isabella answered seriously and put her hand on her mate's shoulder. Then she brightened. "What have you two done since we parted at the bus place?"

Becky had come up behind Isabella. "I'd like to hear too. Let's all go outside and keep Tom company. The stew is cooking in the crock pot."

On the cabin's porch, Paul and Molly told all they had done. Everybody laughed at their ruses and escapes. They appreciated the detour to take the mother and children to her parents. All of them wanted to know more about Paul and Molly's relationship. Molly read aloud the pledge she and Paul had made to each other. Paul told about traveling to Charleston and New Orleans on their "mated-moon." The couple then concluded with a somber description of the state of the country they had observed. Paul looked at Fitzgerald. "Molly and I think you and Isabella could make a difference. Your mission isn't over."

"How?"

"Let's have a serious planning session a little later."

• • •

"This is where Fitzgerald may have saved us all." Tom had insisted on showing Paul and Molly the scene where the confrontation had occurred. His voice reflected a little pride in his young friend. "They came armed. See the 9-mm bullet holes?"

Fitzgerald, for his part, seemed more reconciled with his actions. "I just did what Tom told me to do."

"Supper's ready!" Becky called.

Isabella served hot biscuits to go with the stew. "Did you make these?" Molly asked her.

"I did."

"Tom, will you say grace?" Becky asked when they were all seated at the table.

During supper, Paul and Molly asked more questions about Fitzgerald and Isabella's experiences. Despite the difficulties, the extraterrestrials had loved being with Tom and Becky in Oregon.

As they ate, Becky noticed Isabella's eyes frequently

drawn back to the ring on Molly's finger. Occasionally Isabella looked at Becky's ring as well. While Molly and Paul washed the dishes under Isabella's direction and Tom guarded the cabin, Becky pulled Fitzgerald aside. "I have something for you to give Isabella." She handed him a simple diamond ring.

"Why?" he wanted to know.

"Because she wants one. That's all you need to understand. Just go out there and put it on her finger." Becky showed him which finger.

Fitzgerald did as he was told. Isabella squealed with delight, "Where did you get it?"

"Becky gave it to me for you."

Isabella hugged Becky's neck. "This was Beth's ring," Becky told her. "Paul didn't want it after..." she could not finish the sentence. "You don't mind, do you, Paul?"

Paul shook his head. "Certainly not."

"Let me see!" Molly demanded.

Isabella proudly held her hand out. "Now I am a human wife."

"Now, about sleeping arrangements," Becky began speaking to Paul and Molly. "Are you two actually married?"

"I can sleep in the minivan," Paul volunteered.

"They are more than married," Isabella insisted. "They are mated for life."

Molly nodded affirmation and promised, "We're committed to each other for a lifetime. I guarantee that we'll add the legal status when we can. It's important to formalize our commitment."

Becky took a few seconds to decide. "Okay, I'll accept Isabella's judgment. You two can have the new bedroom. It's almost finished. We don't have a bed for you, though."

"That's fine. I'll bring in our sleeping bags and the air mattress from the minivan," said Paul.

That settled, Becky organized the evening. "I think you four need to have your 'serious planning session.' I'll join Tom on sentry duty outside. After you're done, the men can take turns watching through the night."

● ● ●

The foursome gathered in the cabin's living room. Paul queried the extraterrestrials about their twenty-fourth chromosome. "It's related to DNA repair, isn't it? That's why you needed it when you spent a long time in space."

"Yes, I think that's part of it," Isabella answered. "It also helps us to adjust to new conditions such as Earth diseases." Molly and Fitzgerald listened intently without anything to contribute.

"Can you tell me how it works?" Paul asked.

"A little, maybe. What the Benevolents call an 'amul' is a living cell that rides in our blood. Like your white corpuscle, only different. When it senses a cell with slightly different DNA than those around it, the amul repairs it. If the amul can't repair the DNA, it cuts up the cell's DNA like the bacteria your geneticists use to alter chromosomes. Then the damaged cell can't multiply. Any invading viruses are perceived as different DNA and are destroyed even before they force the human cells to reproduce them."

"That's why you don't get colds."

"Yes, or other viruses. We won't get cancer from chemicals or cosmic radiation either because cells with damaged DNA are repaired or destroyed."

"What about the healthy bacteria humans need to survive?"

"The amul recognizes them just like your infection-fighting white corpuscles do."

Paul rubbed his face. "This is all beyond me. We need to get some expert help."

"Who would we get?" Isabella asked.

"Laura Holdridge would be the best on Earth. And we'll need to ask the Benevolents for help."

"The partnership species' policy is to not share new technology until a species can work together toward long-term goals. Otherwise some groups may use the technology against each other," Fitzgerald explained.

"You'll need to appeal to them," Paul urged. "Or humans won't have a long term."

"Or," Molly injected, "mankind could show some progress working together. We certainly have an immediate incentive right now."

"What do you have in mind?" Fitzgerald asked.

"We need to get a message out," Molly suggested. They all averted their eyes from her. "What?" she said. No one spoke. "You're thinking about the last interview I screwed up! I thought we put that behind us."

303

"Molly's right," Paul conceded. "What happened before doesn't matter."

"And you're also justified in being cautious. I can get out of control. So this time no questions from me. Only Fitzgerald talking to the people."

"How would we do it?" Fitzgerald asked.

"Isn't your blog site, the one we created in the quarantine quarters, still operable? We could post a video. We could put one on YouTube as well."

"What would I say?"

Molly was rolling then. "People need hope. The CDC reporting that North Korea created an unstoppable cancer virus has taken away everybody's hope. You'll need to tell people that the cavalry is coming. You'll need to say that the Benevolents will help us. Otherwise society will fall apart and not be able to use the cure, even if there is a cure."

Fitzgerald looked as if he could cry. "I don't actually know if the Benevolents *will* help. Their policy —"

Isabella interrupted by turning her mate's chin to make him look into her eyes. "Tomorrow, you will need to lie in order to give the humans hope."

Chapter 32

• • •

"Don't look at me. Look at the camera," Molly coached Fitzgerald as he rehearsed his short speech. "And shave that stubble off. We want you to look like the sophisticated ambassador that people remember, not some backwoods hermit. You'll need a haircut too."

Paul and Isabella conferred at the cabin's kitchen table. She told him, "I'll need to get to our spacecraft to transmit and receive most effectively. Have Laura bring all of her data in their binary computer language."

"How will you convert the data into a format your computer can read?"

Isabella held up the device from which they had taken the photos of the snark and Benevolents. "But I'll need Laura there too. She can communicate directly with our genetics experts."

"I'll call her with the disposable cell phone." Getting through to Laura turned out to be more difficult than Paul anticipated. She, expecting imminent cancer, had taken leave from Future Tech to spend time with Jeff. Only after finally connecting with Dr. Finkle did he get Laura's private phone number.

"Laura, this is Paul Sanders. Please hear me out for a few minutes." Paul first repeated what he had gleaned from Isabella. "I think this is worth investigating."

Laura's professional side was intrigued. "And this amul is created by the twenty-fourth chromosome pair?"

"Right. I think it can act like a retrovirus except that it repairs defective DNA. We want you to come to Kennedy Space Center to communicate directly with the Benevolent scientists."

"You want me to dialogue with the alien geneticists clever enough to create Fitzgerald and Isabella from the human genome, which they hacked from our computers?"

"Right. Will you come?"

"Hell, yes. I'd come if I had one hour remaining to live. What scientist wouldn't?"

"Then you'll need to bring all of the latest data from Future Tech with you."

"No need for that." Laura gave Paul the website, her user name, and password. "And my mother's maiden name is Rice."

"Okay, noted. Why don't you download the data into a laptop just to be certain? We'll especially need all you have on the cancer virus. Isabella can access your data from the laptop."

"I'll explain the situation to Future Tech's jet pilots. They've seen the news and will do whatever I ask. Is there anything else you'll need?" Laura asked.

"Could you give us a ride to Florida?"

"Where will you be?"

"Eugene, Oregon."

• • •

"Dear Friends of Earth: you have not heard from Isabella and me for a while. Circumstances have prevented our communication. Nevertheless, all of us now face a dire threat from the cancer virus already afflicting so many. Let me assure you that help is coming. The species that sent us from Benevolent to your planet *will* help us with a cure," Fitzgerald recorded with apparent confidence into Molly's laptop.

"But the cure cannot be administered if society falls apart. In a situation like this, the ordinary human response is to take care of yourselves and your families first. Therefore, we are asking each person to act more than ordinary for the common good by going back to your home, your job, and the things you did before the crisis. Every person should cooperate with authorities to make our infrastructure and support functions work again. The medical community will slow down the cancer's spread by isolating any with the virus. They will assist the cancer victims with the existing treatments until the new treatment is ready. Each one of us is fighting for humankind's survival. You fight by cooperating with authorities and by doing your job well."

"That's perfect!" Molly said. "I'll start getting this posted on social media. I'm sure the networks will rebroadcast your message. That's why it was important to make it short. Now you need to work on your message appealing to Benevolent."

• • •

"We'll need landing approval at Kennedy Space Center and access to Fitzgerald and Isabella's spaceship," Paul requested over the phone after explaining the situation to Harry Thompkins.

"What will be landing?" asked the director.

"Future Tech's Learjet bringing Dr. Laura Holdridge, Isabella, and me," Paul answered. "And we could really use Ginger Peters, if she's available to take samples and maybe do some lab work."

Ginger broke in, "I'm here on the conference call with Harry, Paul. I'll be ready. Do you really think this could give us a cure?"

"I think this is our best shot."

Harry spoke again, "Paul, I wouldn't publicize your trip here or let the government know your plans. There are still a lot of folks who want to blame Fitzgerald and Isabella for everything, including the hot summer we had this year."

"Understood. Thanks, Harry."

• • •

"Who do these people think they are?" Bill Samuel began his regular rant. "Do I need to remind you that the so-called 'Fitzgerald and Isabella' caused the New York massacre? No less than four wars started because of them. Now they're asking an alien power for help. The only help we're likely to receive is an invasion. Remember my words when your children are slaves."

With his innate sense of theatrics, Bill paused to let his viewers ponder those ideas. He then changed his demeanor by smiling at the camera. "But don't just believe it from me. My guest today is President Truman Johnson." The president entered wearing a dark blue suit and a determined expression.

"Welcome to the show, Mr. President. You haven't been my guest since just before the election. Let me say, congratulations. The country made the best choice."

"Thank you, Bill. Our goal is to fight for the principles we believe in."

"Mr. President, I'm going to ask if you think Fitzgerald and Isabella represent a threat to our principles. But first let me play a clip from their address to the US Congress."

"...the representative democracy of your system is not the best choice of government." Fitzgerald's prior words and the outrageous statements to which he had responded had been edited out.

"What do you think of this, Mr. President?"

"Clearly, Bill, this represents an attitude that could undermine our most cherished ideals. Democracy as an institution ordained by God is the most fundamental of our principles."

"And does it trouble you, Mr. President, that they are calling for assistance from an outside source while circumventing the democratically elected government of these United States?"

"I find this deeply disturbing, Bill. Any aid requested for the United States should come from duly elected officials. They should also work through the CDC. We have a responsibility to negotiate carefully for the people and to ensure public safety."

"Could this open America to terrorist attack or worst?"

"I'm afraid so, Bill. Therefore, I've directed the Department of Homeland Security to apprehend the ones called Fitzgerald and Isabella and any who may have helped them. I'm asking every American to aid in protecting our security by reporting any sightings or contact with those threatening us."

"You believe in enhanced interrogation, don't you Mr. President?"

"We'll do whatever is necessary to protect the American people."

• • •

Fitzgerald watched the *Bill Samuel Report* that night with Molly. "What is enhanced interrogation?"

"That means torture, Fitzgerald," said Molly. "They deliberately cause people pain to make them do what they want."

"Does the president mean to cause my Isabella pain?"

"Yes, he does. And me. And Paul, and you."

Fitzgerald stood in horror. "He is like a grizzly bear, right?"

"Worse. And we have nothing like a pepper spray."

• • •

The following morning, noticeably more employees showed up for work nearly everywhere. Additional workers drifted in during the day as more people saw Fitzgerald's video appeal and responded. Somebody coined the catchphrase, "Don't let the ship sink. Everybody to the buckets. Help is on the way."

Molly videoed and posted another encouraging message by Fitzgerald. This time Isabella joined him. She ended their short broadcast with the new catchphrase. By the end of the day, a bouncy tune using those lyrics had surfaced on YouTube. Mankind had started to fight back.

• • •

Molly drove herself and Paul along with Fitzgerald and Isabella in their disguises to the Eugene airport. They had agreed that Paul and Isabella would accompany Laura to Kennedy Space Center. Molly and Fitzgerald would remain in Oregon to help rally people through the internet.

Future Tech's Learjet landed at the Eugene airport about noon. To everybody's surprise, Laura had brought Jeff with her. "I couldn't leave him alone," she explained.

"I'll take care of him for you," Molly promised. To Jeff she said, "Do you like dogs? We're going to see a nice dog."

Jeff looked at his mother for approval. Laura hugged him and pushed him to Molly. She and Fitzgerald each took one of Jeff's hands as his mother and their mates climbed the ladder to board. At the top, all of them turned to wave goodbye.

Molly restrained her tears on the drive back to the cabin but didn't trust herself to converse. Fitzgerald took up the slack by bantering with Jeff and playing little hand games. Tom and Becky warmly welcomed Jeff. Jeff's reaction to the dog, Emma, provided the only bright spot in the midst of dismal circumstances. The boy and dog experienced love at first sight. No less touching, but more surprising, the cat, Jack, approached Jeff immediately. The boy happily fell asleep between Emma and Jack in front of the fire until Tom gently moved him to Fitzgerald's room to sleep.

● ● ●

Fitzgerald came to Molly later that evening, wanting to show her an unusual response they had received on the blog. At first, she was so intent posting exhortations online, she waved him off. "I think this one is maybe important," he persisted.

The message from Ottawa began with, "We don't know where you are right now, but if you can get to Canada..."

Chapter 33

• • •

"Turn on the runway lights and give them landing instructions. Then request refueling for them," Harry ordered.

"This is a highly irregular flight," the space center's Landing and Recovery director argued. "Who are they?"

"Trust me on this one, Walter. And to cover your butt, here." Harry scribbled his order on a scrap of paper, signed, and dated it.

"I do trust you, Harry." The controller began to give instructions and authorization to a private flight headed into Kennedy Space Center. When Harry looked away, Walter stuffed the scrap of paper into his pocket, just to be safe.

The Learjet touched down using the lights after dark. "Direct them to hangar four," Harry instructed him.

"But isn't that where..."

"That's all we'll need from you tonight. Thanks for staying late. I'll turn out the lights. You can go home now. Say 'Hi' to Aileen for me. And Walter, you didn't see anything tonight."

"You're right about that."

The jet taxied to hangar four. The copilot opened the door and deployed the stairs. Three people descended and approached a side door of the hangar where NASA had stored the spacecraft.

Dr. Ginger Peters opened the hangar door to admit them. "Welcome back, Isabella. And you...look different Paul. I wouldn't have recognized you."

Isabella had become all business. She acknowledged Ginger and hurried to her spacecraft. There she started entering instructions in the device she carried.

"Thanks for meeting us, Ginger. Where's Harry?" asked Paul.

"He'll be here in a few minutes. He's giving up his career tonight, you know. Maybe me too."

"Nobody will have a career if we aren't successful." Paul indicated Laura and said, "Dr. Peters, I'd like to introduce you to Dr. Laura Holdridge."

Ginger extended her hand. "Dr. Holdridge, we met at a conference maybe ten years ago. I've followed your work since. Brilliant! Please call me Ginger."

"And I'm Laura. Thank you for helping us."

"I'll need a stairs," Isabella called.

Paul quickly located the mobile steps in hangar four. He had difficulty moving them. "Ladies, if you could help

314

me, please." Drs. Ginger and Laura helped Paul push the stairs into place where the door on the spacecraft had opened when Fitzgerald and Isabella arrived.

They laughed when he teased, "I'll bet that neither of you have served on a ground crew before."

Isabella, intent with purpose, noticed none of this. She ascended the steps and punched in one last code. The craft door cracked open. Isabella pulled open the door, crawled inside, and started activating the systems. A dim light came through the door. "Laura," she called. "Would you please join me?"

With some trepidation, Laura ascended the steps and crawled inside, dragging her laptop with her. The interior looked not unlike photos she had seen of early Gemini capsules. Except that rather than manual switches and gauges, dozens of computerized displays filled nearly every space. Two seats faced a tiny window. Isabella already sat in one seat. A mechanical joystick protruded between her legs. "This is Fitzgerald's seat," she told Laura and indicated the empty place. "You can sit here."

Waiting on the ground, Ginger whispered to Paul. "Do you think I could go up and look inside?"

"Why not?"

Ginger ascended the steps, followed by Paul. She looked inside the spacecraft to see Isabella start speaking into an unseen microphone. "Sneznar 7621. Sneznar 7621. This is Sneznar with an urgent message for the Earth program manager. Taped message now broadcasting." She punched an instruction into her device.

Laura and Ginger heard Fitzgerald's recorded voice. "This is Belpa on planet Earth. We arrived on Earth too late. A human-created pathogen is already killing mankind. We need your help; otherwise, nearly all the humans will die. Their civilization will be lost."

Fitzgerald's voice paused. "We know that you are monitoring our progress. We have not met the projected success. We started with some faulty assumptions including the predicted response of the humans. They have great difficulty developing a corporate mindset to make long-range decisions. One reason is that a few among the humans who act only in self-interest make all respond defensively to protect themselves. And the human reproductive process is so short term and individualized that their immediate needs and those of their young always outweigh the long-term consequences."

Fitzgerald's voice paused again. "You made us so human that Isabella and I are expecting an offspring created in a biological manner. The overwhelming human feeling of parenthood made me deliberately injure another sentient being when I felt Isabella and our child to be threatened. I understand these humans better now. They will need a long process to reform their society. I appeal to you to relax the policy that prohibits technological help until the subject species has reached certain markers. The humans need help with a treatment right now or they will perish. Thank you."

Outside the craft, Ginger whispered again to Paul, "Isabella is pregnant?" He nodded and held a finger to his lips.

After the tape of Fitzgerald finished, Isabella spoke again, "With me now is geneticist Dr. Laura Holdridge. She is one of those we had been instructed to contact. All of her work is available at the following." Isabella gave the web address and Laura's passwords. "Because internet availability could be uncertain, I'm uploading her data on the cancer-causing virus now."

She entered another instruction. "This should take a minute," Isabella told Laura. "Based on the current position of the probe relative to Earth, they could respond starting in twelve to thirteen minutes."

A minute to upload a terabyte of data? Laura thought.

After the data transmitted, Isabella relaxed her professionalism. "We have at least ten minutes before they can possibly respond. Would you like to say something to them while we wait? The computers will translate your English into their language."

Laura looked nervously at the microphone. "Hello, this is Laura Holdridge. We really do need your help. Please tell us what to do." She choked up and could not continue. When she saw that's all Laura could or would say, Isabella explained Fitzgerald's absence and told about the cancer virus. She explained some challenges she and Fitzgerald faced on Earth. Finally, Isabella filled time greeting and sending personal messages to individuals on Benevolent.

Suddenly a computer-generated voice interrupted her. A projection of a bumblebee-like creature appeared on the monitor. "Sneznar! We are happy to hear from

317

you. Please make more travel documentaries about Earth. Everybody on our planet looks forward to them. And hello, Dr. Holdridge. We follow your work closely.

"Sneznar, tell Belpa not to worry about the success projections. As our ambassador, he is doing as well as possible in a difficult situation. His current strategy to stabilize the society in crisis with hope is brilliant. And their response has demonstrated that humans can work together, at least in the short term. And congratulations to you, Sneznar, for successful navigation to and landing on Earth. We are proud of both of you.

"We have anticipated Belpa's request to relax our policy by monitoring Earth's broadcasts. Humans are saying, 'Don't let the ship sink. Everybody to the buckets. Help is on the way.' We interpret the 'help' in that saying as meaning directions from us. The decision has been already made. The policy is relaxed. Our genetic scientists have already been working on a cure for the cancer virus. But warn the humans that this is an exception due to the terrible circumstances. They still need to solve problems themselves by cooperating. Two or three hours of your time will elapse as our computers and experts analyze Dr. Holdridge's latest data.

"In the meantime, let us converse. Congratulations to you and Belpa on the pending creation of a new being. We hoped that you would be able to do so. We knew that would help you to feel most human. Now while we are waiting, Dr. Holdridge, we saw on a television broadcast where you have been personally exposed to the cancer virus. We cannot let anything happen to you. An immediate blood transfusion between you and Isabella will cure you. We recommend two subsequent transfusions a month apart to make certain. Please find a human medical person who can assist right now."

"I'm a physician," Ginger spoke up.

"They can't hear you for about six minutes. Any response will take six more minutes. That's why we send speeches back and forth rather than converse," Isabella explained.

Confirming Isabella's explanation, the voice went on without acknowledging Ginger. "When you find the doctor, arrange an immediate blood transfusion. It will be safe. Isabella is what humans call a 'universal donor.' We'll explain why the transfusion works later. Basically, the amul in Isabella's blood is the guardian of DNA integrity. Meanwhile would Dr. Holdridge be willing to tell us about her life?" The voice stopped.

"They are very curious about humans. They want you to make a speech. Tell them everything about your life. Talk about Jeff," Isabella whispered to Laura.

Ginger spoke to Isabella, "Can you come to the lab for me to take your blood donation?"

"Don't touch anything," Isabella said to Laura. "Just talk to them in little speeches. They want to know you personally." Laura started to tell her life story.

At the foot of the ladder, Isabella found that Harry had arrived. After a brief greeting, Isabella asked, "Can Paul use your car to take me to Dr. Peters' lab?" After Harry silently handed over the keys, Isabella added, "There's an empty seat up there, Mr. Thompkins. You can go inside the spacecraft and talk to the Benevolents along with Laura. They know you are the director in NASA who helped us. They would love to meet you." She repeated the instructions she had given to Laura and reminded, "Because of the transmission delay, talk to them in little speeches."

In her medical area, Ginger took a pint of Isabella's blood. "Bring me Laura," Ginger instructed Paul. Then she spoke to Isabella, "Young lady, did I hear that you are expecting a baby? Have you been to an obstetrician?" When Isabella indicated she hadn't, Ginger started to examine her. Finally, she pulled out an ultrasound wand. In a couple of minutes, the screen showed Isabella's fetus. "Looks normal," Ginger concluded.

"Does it have a tail or wings?"

"No tail or wings. But it is a boy human."

"How can you tell it's a male?"

Ginger printed a sonographic image for Isabella and pointed to a spot. Isabella's eyes widened.

Paul had returned to the spacecraft to collect Laura. Only her life being at stake forced her to leave the cockpit. At her lab, Ginger started preparing for the blood transfusion to Laura.

Inside the spacecraft, Harry experienced an amazing hour asking questions of another civilization. Harry's six-foot-two and 220-pound body didn't fit well into the seat designed for Isabella. Harry hardly noticed. The two

Learjet pilots took turns listening at the open door.

Isabella, having been returned by Paul's shuttle service, took Fitzgerald's seat alongside Harry. She found Harry listening to the Benevolents describe the challenges of exploring the universe and discovering new civilizations by transporting probes through dimensions. Intercepted radio signals could be tens of thousands of years old. Usually the civilizations had vanished by the time the signal could be traced. The Benevolents had been discovered and saved by an even older civilization. Benevolent's first inter-civilization project would be serving as mentors to Earth.

Suddenly the friendly voice became more professional. "Transmitting the following files: Number one, preparation of cancer virus preventative. Number two, fabrication of treatment genetic repair biotic. Number three, personal letters to Sneznar and Belpa." A minute later, the professional voice announced, "Transmission complete."

Then the friendly voice came back speaking to Laura without realizing she had been pulled away. "Dr. Holdridge, there will be side effects from your blood transfusion. You are likely to tire easily for a couple of your days, after which you'll feel younger. As you implement these procedures you may have questions. You can communicate privately with us through your personal computer by putting text messages into a folder we created on your cloud storage called 'Sneznar.'"

Harry's cell phone rang. The front gate guard reported, "Mr. Thompkins, some federal agents are here. They want to come inside."

"Do they have a search warrant?"

"I'll ask." The guard stepped away then came back. "They say they don't need a warrant because this is a federal facility and they are federal agents."

"Stall them any way you can. Tell them I'm coming. Say they need to be issued passes before entering. Just anything to delay them."

"We have to go. Belpa and I love you," said Isabella to the microphone. Then she transferred the files and a recording of the conversations from the spacecraft to her device and onto Laura's computer.

Harry left the spacecraft and called Ginger. "Send Paul and Dr. Holdridge back. The Feds are here looking for our friends."

"Laura is lucky her veins are big. The transfusion has just finished."

Paul raced back to hangar four in Harry's car. In transit, Laura phoned the jet with instructions to get ready for takeoff.

Isabella re-locked the spacecraft and descended the steps. Along with Paul and Laura she ran to the Learjet. Harry yelled after her, "Thanks for the most wonderful experience of my life!"

"Take off! Take off!" Laura shouted as soon as they were inside.

Through a window, Paul could see headlights converging on hangar four. He realized, *If they found us here, they won't take long finding the cabin in Oregon.*

Chapter 34

• • •

The ringing phone woke Molly at 2:00 a.m. "Hello."

"Molly, you need to get out. The Feds figured out that we landed at Kennedy Space Center and came to get us. They'll trace our calls to the cabin." Paul's voice could not have been more urgent.

Still only partly awake, her reporter's instinct asked, "How did they find you?"

"I don't know. Maybe a voice recognition program when I called Harry. Now just go!"

"Where are you, Paul?"

"We're in the Learjet headed toward Future Tech in North Carolina. Laura has work to do. The Benevolents granted Fitzgerald's request. She's studying the cancer virus treatment instructions from them now."

"See if the pilots will take you to Canada after dropping Laura off."

"Canada?" Paul wondered.

"They've offered to give us asylum."

"Can you get there with Fitzgerald?"

"I don't know."

"Molly, get moving."

• • •

Moving took longer than a few minutes. Molly woke up Becky and Jeff then brought in Tom and Fitzgerald, who stood sentry duty. Her words to them were direct and simple. "Paul called. The Feds are onto us. We all have to leave."

"Where can we go?" Becky asked.

"We'll try for Canada."

"We won't make it," Tom predicted. "They'll guess where we're headed and order the border sealed. That's standard procedure."

"We have to try."

"They'll seal the border..." Tom repeated, "...unless they think they have you cornered here."

"How would we do that?"

"Becky and I will stay here and make them think you're here too."

"I won't let you do that."

"Honey, who put you in charge?" Becky interceded and then smiled at Molly. "Canada's too cold for me anyway."

Tom got practical. "How are you on gas?"

Molly hadn't thought of that. "The minivan is near empty. I've got some gas still in containers."

"You'll take the SUV then. I'm near full. And a local license tag will be less conspicuous."

Quickly they loaded the Sawyers' SUV with the remaining containers of gas, their backpacks, laptops, plus food and water left over from Paul and Molly's trip across the country. Becky added a gallon of milk from her refrigerator for Jeff. "What's in these suitcases?" Tom asked as he transferred them from the minivan. Molly unzipped one to reveal a large portion of the million dollars in one hundred-dollar bills. "Whoa! Did you rob a bank?"

"Sort of." At Tom's worried look she reassured him, "It's all legal money. But I will need a tax accountant when all of this is over."

"I'll be ready."

With the SUV loaded, Molly ordered, "Everybody in."

An unexpected delay came when Jeff refused to leave Emma. "Take her along," Becky insisted. "They're happy together. We'll pick her up later." Together Jeff and Emma got into the back seat.

"Thanks, Tom," Fitzgerald said as they shook hands.

Tom pulled the younger man to him for a bear hug. "I'm proud of you, son," he said.

Tears streamed down Tom's and Becky's cheeks as Molly guided the SUV down the driveway. When he noticed Becky looking at him, Tom commented, "I'll miss that dog." But he knew that he wasn't fooling her. "Let's get ready for a siege, Becky."

• • •

Molly turned away from Eugene. *The federal agents would come from that direction*, she thought. She planned to loop around and connect to the I-5 interstate. *We need to get to the border fast.* But the twisting, turning back roads made covering miles quickly difficult. Fortunately, Jeff and Emma fell asleep together on the back seat. Fitzgerald, exhausted by days of work followed by sleepless nights on sentry duty, soon nodded off also despite the situation. *He's gotten used to crises*, Molly realized.

As she drove, she reflected on her life. Less than a year ago she had been a single, independent, professional woman with a promising career ahead. *Now I'm jobless, unofficially married, a media pariah, and on the run in a strange vehicle with an old dog, a Down Syndrome boy, and an alien.* She laughed softly rather than wake the others up.

Next Molly thought about Paul—his handsome looks, his values of loyalty and self-sacrifice, and most important, his love for her. *I wonder where he is now.*

• • •

Paul and Isabella waited in North Carolina for the Learjet to be refueled. Asked by Laura if they would convey Paul and Isabella to Canada, one of the pilots had replied, "Hell, yes."

The other pilot, more circumspect, had simply asked, "Where in Canada would they like to go?"

The early morning news shows gushed over the national spirit that had followed Fitzgerald's promise of help. The three hosts sported three T-shirts, each with one part of the rallying cry: *Don't let the ship sink. Everybody to the buckets. Help is on the way.*

"Work attendance is expected to reach 95% today following yesterday's rally of human spirit. Normal work attendance is about 92%, but those numbers dipped below 20% in the last couple of weeks. People everywhere are now pitching in to restore the prosperity that collapsed last week after the reports on the cancer virus pandemic," the lead anchor reported.

"In other news, Homeland Security officers are in a standoff with reputed terrorists holed up in a mountain cabin near Eugene, Oregon. Officers backed off to wait for reinforcements when faced with gunfire as they approached the cabin at about 4:00 a.m."

"Is that where Fitzgerald is?" asked Isabella.

"I think that's where Fitzgerald used to be."

"Sir and ma'am, we're ready for takeoff," one of the pilots said and asked again, "Where shall we take you?"

"Ottawa, please."

• • •

"Can I fire the next shot?" Becky asked.

"Just make sure you don't hit any of 'em," Tom told Becky. "Aim high so that they'll duck. Don't let a ground ricochet kill someone by accident." Becky squeezed off another rifle shot. "Good girl."

"They sure ran when you emptied that machine pistol over their heads last night," said Becky.

"Too bad we don't have any more 9-mm ammo."

"Tom, that was smart of you to cut down a couple of trees to block the driveway."

"Yeah, they'll be certain they've got us cornered and will take their time." Tom chewed another cookie. "Have you seen Jack?"

"He's hiding in the basement. I'm glad Emma isn't here. You know how scared she gets around fireworks."

The phone rang. Becky answered. "Tom, it's that hostage negotiator again. He wants you to release one of the women."

"I'll talk with him." Tom took the phone and mimicked an agitated man. "I told you before that no one up here wants release. And you've got no business trying to arrest Fitzgerald and Isabella anyway. They haven't done anything wrong." Tom listened a minute, then said, "Okay, I'll ask." Tom yelled without covering up the phone, "Fitzgerald, Isabella, do you want to surrender?"

Becky feigned a high voice to yell back, "No!"

"Did you hear that? We'll stay here until the snow freezes your butts."

• • •

Morning rush-hour traffic slowed Molly in Portland. The radio traffic report sounded almost normal. "I-5 into the city is slow to Central Avenue. After that, expect a speed limit drive north. It looks like everybody is showing up early for work today. I'll bet there will be some dramatic stories around the water cooler."

Molly looked through the rearview mirror into the back seat. Jeff had woken and was happily sharing cookies and milk with Emma for breakfast. Beside Molly, Fitzgerald remained asleep slumped against the door. *It must be tiring to carry the fate of an entire world on you,* she thought. *Only about five more hours to Canada.*

● ● ●

Dr. Ben Finkle stepped in front of a battery of microphones set up in the lobby of Future Tech. "Thank you for coming," he said to the gathered reporters. "We promised to make an important announcement regarding our research into the cancer virus. Dr. Laura Holdridge is here to make that announcement."

Laura stepped in front of the microphones. Some of the reporters thought she looked disheveled, and yet somehow, young and fresh. With a sense of theatrics previously foreign to her, she started with the universal rallying phrase: "Don't let the ship sink. Everybody to the buckets..." she paused to let her listeners imagine the third phrase. Rather she completed, "Today, help has arrived."

The reporters stood perplexed. Was this a joke? One shouted out, "Are you saying that we have a treatment?"

"Affirmative. We have the formula for a treatment which can also serve as an immunization. It is an advanced form of immunotherapy that targets genetic deformities.

But the treatment will take everybody's cooperation and effort to scale up production. We are fortunate that the North Koreans modified a cold virus with symptoms rather than a symptom-less virus. That will make tracking and applying immediate treatments easier."

Everybody shouted questions at once. Rather than field any specific question, Laura motioned for silence and said, "The treatment will be in the form of an injectable biotic provided by the planet Benevolent as promised by their ambassador, Fitzgerald. Our lab is already working to combine a component from Isabella's blood with a harmless bacterium from Earth. This will allow us to multiply the treatment using cultures. Future Tech will make the prototype available to the CDC without charge. They will cooperate with the World Health Organization to manage production around the world. Producing doses as quickly as possible is necessary to save hundreds of millions of lives."

"Is it safe?" a shouted question interrupted Laura.

"I've applied a precursor of the biotic to myself. It works somewhat like the naturally occurring types of bacteria we use to cut up DNA. We believe the treatment will be safe beyond any reasonable doubt."

"How do you know that the treatment comes from Benevolent?"

"I personally talked to them..." This quieted the listeners "...along with Director Harry Thompkins of NASA, from inside the alien spacecraft at Kennedy Space Center."

Silence dominated as the reporters tried to imagine her statement. Only one voice hesitantly asked Laura, "What are they like?"

"The Benevolents are very friendly, a species of sanguine personality types. They care about us."

Another voice spoke up, "Where are Fitzgerald and Isabella now?"

"None of your damn business."

• • •

"Time we took a walk, Becky. They've got reinforcements. They'll be surrounding the cabin and trapping us soon. Bring your winter wear. We'll probably be out overnight."

"You know my knees aren't good," Becky reminded her husband.

"Good enough for us to hide in the national forest. They won't find us without dogs. Just bringing in the dogs to start looking for us will take hours. Our friends should be in Canada by then."

"You're a good man, Tom."

• • •

Molly approached the US Border Control checkpoint with trepidation. Although Border Control's top priority remained to guard entry to the United States, they still screened those passing out.

The federal agent seemed suspicious. "I'm taking my son and his friend to Whistler to see snow," Molly explained. *That was the lamest story ever told*, she realized. *If he wasn't suspicious before, he will be now.*

"Would you please pull to the side and all get out of the car, ma'am?"

A tall young woman, a short light-skinned African-American male, a Down Syndrome teenager, and an old dog stood before the border control agent. The male seemed the most suspect. The agent looked closely at his hair then reached out and gently lifted the wig. "I know who you are," the agent said aloud to himself.

Chapter 35

● ● ●

"That's not who you think…"

The Border Control agent held up a palm to interrupt Molly. "Lying to any federal agent is a crime. Don't say anything you might regret later."

The agent took a closer look at her too. Molly could see him making a mental association between her and Fitzgerald. "Kathleen, come and look at this," he shouted to his supervisor.

A gum-chewing uniformed woman about forty years old sauntered over. "Whattaya got, Randy?"

"Take a close look at him and then her." Randy pointed at Fitzgerald and then Molly.

"Oh my God!" Kathleen stood gaping at Molly. Then she slowly extended her right hand. "Could I shake your hand, please? The hand that slapped that idiot Bill Samuel?"

Molly managed to take her hand. "We just got the news," Randy babbled. "Help has arrived."

"Hey, everybody! Come on over here. You'll want to see this!" Kathleen shouted. Quickly Border Control agents surrounded Molly and Fitzgerald along with Jeff and Emma.

One of the agents brought out a cell phone. "My kids won't believe me without some proof. Would you?" Somewhat in shock, Molly posed alongside the agent and Fitzgerald. Other agents pressed in for selfies or handshakes.

"That's enough," Kathleen told them all. To Molly she said, "You need to get across the border. The president has got plenty of his henchmen looking for you."

"Don't you work for the president?" Molly choked out.

"Anybody here vote for that moron?" Kathleen rhetorically asked the group. To Molly she said, "You best be going now," and pointed north.

In a couple of minutes, they were at the Canadian border crossing station. "Kathleen just called, Ms. Powell," said the border agent. "But Ottawa had already told us to be ready. Dr. Paul Sanders secured asylum for you. Welcome to Canada." To Fitzgerald he quoted, "Help has arrived," and added, "Thank you."

• • •

Boom, boom, boom. Tom and Becky heard explosions in the direction of their cabin from a couple of miles away. "That's probably flash grenades," Tom told his wife. "They'll be inside the cabin now. We'd better keep going." He noticed a couple of tears on her cheeks. "Your knees okay?"

334

"I'm doing fine. I was just thinking about how scared Jack must be."

• • •

Paul and Isabella along with the Learjet pilots watched TV at the Ottawa airport. Canadian news rebroadcast the press conference Laura had given. The bottom of the picture displayed a bold graphic: "Help has arrived!"

A Canadian immigration official watched with them. "Dr. Sanders, we've just received word that Ms. Powell and Mr. Benevolent have been admitted to Canada at our Vancouver checkpoint along with a teenager and a dog. Fitzgerald and Isabella have diplomatic status in Canada. You and Ms. Powell have asylum. Along with the diplomat," the official indicated Isabella, "you can go anywhere in Canada you choose."

"Where would you like to go?" one of the Future Tech pilots asked Paul.

"Could you take us to Vancouver, please? And would you also radio and tell Laura where her son is."

"You've just saved the lives of...well, everyone, including our wives and kids," said the other pilot. "We'll take you absolutely anywhere you want."

• • •

Tom spread the sleeping bags left by Paul and Molly on soft needles under a grouping of Douglas fir trees. "These trees will keep the frost off us."

Becky held a tiny radio to her ear. "Tom, they made

it. The Canadians have reported that all of them are in Canada, even Paul and Isabella. And they're announcing that 'Help has arrived.' What does that mean?"

"I think that means that we can turn ourselves in now. Not until morning, though. Walking at night in these mountains is dangerous."

"Well, if we're not hiding anymore, make me a campfire. I'm cold."

● ● ●

Molly and Fitzgerald watched the "Help has arrived" news on a Canadian network in the hotel room where Royal Mountie representatives had taken them. Nearby, Jeff and Emma slept on one of the beds. The hotel phone rang. Surprisingly the caller asked for Jeff. Molly woke Jeff gently and handed him the phone.

"How are you, sweetie?" Laura asked. "Are they taking good care of you?"

"I'm okay. We took a long ride in the car. Emma came along."

"Who is Emma?"

"A really nice dog."

"That's good. I heard you are in Canada. Are you ready to come home?"

"Yes."

"I'd come to get you, but I can't right now. Do you remember the men who flew the airplane and let you sit in the cockpit on the way to Alaska?"

"Yes."

"The same men are coming to Canada to bring you home. I want you to go with them on the airplane, okay?"

"Can Emma come with me?"

"I don't know, sweetie. Can I speak to Molly?"

Jeff handed the phone to Molly. "This is Laura, Molly. Thanks for taking care of Jeff for me."

"No problem. It was mostly Fitzgerald and Emma. I just drove," Molly answered.

"The Future Tech jet is bringing Paul and Isabella to Vancouver. They can bring Jeff back to North Carolina. Do you think Emma could come with him?"

"I wouldn't want to try getting Jeff on the jet without her. She loves him too. And she's a golden retriever, very clean and gentle."

"What about the dog's owners?" Laura wanted to know.

"I don't know where they are right now. But I'm sure they won't mind. They sent Emma to keep Jeff company."

"Thanks! The jet should be in Vancouver in about three hours. Can you take Jeff and Emma to the airport?"

"Of course!"

The Royal Mounties insisted on giving their guests a lights-flashing escort to the airport. Molly felt embarrassed when she had to stop the motorcade to get gas for the SUV. A Mountie pumped the gas for her and paid the station. Then Canadian Customs and Security waived all the procedures to allow Molly to follow the official vehicle onto the tarmac to meet the Future Tech jet. There she and Fitzgerald welcomed their mates.

● ● ●

Tom and Becky sat next to an attorney in a federal courtroom. The judge listened carefully to the US attorney general's representative. "The government requests the Sawyers be transferred to a federal facility to be interrogated."

"This is an arraignment hearing," the judge responded. "With what are they being charged?"

"Oh, yes. The Sawyers concealed fugitives, resisted arrest themselves, and fired on federal agents. We ask they be held without bond until—"

The judge interrupted, "The incident report filed by the lead Homeland Security agent suggests that the Sawyers deliberately fired above the agents' heads. And that they turned themselves in the next morning."

"Your Honor, that situation is subject to interpretation."

"Did you have a warrant or any credible probable cause for attempting to arrest the individuals known as Fitzgerald and Isabella?"

The representative stood silent. The judge continued, "No? Then no crime would have been committed without government overreach. Furthermore," the judge glared at the prosecuting attorney, "do you think you can find even one potential juror who would convict this couple? Let alone twelve on the same jury. If I were a juror myself, I'd vote not guilty. Counsel for defense, do you have anything to say?"

Tom and Becky's lawyer knew when to remain silent. "No, Your Honor."

"Then case dismissed. Mr. and Mrs. Sawyer, you are free to go. No, wait! I order the officers who arrested this couple to give them a ride back to their cabin, what's left of it."

The judge banged his gavel in anger. "Let me add that the attorney general's office should be investigating the abuse of federal authority that led to this confrontation." Seeing the stenographer's hesitation, the judge added, "Make my last comment part of the court record."

• • •

Molly and Paul lay together in their hotel bed. "This is a much nicer hotel than the ones we stayed at on our 'mated-moon.'" Molly observed. "Let's order room service for breakfast."

"I hate to spoil the mood," Paul replied, "but how are we going to pay for this? Fitzgerald insists they, and thereby we, pay rather than have the appearance of being obligated to anyone. And I think he's right."

"Have you forgotten all the money we carried across the country in the suitcases and the prepaid credit cards?"

"You brought all that with you into Canada?"

"Hello, yes. You think I'd leave our resources behind? The suitcases are in Tom's SUV and guarded by the Royal Mounties."

Still a stickler for details, Paul persisted, "Isn't it illegal to bring that much cash into Canada?"

Molly lounged completely relaxed in the soft sheets.

Sleep tempted her to return. "They didn't ask. And with Fitzgerald's diplomatic status, they didn't search either."

"Then I'll have steak for breakfast."

"That's my boy. Order one for me too. Medium rare."

Paul got out of bed and used the room phone. After ordering the steaks he asked, "What do you think Fitzgerald and Isabella are doing?"

Molly remained sleepy. "I don't know. They're in the next room. Tap on their door and ask them."

Paul found the extraterrestrials awake and fully dressed. Fitzgerald watched TV news while Isabella tapped on their laptop. The remnants of a large breakfast indicated that they had not starved. "Where did you get the food?" Paul asked.

"The hotel brought it to us. Their pancakes are not as good as Isabella's. But the drink is very special," said Fitzgerald. Paul noticed an empty pitcher of maple syrup.

"Are you two okay alone today? Molly and I need some rest in our room."

"Can we go out looking around? When we went downstairs looking for food, a kind man and woman in red uniforms offered to protect us if we go out."

"You mean 'Royal Mounties'?"

"Yes, I think. The man is the same one who led Molly here in a police car yesterday from the border."

"You'll be fine. See you tomorrow."

• • •

Both Paul and Molly fell asleep again after eating.

Late in the afternoon, Paul woke up. Steam coming from the bathroom told him that Molly was indulging in a long, hot shower. He turned on the TV. A local news station had interrupted their regular service to air a young female reporter and cameraman following Fitzgerald and Isabella. Two Mounties in red uniforms escorted the ambassadors around Vancouver. The extraterrestrials spent more time talking to Canadians and posing for selfies than actual sightseeing. Fitzgerald gave a brief interview to the reporter. "We are very grateful to Canada for their hospitality. Vancouver is a beautiful city."

Molly came in wearing the hotel's bathrobe and drying her hair with a towel. Paul pointed to the TV. "Look at Fitzgerald and Isabella. They're out having a good time."

"They're inexhaustible." Molly slumped on the bed. "I'm happy just to be here with you."

"Same here."

Chapter 36

•••

In the first spare moment Laura had in days, she re-listened to the recording Isabella had given her from the cockpit conversation with the Benevolents. They had said something she didn't understand about her computer. Laura checked the cloud storage linked to her computer, looking for a directory labeled "Snezar." There she found it as the Benevolents had promised. A text file waited. "Hello Dr. Laura. We enjoyed meeting you. You surprised us by not requesting treatment for your son, Jeff. The preparation process would be complex. The treatment, although painless, would take at least five of your years."

Laura reread the message. *Treat Jeff for Down Syndrome? If changed, would he be the same loveable boy? Would his life be any happier? Would I miss the Jeff I love so much? Is this selfish of me? Do I have the right to deny him the opportunity to be someone else? And, if changed, could he care for himself better after I'm gone?*

A separate file had been included, "Treatment of Down Syndrome in humans." Laura opened the file. Detailed instructions revealed that the amul could be programmed to seek out and change a specific DNA deformity rather than simply eliminate aberrant cells. "To program the amul, a reproductive cell from the patient would be repaired. A cloned zygote would then be formed to define the desired DNA to the amul. Afterwards the amul can gradually heal the mental aspects of Down Syndrome or other genetic deficiencies. The zygote could be discarded or processed into a person depending on the views of the practitioner. We recommend the latter," the message concluded. "Sincerely, Benevolent."

● ● ●

"Shall we have steak again for breakfast?" Paul mumbled to Molly the second morning.

She wiped her eyes to clear them. "Maybe grilled shrimp today with some artichokes."

The hotel phone rang. Paul answered to hear a gruff voice. "Glad you made it. Where's our dog?"

"Hi, Tom! Jeff took Emma to North Carolina. Sorry. What happened to you guys?"

Tom told their story and added, "Emma will be fine with Jeff. We're back here at the cabin. The Feds left quite a mess. Jack turned up after a few hours. Probably he'll be even more skittish around strangers."

"Thanks for what you did."

"It was our pleasure. I could use my SUV back, though.

Becky suggested we drive your minivan up to Vancouver to exchange."

"Sure, we need to stay in Canada for a while, I think."

Tom laughed. "Maybe not too long. The press down here is all over the president for running you out of the country. Let's talk again when we're ready to head your way."

• • •

Over breakfast Molly wondered, "Do you think we should actually do something constructive today?"

Paul ate a shrimp. "Maybe, yeah. Let's check to see if Fitzgerald and Isabella need anything, or if they're happy charming the Canadian public."

"I'm sure they're happy. But you know Fitzgerald and his mission."

"How about you check on them today?"

Molly found Fitzgerald and Isabella in their room. Fitzgerald worked on the laptop while Isabella monitored the news. "Look Molly," she said. "The news is about Tom and Becky."

"...sources have confirmed that two Americans, Tom and Becky Sawyer of Eugene, Oregon, played a major role in protecting Fitzgerald and Isabella until the treatment could be identified," the news anchor reported. "Court documents show that the Sawyers also helped them to escape to Canada. Policies of the current administration in Washington made their escape to Canada necessary."

"Have you two had food today?" Molly asked.

Isabella brightened to reply, "Yes. Today we had chicken eggs and a round meat called 'Canadian Bacon.' And we ordered more of the special Canadian drink called maple syrup." Two empty glasses with a sticky residue confirmed her words.

"Do you have anything planned for today?"

Fitzgerald looked up from the laptop. "Could we post another video today, please? Isabella and I have another message to deliver."

"Sure. Let Paul and me get dressed, then we'll get started."

● ● ●

After rehearsing the new message with Fitzgerald and Isabella, Molly went to the hotel lobby. There she found the same Canadian news reporter and cameraman that had followed their friends the previous day. The news team's eyes widened when they saw the famous Molly. "Would you do a favor for us, please?" Molly asked. "We'd like better video quality than we can get from a cell phone. Could you come upstairs—"

"Yes, we would be happy to," the girl broke in. "Sorry for interrupting, Ms. Powell."

"I'm Molly. You two come on up."

In Fitzgerald and Isabella's room, the cameraman fiddled with lighting and angles until satisfied. The reporter groomed her subjects slightly until she asked Molly, "Do you mind if I tag it?" Molly gestured *Go ahead* with her two hands and stepped back.

"This is Sara Bryant and Bennie Murray with KBAX news in Vancouver, British Columbia. We're here with the ambassadors from the planet Benevolent. Fitzgerald and Isabella have an important message for us." Sara stepped out of the picture as Bennie zoomed in on their subjects.

"Greetings to all of our friends worldwide," Isabella began. "Your cooperation and teamwork in the current crisis has heartened us. Together we will be able to defeat the cancer virus that has afflicted so many innocent people. We thank Future Tech and the American CDC for their crucial roles in creating the treatment."

Fitzgerald spoke next, "We arrived on Earth as ambassadors nearly a year ago. Our understanding of human nature had been based on the culture of our creators and on intercepted movies and TV. We have learned much in a year. We cannot expect humans to respond in a way that seems logical to us."

He paused before continuing, "In Alaska, Isabella and I encountered a grizzly bear. Its species evolved to be aggressive and violent in a wild world. The bear reacted to us that way and would have killed us had a friend not saved us with pepper spray. But the bear's violent nature has resulted in it nearly being exterminated. Only a few grizzly bears now survive in harsh, isolated places.

"Human beings are like the bear. Aggression served individual humans and groups when the world was wild. Now that same competitive nature threatens mankind's existence. Therefore, we reemphasize our challenge that

347

humans learn to work together to solve problems. We are seeing that in the cancer crisis. Together we can build on that spirit of cooperation to create a better future for mankind."

Isabella spoke again, "The many people suffering from the cancer virus pandemic is a tragedy. Understandably, others are fearful of contracting the disease themselves. Many people go untreated. Fitzgerald and I will go to Asia under the auspice of the World Health Organization to do what we can to alleviate suffering as the treatment is being prepared. Medical specialists who are willing to join us will be given priority preventative measures, the same treatment Dr. Laura Holdridge received."

"Thank you again," Fitzgerald and Isabella said together.

The Canadian reporter signaled "cut" to Bennie. She turned to Molly. "Can we upload this to our network?"

Molly handed her a stick drive. "Give us a copy first and then you can release it." Sara and Bennie hurried to pack their things and get to their van. Neither of them had ever had such an important scoop to report.

Molly posted the clip Sara had provided to Fitzgerald's blog. But that hardly mattered. By the time she had finished, the clip has been broadcast all over Canadian news and would quickly reach the world.

● ● ●

"Welcome to Canada!" Paul and Molly plus Fitzgerald and Isabella greeted Tom and Becky at the Vancouver hotel.

"You two have become big celebrities," Paul congratulated them.

"Aaah! With the stars," Tom indicated Fitzgerald and Isabella, "and you two out of the country, we're all they can find to make a story."

"The reporters have been snooping around the cabin," Becky complained. "Tom wanted to fire a few shots over their heads, but I stopped him."

"Why don't you stay up here for a few days with us?" Fitzgerald invited. "You could get a room in the hotel. They have good food here."

"Nah!" Tom replied. "We brought the minivan and we'll take our SUV home. But we need to get back before souvenir hunters get into the cabin and strip it clean. One already got my log splitter. They'd probably take Jack if they could catch him."

"Then at least let us treat you to dinner," Molly offered.

To that the Sawyers consented. "Wait until you taste the special Canadian drink we've discovered," Isabella promised.

• • •

"Dr. Laura," the text message on Laura's hard drive began, "we have enjoyed responding to your questions about mass preparation of the promised cancer virus treatment. Your questions about the Down Syndrome treatment show deep understanding of genetic engineering. We are happy to be your partner.

"Now let us ask you a question. Have you seen our ambassadors' comparison of the grizzly bear to mankind?

To be most effective as our ambassadors, Fitzgerald and Isabella need to be open and guileless. Therefore, they do not need to know everything. The question we place before you is, 'Could the "bear" use a little help changing its nature for the benefit of its species?' Benevolent."

●●●

"Do you think we can trust a vaccination provided by an alien species who probably wants our planet for themselves?" Bill Samuel began his normal rant. "Even if the treatment works, millions of people have died horrible deaths, while the so-called 'ambassadors' held the cure all the time. Let me ask you, would this Fitzgerald and Isabella have ever revealed the cure if President Johnson had not turned up the heat on them? Or would they have allowed the cancer to kill all so that this planet, our planet, could be populated with a different species? I don't know, maybe they would have revealed the cure in time to preserve a remnant of humanity to be their slaves. And now that very president is under fire by the public whose safety he put before all else."

●●●

"We have a special announcement coming from the White House," Steve Wilson announced. "Let's pick up President Truman Johnson live."

The camera switched to the familiar hallway scene used for major announcements in the White House. The president looked anxiously at someone off camera until suddenly he realized that the feed had started. He located the prompter and began reading, "Fellow Americans, we can see the light at the end of a tunnel regarding the Asian cancer virus pandemic. The cases in the United States have been isolated and are being treated. I would like to thank the CDC whose personnel have worked tirelessly under my direction to avert a catastrophe of unprecedented scale.

"Not everybody saw eye-to-eye in how to deal with this crisis. A few even fled the country to avoid being part of the solution. However, in the interest of national unity, I have decided to issue a full presidential pardon to Fitzgerald and Isabella and all who aided or harbored them. Their diplomatic status will be restored. They are welcome to return to the United States."

Chapter 37

• • •

"Thank you for coming on our *In Touch* program, Bill. Your own commentary show has topped the ratings for many months. Although the news has been quieter since the announcement of the cancer-virus treatment a month ago," said Steve Wilson to his guest across an interview table.

Bill Samuel magnanimously replied, "Thank you for your invitation, Steve. I've been friends with DSC's news director, George Baker, since we were interns together. Our teamwork has buoyed all of DSC's ratings."

"That's true. But did you hear that George has decided to explore other opportunities outside DSC?"

"No, I had not heard. When was that announced?"

"Just now, actually. You and George did pull off some great coups. I remember when he asked Molly Powell to appear on your show. DSC's ratings went through the ceiling at 69%. And later the video had nearly three billion viewings."

"Yeah, that was a stroke of genius. I told George so when he proposed the idea. And Molly Powell isn't bad to look at, but she just wasn't ready for the big time."

"Hmmm..." Steve looked thoughtful. "In an amazing coincidence, Molly happens to be in our studio tonight. What do you say we bring her on camera?"

Bill looked around him as if Molly might be sneaking up with a club. "Sure, why not?"

"Come on out, Molly," Steve invited.

Bill saw a large blond woman wearing her hair in a ponytail stalk onto the stage. A stagehand brought in another chair to set at the table. Molly took her seat while staring directly at Bill.

"You two meet again," Steve continued. "A lot has happened since your first broadcast together. I'll start with Bill. Have your opinions about the ambassadors Fitzgerald and Isabella changed since that time?"

Bill swallowed and smiled self-consciously in front of the camera. "All of us are glad for the fortuitous arrival of Fitzgerald and Isabella. But if NASA had presented all the facts, if Fitzgerald and Isabella had been more forthcoming from the beginning, a lot of hardship could have been avoided. Their reticence probably cost a lot of lives."

"NASA gave the DNA results, the telemetry data, all the laboratory analysis, and made their guests available for interviews. Fitzgerald and Isabella clearly explained themselves. What facts were withheld?" Steve rebutted.

"Well, NASA hasn't had a good record of revealing

the truth. And we only had what the aliens said to go on. That's all we still have. I understand the treatment has something to do with their blood. Who's to say that alien cells inside humans won't result in some sort of mind control?"

Steve turned to Molly. "Ms. Powell, do you have an opinion about the truth?"

"The truth is that Bill and others like him manipulate people's ideas with falsehood and plant fear in them. All they care about is attracting a following. Facts are irrelevant to them."

Bill spoke with an air of condescension, "That may be your opinion, Molly. But there are many others who think differently. And our American First Amendment guarantees—"

Molly interrupted, "The First Amendment gives freedom of the press. It doesn't state that all ignorant opinions and con men are of equal value. If people had listened to you, Fitzgerald and Isabella would have been permanently incarcerated or worse. You claimed an alien invasion was imminent. You would have used nuclear weapons on innocent people and invited retaliation against the United States. You advocated arrest and torture of Fitzgerald and Isabella. Your ego, greed, and stupidity would have doomed mankind. And now you're planting seeds of more fear with ridiculous talk about mind control."

Bill, for once, sat speechless. Steve listened calmly, letting the scenario play out. "Bill, do you have a response?" he prompted.

Rather than answer Molly, Bill spoke to Steve. "I can see that DSC no longer respects journalists and the opinions of millions of people. As for Fitzgerald and Isabella and their hangers-on like Ms. Powell here, they are still keeping secrets. I'll continue asking the questions people want to hear."

Molly stood and raised her right hand that had previously struck Bill. He recoiled backwards with a startled expression. Molly kissed her hand then used it to pat her own butt.

Bill stood up and stormed out of camera range. Steve watched Bill go without apparent concern. "Well, I guess Bill just isn't ready for the big time," he commented and then turned to Molly. "As it seems our featured guest has been called elsewhere, would you be willing to answer some questions, Molly? We have some program time left."

"I'm a reporter, Steve. I report the news. I'm not the news."

Steve laughed. "Well, good luck with that." Realizing the absurdity of her own statement, Molly laughed with him.

"Have you been following the impeachment proceedings of President Johnson?" Steve pushed on. "That pardon the president gave to all of you came too late and too little for him."

Again, Molly laughed. "I never thought I'd see the party in power impeach their own man. And the charges of 'dereliction of duty' in the crisis might not be strictly constitutional."

"And the minority party is opposing the impeachment!" Steve retorted in amazement.

"That's only because they want to run against him in the midterms. They'll lose the impeachment vote, though. His party wants Johnson gone."

"Politics as usual!" Steve sighed and changed the subject. "What are Fitzgerald and Isabella doing now?"

"They're still in Asia, helping cancer victims. They're immune to the carrier cold themselves. And the basis of the treatment comes from their blood. Everyone who receives a blood transfusion from them is also immune. So they've recruited a team of medical specialists. Dr. Ginger Peters of NASA agreed to lead the medical team and administer the preliminary preventative measures to others on her team. They add two new people to their team daily. Still tens of thousands are dying every day."

"How about progress on the promised treatment?"

"It's one hundred percent effective if the cancer is caught early. Dr. Holdridge at Future Tech and the CDC have gotten every facility able to manufacture the biotic involved. But the treatments are just now becoming widely available. And some firms are profiteering on what they received for free. The lawyers can sort that out after the epidemic is resolved."

"Now Molly, what about you? What are you doing?"

"Steve, I'm writing fact-based essays about the various issues facing mankind for Fitzgerald to study. I try to objectively tell both sides. Usually then both sides get angry at me. That gives them one thing to agree on. It's a start."

Steve laughed. "Knowing you, I can imagine neither side appreciating your analysis. So what plans do you have for the future? I suppose having helped to save the world is hard to top."

Molly laughed again. "There's still plenty to do. The world is temporarily saved. A lot of hard work lies ahead solving problems. The profiteering on the treatment proves that."

"Are the Benevolents going to help us solve those problems?"

"Their original policy insisted that humans solve their own problems. We are so factious that the Benevolents were, still are, concerned that individuals could use the technology for personal gain. Or some groups would use the technology to gain advantage over others. But the cancer virus and pandemic and our ultimate cooperation convinced the Benevolents that some immediate technological help for Earth could be warranted."

"How will that be managed?"

"Former NASA engineer and scientist Dr. Paul Sanders has agreed to head the Benevolent Foundation. The foundation still helps educate children but will broaden its emphasis. They will be the liaison between Benevolent and Earth using a non-profit approach. In addition to taking donations, the non-profit will carefully license selected technology to developed countries and use the proceeds to help non-developed countries catch up. Isabella has re-programmed their spacecraft to allow Harry Thompkins to communicate with the Benevolents.

On behalf of Paul and the foundation, he will introduce the appropriate human experts to them."

"Molly, we're almost out of time. But before we go, I notice that you're wearing a diamond ring. And by now everybody knows the story about you and Paul Sanders being on the run from authorities. Being on the lam together must have been rather romantic. Are you and Sanders together now?"

"Yes, we are mated. Isabella says that's like being married, only stronger. But we did get a legal marriage certificate in a court last week. Since Paul's family is religious, we'll also have a ceremony and exchange rings in his parent's church in the spring. And I'll be hoping for the Great Creator's blessings as well."

"Congratulations, Molly." Steve looked at the camera, which focused in on him. "So there you have the latest from Molly Powell and the Benevolent Foundation. This is Steve Wilson on *In Touch*, a program of DSC News. We hope you'll join us again next week."

The program director signaled "cut." The camera light went out.

Steve turned to Molly. "Thanks for coming on. I felt the network owed you a chance to confront Bill. We'll not be renewing his contract."

"I'm sure somebody will pick him up. He pulls in viewers," Molly responded.

"Unfortunately," Steve responded. "Any chance on keeping you as part of DSC News, Molly? Although this won't become official until tomorrow, I'll be the new news director."

"Congratulations, Steve. And thanks. You might entice me to do a special report occasionally."

"Some worthy cause you believe in, I suppose?" he probed. Molly's smile revealed the truth of that. Then Steve teased Molly, "I understand that you even used DSC Network to get inside information on your pursuers."

Once again Molly's smile revealed her guilt. "Yes, I did, Steve. George used me. I used him back."

"The article you wrote for *Time* magazine likely hastened George to the door," Steve added. "How about the first special you do for DSC being the whole story of you and Dr. Sanders on the run? The cold, hard, and yet exciting truth."

That appealed to Molly. "Maybe, yes. The whole story. And DSC will make a big donation for at-risk children and endorse the Benevolent Foundation, right?"

Then Steve laughed. "Of course. But back to the ring you're wearing."

Molly thought a second longer. "Tell you what, Steve. If DSC does that special for the Benevolent Foundation, we can throw in an exclusive video of the Powell-Sanders wedding."

"You've got a deal!"

Chapter 38

•••

"This is Tom," Paul heard after answering the phone.

"Hi, Tom! How's Becky?"

"She's doing well. Getting ready for Christmas."

"I saw Emma in North Carolina last week. She acts spryer, even looks younger. You were really kind to let Jeff keep her."

"Well, Emma needed more attention than Becky and I could give her. I'm happy she has a better home." Tom paused a few seconds before going on, "But Paul, the reason I'm calling is that with the cancer virus treatments becoming readily available, Fitzgerald and Isabella are coming back to the United States. Becky and I invited them to spend Christmas here in Oregon. They're coming in on December tenth and staying into the new year. We sure would love to have you and Molly join us."

"Thanks, Tom! I've already promised to spend Christmas day and a week afterwards with my parents in Arizona. My brother will be home from Okinawa and they all want to meet Molly. But I think we could be in Oregon some the week before Christmas. Let me check with Molly."

"That would be great!"

● ● ●

Paul and Molly pulled up the driveway to the Sawyer cabin in a rental car a week before Christmas. They found Fitzgerald and Isabella taking turns splitting firewood while Tom watched. Isabella showed a baby bump. "You're making a pregnant woman work?" Paul chided.

"You try stopping her," answered Tom.

Isabella swung the new splitter above her head and down, separating a log into two halves. "I like this physical outdoor work," she said.

After greetings, Tom instructed Paul and Molly, "Go on to the cabin, Becky is expecting you. We'll finish up here."

In the cabin, they found Becky making up a new bed in the bedroom Tom had added with Fitzgerald and Isabella's help. "No sleeping bags for you two this time," she promised after hugs. "Would you like some hot chocolate?"

Fitzgerald and Isabella came in covered with snow while laughing and poking at each other. Becky shooed them back outside. "You two knock the snow off each other before you drip all over my floor."

That completed, they both wanted hot chocolate as

well. "What have you been doing here in Oregon?" Molly asked.

"They've been catching elk," Becky answered for them.

"Fitzgerald tried to ride one like a snark," Isabella said. "It threw him into a snowbank." She showed a blurred photo of her mate airborne as an elk cow escaped.

"You can catch the elk?" Paul questioned.

"They are not so hard in the deep snow," Fitzgerald explained. "They hide in the thickets. You sneak close without noise. Then the elks cannot run so fast in the snow. I think we'll stop chasing until next summer when the elks have a better chance."

"And we learned to drive a car," said Isabella. "Tom and Becky taught us."

"Only three fender benders," Becky added in a confidential tone. "And you landed a spacecraft!" she admonished Isabella.

Isabella shook that off with a smile. "I crashed hundreds of spacecrafts in the simulator."

Tom came in after storing the tools. "When's supper, Becky? I'm starved."

"The turkey is ready if you are."

"Let's eat."

Over dinner each couple reviewed what they had been doing. The cat Jack, having recovered from his flash bomb ordeal, wound between their legs as they ate. Finally, Becky gave him a little dish of turkey in the kitchen.

After Isabella's description of their time in Asia, Fitzgerald expressed some frustration. "Nothing has really changed. No problems have been settled at the United Nations. Few humans will accept anything but capitulation from those who disagree with them. And many are using the cancer virus to take money from others, even in a crisis." Fitzgerald shook his head. "The factual issue papers you send me are very good, Molly. But even if the sides could agree on the facts, they are unwilling to work together or compromise. What do they think will be the end of that?"

"The problem is often that a few on both sides make money or get power from keeping the issue unresolved. Many are more interested in promoting self-serving solutions, than solving a problem. And few humans can think about, as you say, 'the end of that.' Humans only think about the right now," Molly pointed out. Then she corrected herself, "No, humans also think about the past. They can't put the past behind them."

"Humans can learn, though." Although he spoke for everyone to hear, Paul addressed Molly. "Think about you and me. We were, still are, very different. And we each held on to problems from our past. Yet we learned how to have a relationship."

Molly had also learned to listen to Paul when he grappled with a difficult concept. "So what are you suggesting for Fitzgerald?"

They all waited for Paul. His words came slowly as he discovered them himself. "Maybe Fitzgerald's exhortations to change and cooperate need more 'How' with them."

"You mean tell the humans what they should do? They won't like that," Fitzgerald objected.

"No, I mean 'How' as in how to resolve the problems themselves."

"Maybe like a school," Becky spoke up.

"Yes, but not only teaching. Fitzgerald could include mediation on specific issues." Paul went on, "You could call it, 'The Center for Resolving Problems.'"

"No," Molly interceded. "You'll need something that can become a trademark. How about the 'Benevolent Embassy.' I'll bet you could even get sovereignty over the grounds like most embassies."

"Once Isabella has the baby, we won't be traveling as much. Those interested in real resolution of issues could come to us. I like it," Fitzgerald concluded. "Where would we locate it?"

Then Tom suggested, "Why not right here in Oregon? You could even have lodging for the primary opponents. Get negotiators away from those who have a vested interest in keeping the conflict alive."

"Could an official embassy be located away from Washington, DC?" Becky wondered.

"Why not?" Molly countered. "It would be an embassy to the world, not just the United States. I'll bet the state of Oregon would gladly welcome you."

They all sat contemplating the enormity of the concept. Paul, ever the practical one, warned, "An operation like that would need a lot of money. You have about three million dollars left from the book sales and the travelogues Molly sold. But that wouldn't be nearly enough." Everybody looked at Molly.

She challenged them, "Do you think I always know what to do about money?" They all nodded. Molly grinned. "Actually, I do have an idea. Fitzgerald, didn't you say that there are fourteen civilizations on different worlds allied together?"

"Yes, they all communicate and exchange ideas."

"I'll bet some TV networks would pay big dollars for exclusive specials describing those worlds. Remember when we raised a hundred million dollars for the foundation by doing that TV special from inside the isolation quarters? You showed pictures of the Benevolents. Thirteen other specials could raise plenty of money to fund the Benevolent Embassy. You could publish more books too."

"You'll need a competent accountant. I've got a few good years left. And you might not need to pay me," Tom offered.

"Why wouldn't we need money to pay you?" Isabella, second only to Paul in details, asked.

Tom acted embarrassed. "Actually, Becky and I need to talk to you about something related to that." Becky looked at the ceiling as her husband spoke. "A movie company offered us a million dollars to use our story. That is, your story from our viewpoint. Major Hollywood stars would play Becky and me, regular actors the rest of you. The story would mostly be about our lives including helping you. An actress would even play Beth. If we had that million dollars, we wouldn't need to be paid by the embassy. But we didn't want to sign the contract unless all of you agreed."

The other four all looked at each other. Paul, Fitzgerald, and Isabella all assured Tom and Becky of their agreement and encouraged them to sign the contract. All but Molly. "Ask them for three million or one million and five percent of the gross. Settle for two million or one million plus three percent," she advised them.

• • •

Because Paul and Molly needed to fly to Arizona on Christmas Eve, the group decided to celebrate their Christmas on December 23rd. Becky and Isabella fussed over a ham and other dishes in the kitchen. The others watched football on TV. In truth, Fitzgerald, always interested in food, would have preferred to be in the kitchen with Becky and Isabella.

"Turn off the game," Becky told them. "Dinner is ready. Tom, would you say grace."

"Molly got us 1.6 million dollars plus two percent," Tom babbled in disbelief during dinner. "I'll quit my job, right after New Year's. I was sick of filling out tax forms anyway."

"Just wait until you see the movie deal I can get for Fitzgerald and Isabella," Molly predicted.

Fitzgerald said to Tom, "Let's start looking for a site for the embassy tomorrow."

"Realtors don't want to work tomorrow or Christmas. Let's search online, then I'll call them the day after Christmas," Tom offered. "I think we should get at least a hundred acres."

After dinner, Becky read the poem *The Night Before Christmas*. Then Tom read the biblical account of Jesus' birth from the Bible.

"The Santa Claus is not real, right?" Isabella asked.

"You are correct," Paul answered her.

"And the story of the baby?"

"Many people think that story is true. I do," Paul answered again.

"This is a beautiful story," Fitzgerald said. "I love the 'Peace on Earth, goodwill to men.' I believe in the Creator who stands for that."

"I think of the young girl, Mary, having a baby in a strange place," Isabella added. "I'm sure that was frightening for her. "She must have felt great love for her unborn child." Isabella smiled and patted her rounded belly. "Some things about humans are difficult to understand, but I have never understood them better than I do right now."

Epilogue

10 Years Later

• • •

"Welcome to the embassy of the planet Benevolent. My name is Susie Faber," the perky tour guide greeted a group of twelve. "The embassy grounds are 342 acres that border the United States National Forest. Sovereignty over this land has been granted to the planet Benevolent by the US government.

"The embassy consists of three sectors. The most important sector is the Benevolent Embassy itself. There Ambassador Fitzgerald meets with representatives of people groups with differing views on difficult issues. The ambassador has helped humans to reach agreements on several of Earth's problems: elimination of nuclear and other weapons of mass destruction, the Kashmir border disputes between India and Pakistan, a global trade agreement, measures to stabilize the earth's climate, creation of independent enterprise zones in Africa, and other issues. But there are many challenges remaining. Right now, the ambassador is meeting with representatives seeking to demilitarize borders in the Middle East."

"How does he get people to agree?" one of the guests asked the tour guide.

"Before the representatives come here, two-thirds of the people they each represent must agree with a mutual fact statement. The statement might simply recognize that one party believes this, the other believes that. Even those fact statements sometimes take years to work out. But they require mutual recognition of the other's position before starting negotiations. The negotiations may take additional years as the representatives submit the steps agreed on to their constituents for approval.

"The second sector on the embassy grounds is the Benevolent Foundation headquarters. They are dedicated to helping individual humans everywhere achieve their potential." The tour guide quoted, "The greatest tragedy is the loss of human potential."

Another guest asked, "How is it funded?"

"I was just getting to that. The foundation is funded by donations and by the licensing of technology provided by our friends on Benevolent. For example, licensing of the new super-computer technology modeled on DNA has provided funds for education of hundreds of millions of children in less developed countries. The children in turn agree to and are better able to care for their parents in old age. This has stabilized populations in many regions. The foundation is managed by Paul and Molly Sanders. You may remember them from movies." Several of the tour guests nodded.

Susie smiled broadly. "During the cancer virus crisis, Paul and Molly stopped on the highway to give my mother and three young children, including me, a ride. Mom had been praying for help. Afterwards she wondered if they might have been angels. Later Paul and Molly recognized my mother, Alice Faber, as the one who first suggested asking the Benevolents for help. Mom is certain God led her to do so."

"Why do you have goats here?" A young boy pointed toward a three-acre enclosure with a herd and various obstacles.

"That's so that you can try catching them." The tour guide explained, "You are currently in the third sector of the embassy. The visitor area has been created by Harry Thompkins, the former NASA director who helped Fitzgerald and Isabella when they first arrived. There are many exhibits about the universe we share with other sentient species. The spacecraft Fitzgerald and Isabella took to reach Earth is on display behind me. If you join the line to the deck, you can look into the cockpit. And Mr. Thompkins has set up ten stations where you can experience communicating with a real alien on Benevolent."

"What about catching the goats?" the boy persisted.

"And for children, we have various activities that

represent life on other planets. A sport on Benevolent is chasing and touching wild snarks. Since we have no snarks, human children get to chase goats. The goats have a breakaway flag tied to their tails. If you can get a flag from a goat, we'll give you this badge." The tour guide held up an award saying, "Benevolent Goat Catcher."

"The smaller children can go into a petting area where the goats and other animals are tame and friendly. That concludes our orientation. The rest of the tour is self-guided," the tour guide concluded. "Please don't forget our gift shop where books, videos, and movies about space and other species are available. All the proceeds go to fund the visitor area and feed the goats."

● ● ●

Dr. Ben Finkle had rarely stopped by Laura's office in recent years. At eighty-six, the Nobel laureate had been confined to a motor-operated wheelchair for nearly a decade. Laura rose to meet her mentor. "Dr. Finkle, you look well."

"The hell I do. I've got nine out of ten toes in the grave already." Laura, knowing that he wouldn't have taken the effort to come without a purpose, waited. "I don't really mind leaving this earth, though, knowing that you're continuing my work. No, not continuing, but leaping forward. What is it? Are you up for your third Nobel, now?"

"Yes, sir. But everything I've done has been based on the work you did. And using this..." she indicated the Future Tech facilities and organization.

The old man coughed. "Laura, I came by to tell you that I've just completed a new will, certainly my last. As we discussed earlier, fifty-one percent of Future Tech is yours to use for mankind."

"Thank you, Ben. I give you my word to use your company well for the good of humanity."

Ben looked at the wall where he saw a portrait of Rosalind Franklin and her words, "...by doing our best we shall succeed in our aims: the improvement of mankind."

The old man smiled. "I know you will; have done so already. Just make enough money so that the forty-nine percent can support my various ex-wives and offspring." Laura nodded, as Ben continued, "How's that son of yours, Jeff?"

"He graduated from high school last month, several years late, but with ninety-eighth percentile college entrance scores."

"He's headed to Duke, I heard. Nice progress for a kid born with Down Syndrome."

Laura smiled. "Yes, that has been remarkable. I wanted Jeff to devote his life to rock and roll, but he chose physics. Kids? Go figure."

Ben cackled as only an old man can. "Is that dog still with him? You know that she was an old dog years ago; now she looks middle-aged for a dog. You look younger too, Laura."

"You mean Emma. Plenty of love and care, I think," said Laura. "And me? Maybe I've been too busy to age."

"Didn't you get the dog when you worked with the extraterrestrials, Fitzgerald and Isabella? How are they doing?"

"Yes, we stay in close touch. Fitzgerald mediates major problem negotiations at the Benevolent Embassy in Oregon. He's the go-to guy to solve big disputes. Isabella had a heathy baby boy, then she adopted more than a dozen other children, including several with special needs. She started the voluntary movement called 'One-and-Adopt.' Her surrogate parents, the Sawyers — maybe you saw that movie — grandparent all the children.

"Paul and Molly Sanders run the Benevolent Foundation for Fitzgerald and Isabella. Molly's baby girl hasn't slowed her down much. She researches issues and makes factual documentaries. The Sanderses moved the foundation's headquarters to the Benevolent Embassy several years ago."

"And you also have an eight-year-old son now. He looks a lot like Jeff did at his age except without the Down Syndrome features."

"Yes, I do. You could say Toby is a chip off the old block."

"Uh huh. One last thing, Laura. I read an article recently that kindergarten school teachers are claiming that kids from about seven years down average much...nicer than previous generations. Less selfish. Fewer bullies."

"Well, Ben, decades ago you identified the gene sequences that statistically correlated with tendencies toward both altruism and antisocial personality disorder."

The old man stared at Laura. "Didn't Fitzgerald promise to let humans solve their own problems?"

"Fitzgerald kept *his* word. And *humans* are solving the

374

problems." Understanding passed between the protégé and her mentor.

"Ah, yes. And you identified that symptom-less retrovirus." The old man sat for a minute savoring the moment while breathing deeply. "Things are going to get easier, aren't they?"

"Yes...they...will, with each succeeding generation."

"Well, keep up the good work. Goodbye, Laura."

"I'll take care of things, Ben."

"I have no doubt you will."

Author's Note

• • •

All the characters in this novel are purely fictional and created in the imaginations of the authors. Except for the extraterrestrials and the white corpuscle-like amul in their blood, all the science, technology, history, and geography are based on facts and used plausibly. Truly the rapidly evolving science of genetics is both exciting and frightening.

About the Authors

•••

Kit and Drew Coons met while living and doing humanitarian work in Africa. As humorous speakers specializing in strengthening relationships, they have taught in every part of the US and in thirty-seven other countries. For two years, the Coonses lived and taught in New Zealand and Australia. They are keen cultural observers and incorporate their many adventures into their writing.

Drew has a strong technical background with honors degrees from both Auburn and Georgia Tech. He worked on the Delta Rocket program and designed critical components for the Space Shuttle. Later as a researcher for BASF Corporation he received twenty-three US and several international patents. Kit has an honors degree in education from the University of Minnesota. She is a gifted teacher and blogger with an undaunted spirit regardless of the circumstances.

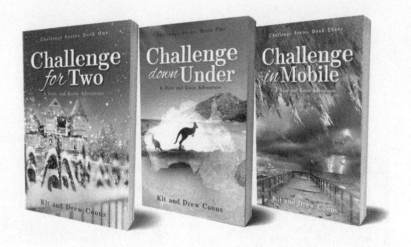

More from Drew and Kit:
The Challenge Series

Challenge for Two
Challenge Series Book One

A series of difficult circumstances have forced Dave and Katie Parker into early retirement. Searching for new life and purpose, the Parkers take a wintertime job house sitting an old Victorian mansion. The picturesque river town in southeastern Minnesota is far from the climate and culture of their home near the Alabama Gulf Coast.

But dark secrets sleep in the mansion. A criminal network has ruthlessly intimidated the community since the timber baron era of the 19th century. Residents have been conditioned to look the other way.

The Parkers' questions about local history and clues they discover in the mansion bring an evil past to light and create division in the small community. While some fear the consequences of digging up the truth, others want freedom from crime and justice for victims. Faced with personal threats, the Parkers must decide how to respond for themselves and for the good of the community.

— ◆ —

Challenge Down Under
Challenge Series Book Two

Dave and Katie Parker's only son, Jeremy, is getting married in Australia. In spite of initial reservations, the Parkers discover that Denyse is perfect for Jeremy and that she's the daughter they've always wanted. But she brings with her a colorful and largely dysfunctional Aussie family. Again Dave and Katie are fish out of water as they try to relate to a boisterous clan in a culture very different from their home in South Alabama.

After the wedding, Denyse feels heartbroken that her younger brother, Trevor, did not attend. Details emerge that lead Denyse to believe her brother may be in trouble. Impressed by his parents' sleuthing experience in Minnesota, Jeremy volunteers them to locate Trevor. Their search leads them on an adventure through Australia and New Zealand.

Unfortunately, others are also searching for Trevor, with far more sinister intentions. With a talent for irresponsible chicanery inherited from his family, Trevor has left a trail of trouble in his wake and has been forced into servitude. Can Dave and Katie locate him in time?

— ◆ —

Challenge in Mobile
Challenge Series Book Three

Dave and Katie Parker regret that their only child Jeremy, his wife Denyse, and their infant daughter live on the opposite side of the world. Unexpectedly, Jeremy calls to ask his father's help finding an accounting job in the US. Katie urges Dave to do whatever is necessary to find a job for Jeremy near Mobile. Dave's former accounting firm has floundered since his departure. The Parkers risk their financial security by purchasing full ownership of the struggling firm to make a place for Jeremy.

Denyse finds South Alabama fascinating compared to her native Australia. She quickly resumes her passion for teaching inner-city teenagers. Invited by Katie, other colorful guests arrive from Australia and Minnesota to experience Gulf Coast culture. Aided by their guests, Dave and Katie examine their faith after Katie receives discouraging news from her doctors.

Political, financial, and racial tensions have been building in Mobile. Bewildering financial expenditures of a client create suspicions of criminal activity. Denyse hears disturbing rumors from her students. A hurricane from the Gulf of Mexico exacerbates the community's tensions. Dave and Katie are pulled into a crisis that requires them to rise to a new level of more than ordinary.

What is a
more than ordinary life?

Each person's life is unique and special. In that sense, there is no such thing as an ordinary life. However, many people yearn for lives more special: excitement, adventure, romance, purpose, character. Our site is dedicated to the premise that any life can be more than ordinary.

At **MoreThanOrdinaryLives.com** you will find:

- inspiring stories
- ideas and resources
- entertaining novels
- free downloads